Memoir of a Mermaid

When, At Last, He Found Me

Heather,
Thanks for reading!

BOOK ONE IN THE MEMOIR OF A MERMAID SERIES

Memoir of a Mermaid

When, At Last, He Found Me

ADRIANNA STEPIANO

This is a work of fiction. Names, characters, places, and incidents either are the product of the author's imagination or are used fictitiously, Any resemblance to actual persons, living or dead, events, or locales is entirely coincidental.

༄

Text and illustrations copyright © 2012 Adrienne C. Stepaniak

All rights reserved.
Published by Adrienne C. Stepaniak, Wyandotte, Michigan 2012
www.memoirofamermaid.com

ISBN: 0615626254
ISBN-13: 978-0615626253

First Edition

For Tyler and Isabel
Let your imagination forever be untamed

※

After the summer I had, I'm finding it difficult to receive normality. My mind, heart, and body are so very different compared to when May flowers were first in bloom. The Earth calls to me but I refuse to listen for it is not the wandering life that I desire. Roots strong enough to hold when the tide pounds the land are the things I seek.

I write, not to document but rather to be convinced of the impossible net reality has tangled me in.

-S.O.S

※

ONE

A feeling of awareness is the only way to describe it. When my head clears from all the daily nothingness and for a moment I know. I know. I KNOW—that I exist and that one day I will no longer exist; at least not in the flesh. I'm sure most people have similar moments of clarity. It's the random seconds where life seems real—implausibly existent.

It used to happen only when the thought of death crossed my mind. Then, it started happening more frequently. When I became angry or upset—overwhelmed or confused; my mind would turn off. It literally went into total shutdown mode. Calling it an inconvenience was putting it lightly.

Things didn't begin to turn around until the day of my high school graduation. I was forcing myself upon the day. Not only did I want it to be over, I wanted it to be different. And in many ways it was.

The temperature was a scorching 98 with 70% humidity, which was unseasonably hot for Maine in June—a side effect of global warming, no doubt. I regretted, almost immediately, wearing my hair down. It is thick and to make matters worse, it's dark brown. I was sweltering.

As I stood in line waiting behind the students with last names beginning A thru S—I grew anxious. Stress filled my thoughts when I caught a glimpse of the onlookers. A fast wind whipped through the football stadium. A few students lost their caps to its strength. I gripped the brim of mine. The wind was out of place but I didn't notice, I was too focused on what was about to occur. I began to silently panic.

The moment of awareness washed over me. I tried to ground myself to the situation. Everything is fine. Settle down; settle down; settle down. I repeated the words in my head; unconvincingly. Nothing was fine. It was the beginning of the rest of my life and I knew naught where it was going.

The beating of my heart was all I could hear. Stars began to cloud my vision and my head grew light. The last thing I wanted to take place that day—in front of all those people—was happening and I could do very little to control it. My consciousness began to fade and I fell.

The blackouts started soon after my father died. Looking back, it all makes perfect sense but at the time, it was simply unbearable. Sadly, these meant more than just waking up humiliated. It was also inevitable that I had to endure the worst day of my life once more. While I was out cold, one scene played like a movie clip in my brain—leaving me clues to a seemingly endless mystery.

The memory was clear; I stood on the beach talking to my friend whose name I don't even recall. She already knew I was not permitted to go into the ocean but still she dared.

"Leaving information out isn't lying. Seraphin, if you don't tell your Dad that you went in the water, how will he know?"

"He said he would know. Besides, I don't want to go in the water, the waves are too high and the tide is coming in." This was the same excuse I used a thousand times but the truth was, deep down, I didn't want to disobey my father's wishes.

"I'm leaving, my Grandma should be home soon and she'll be upset with me if she knew I was here."

"You are so boring." My friend said.

I watched myself stand up, but instead of climbing the steep hill to my house, I walked towards the ocean. My friends began to cheer when they realized what I was doing. My heart was racing with excitement and so was the water—wave after wave pounded at the sand. The sound of the water was calling.

My foot touched the fresh wet sand and I knew there was no turning back. I was going to deliberately disobey my father. He told me countless times to stay out of the ocean, saying it was too dangerous.

I let the water wash over my toes as it pulled for me to go further. I spoke confidently, trying to hide the fact that I was terrified. "What's the big deal anyway? I'm ten now and I'm a great swimmer. I should be allowed to have fun." Then, I did it—I dove into an oncoming wave—with near perfect form, I might add. I felt my body move through the heavy salt water. I remember feeling alive that very moment—all my senses were heightened—I could have stayed under the surface forever but instead I resurfaced. The not-so-great friends cheered at my defiance.

Now, I knew very well that I was going to get in a heap of trouble when my father found out. At the time I thought it lucky that he was out of town that day for work. I thought I had at least 24 more hours of freedom before he grounded me—for the rest of my life. If only that had been the case—I would give anything to hear him holler. Instead, reality played in my unconscious mind.

My faulty friend so graciously reminded me of how much trouble I was going to be in. "You are so gutsy. I would never go against your Dad. He's intimidating."

"Well, luckily he's out of town and won't know." I said, knowing perfectly well that wasn't true.

Then, I decided I was going to confess—right then—while I stood waist deep in the Atlantic Ocean. I called out my father's name. "Samuel Shedd, look at me, I am in the OCEAN!" At the mention of my father's name, I had a dark feeling in the pit of my stomach.

Then, I could actually hear his panic stricken voice in my head. "Seraphin, get out of the water!"

I knew I had to do what he said. Somehow I knew that both he and I were in danger. I could feel the threat. It was too late though—there was nothing I could do. I tried to swim towards the shore but my body grew heavy and weak. My arms and legs were impossible to move. My friends were shouting and running to the water.

"*Seraphin, Seraphin!*" They were screaming.

"*Seraphin, Seraphin*, are you with us?" The Superintendent was staring down at me, along with roughly 1500 people set up in rows of metal folding chairs on the football field. The band had stopped playing *Pomp & Circumstance* and a baby was crying. A man sneezed which caused a skittish woman in the front row to flinch.

As if that moment was shocking to anyone; I was considered a freak at that school and I had been for eight long years.

Just like always, humiliation was at its peak. I slowly got to my feet, nodding to the Superintendent. It was a small gesture to let him know that my mind had returned to its rightful place, the present. Into the microphone he spoke with a hint of disgust, *Seraphin Olivia Shedd.*

The football stadium was silent. With a deep breath I crossed the stage to accept my diploma.

Just like my grandmother had planned, an attorney was waiting. He handed over the key to the Shedd family estate. I held up my end of the agreement. Before my Grandma passed away I promised her I would not live alone until school was finished. I may not have known where my life was headed but I knew one thing, after 5 months, I was finally going home.

"Ms. Shedd, it was a pleasure doing business with you and your grandmother." The attorney shook my hand. "Congratulations."

It may sound strange that a girl of only 18 wanted nothing more than her family estate but it was true. I didn't know it at the time—maybe it was subconscious—but that house was more than just a place to hang my hat.

☙

I had been living with the Cottington family. Grandma was my last surviving relative, before she died, she asked Gomer Cottington and his wife Mara to make sure I was taken care of until after graduation. They kept their promise. Gomer was a friend to my father and he was always very welcoming. Unfortunately, he took a job in Detroit and had to relocate soon after I moved in. Sadly, his wife, who felt no obligation to care for me and only harbored resentment, was forced to stay behind on my account.

Mara was anything but pleasant. She had been packing with a firm departure date of that very day. There was no hiding the fact that she was ecstatic to finally be rid of me. It was surprising to not hear her cheering from the bleachers when I crossed the stage. She could barely contain her excitement earlier that morning as I carried my bags out to the car. Although, she probably didn't want someone to realize she was with me. Those public displays of instability on my part were enough to drive anyone away. Honestly, I can't say I would lay claim to myself if put in the same situation. Perhaps, I shouldn't have been so hard on her. Conceivably, under different circumstances, I was somewhat sure she would have been more welcoming.

I still had not made up my mind about the Cottington's son, Ethan. Mara made it impossible for us to get to know each other. I searched the crowd for him, worried he would leave before I had a chance to say goodbye.

He found me first. "Phin, my Mom wants to make sure you have everything from our house." Ethan shouted as he ran down the bleachers to where I stood.

"Yes, I have everything in my car. Tell your Mom thanks and have a safe trip." I leaned in, giving him a hug. It seemed like the right thing to do, but I was wrong. He awkwardly kept his arms down. Immediately, I regretted my demonstration of friendliness. It was the first time I had ever shown him any affection and it was every bit as strange as I thought it would be.

"I told you this morning, I'm finding a way out of this move. I'll be 18 in December and then I won't have to live with them." Ethan, unlike his mother, did not intend on moving away from Maine.

"Your Mom is leaving now. I think you've run out of time."

"Nah, I have to find Ms. Z." He looked over my head, into the crowd. "I'll see you around."

Even though I lived with Ethan, I really didn't know him. We didn't hang out with similar crowds. Actually, the truth was, he had friends and I didn't. The guy was nice enough, but hardly ever around. When he was home, he locked himself in his man-cave of a bedroom and only came out for food. I got the feeling that he didn't like his parents very much and I couldn't blame him, his mother was like talking to a raging bull. At school, he was always surrounded by football players and swooning girls. I couldn't figure out why they swooned over him either. In my opinion, his head was too square and his face was too flat. He looked just like Mara and that drove me away, for obvious reasons.

The field cleared and the student volunteers were almost done folding up the chairs, but for some reason I felt it difficult to leave. I sat on the bleachers playing with my car keys for close to an hour. My 1972 black Ford Gran Torino was shining from far across the parking lot. It was my father's car and he loved it almost as much as he loved me—and he loved me a lot. When I was a kid he would park in the furthest, most remote parking spot in an attempt to protect it from door dents. It was silly to me but I felt I must do the same since it was all I had of him.

I couldn't bring myself to leave. I stood a few times but sat back down. I was suddenly scared to go home to an empty house.

Luckily a voice came up behind me. It was the voice of a friend. This was perhaps the only person that seemed to care for me despite my social awkwardness. A smile crossed my face when I heard her speak.

"Congratulations on your graduation Ms. Shedd." I turned to find Ms. Doreh Zebedee, my biology teacher whom I adored and who everyone lovingly referred to as 'Ms. Z'. It sounds sad but she was probably my best friend and that's not saying much because I only saw her at school.

In her arms was a large box overflowing with books. I remembered that Ethan had been looking for her and wondered why, but decided not to bring it up. "Thanks. Can I carry those for you?" I asked.

"Why do you think I came over here? As always, I have motives. I was hoping I could persuade you to help me with some things." She said with a chuckle and handed me the heavy box of books. She continued to stack additional books from her arms into mine until she was only holding her car keys.

I followed, struggling to keep up. For such a round little woman she was quite fast. Her short legs took two strides to my one and yet, I was still a few steps behind. A bead of sweat ran down my forehead, dripping onto a hardcover copy of *Deadly Ocean; An Educator's Guide to Adventure*. I smiled at the thought of Ms. Z battling sharks armed with nothing more than her yardstick.

"What is all this stuff?" I asked.

"You're not the only one leaving the school this year. I am starting a new job. I have to get everything out of the classroom." She took the books, tossing them into the back of her already overloaded car.

My heart dropped. The thought of her not being around had not crossed my mind until that very moment and it was upsetting.

"Where is your new job? Nearby I hope."

She ignored my question and changed the subject, which meant that it was probably not close to Bar Harbor. "What are you still doing here?"

Pausing for a minute to think, I wasn't sure what to say. "I was just trying to figure some things out."

"Anything I can help with?" She would have been concerned if she knew I was worried to go home. Clearly, it was a busy day for her. My issues didn't need to cloud her mind.

"I'm fine. Is there anything left in your classroom or is this the last load?"

"I have more," She said with a sigh. "Do you have time to stick around this afternoon?"

"Sure," I followed her into the school since the truth was; I had nothing but time. Earlier, all I wanted to do was go home. When faced with the reality, I found myself avoiding it for as long as possible.

We entered the school through the gymnasium doors, it was empty and our footsteps echoed as we walked across the gym. "We'll have to cut through the locker room and pool. The floor in the main hall is being polished."

"Okay," I said nervously.

We reached the pool door and the smell of water and chlorine filled my nose. The air was humid with the slightest scent of mildew. Ms. Z held the door open and I reluctantly stepped into the room. The heavy metal door slammed behind me and immediately I had to hold back a rush of panic.

Four years earlier was the first and last time I was in that pool. Despite the fact that my 9th grade guidance counselor had been warned about my water phobia, he still put swimming on my schedule. On the first day of swim class, as the rest of the girls gathered, shivering from the cold air and complaining that they were going to get their hair wet, I stood still and silent. Mr. Marsh our swimming instructor ordered everyone into the water. Gripping the edge of the pool tightly, I lowered my body in. At about waist deep, I blacked-out and sank to the bottom. Mr. Marsh had to dive in and save me from drowning. It only took 15 minutes for me to regain consciousness. During that rather short time, he went to my guidance counselor and demanded my schedule be changed. If the counselor had listened in the first place, the whole ordeal could have been avoided.

"You can't stay terrified of water forever." Ms. Z was standing across the pool deck, her voice echoed around the room. She knew my history. The school district hired her when I was in the 4th grade, the year my father died.

The water was clear and motionless. The mosaic at the bottom of the pool could be seen in its entirety; the design was created out of green, blue and white tiles. It featured a merman and a mermaid with their backs to each other appearing powerful and confident while battling a sea serpent. Their tails were crossed and their arms outstretched.

"There is no reason for me to go in water, other than to take a shower." I stepped closer to the pool, focusing on the mosaic. "Who are they?"

"They represent the Guardians of the Sea. Do you believe in the Legends of Merfolk?" Ms. Z asked.

"Do you mean mermen and mermaids?" I laughed a little. "Are you asking if I believe they used to exist?"

"No."

"Good because I was beginning to—"

She cut me off. "Do you believe they exist in the world we live in today?"

"Of course not," feeling the water's pull. "Can we go to your classroom now?"

She ignored my request to leave. "The Legend of the Guardians dates back over 3000 years. They, the ones you see featured in this mosaic were the last Guardians and that was almost 500 years ago. They brought great balance to the waters of the Earth. That balance lasted many years but sadly, due to much pollution and corruption in our world, the waters are no longer a peaceful place for marine life."

It was the craziest I had ever heard Ms. Z sound. I mean, she was a bit odd most of the time but this was a whole new level. She spoke as if it were all true. Well, I suppose the part about the world being polluted and corrupt was true. Believing in mermaids though, made *her* sound a bit out of *balance*.

She continued. "As you can see in the mosaic, the female Guardian is wearing a carcanet around her neck and the male Guardian has a cuff around his wrist. Both of these relics are said to be the most powerful on Earth and serve to enhance the Guardians already incredible gifts. Neither has been seen for centuries. From what my research tells me they are to be handed down from generation to generation in the form of a family heirloom, not taking their true form until new Guardians seek their power."

Ms. Z was in a trance, staring down at the mosaic intently, I half expected her eyes to start glowing and a prophecy to shoot out of her mouth. I could see the carcanet around the female figure's neck and the cuff around the male figure's wrist. The female held the Earth in the palm of her hand. She wore a green seashell bra and her hair was spread out in long blue swirls. The male held the Moon in the palm of his hand and the burst of bright white tiles that surrounded them both seemed to be emanating from his cuff. It was indeed a lovely design but it scared me to be that close to water and I wanted to leave. I began to walk towards the door.

"You know, Ms. Shedd, they say a new Guardian has been born with the Rune of the Sea?"

"No, I didn't know that," unsure of the exact meaning of a rune. I answered.

"Yes. If it is so, the first-born must find the second born and when that happens they will cleanse the waters and the land as well. They will protect all those loyal and destroy the enemies. Balance will again be restored."

I felt like laughing. Was she playing a joke on me? She sounded ridiculous. After a few moments of awkward silence, I tried to move us along. "Okay. Well, Ms. Z, we have a lot of work to do in your classroom, right?"

"Oh yes." She seemed to snap out of whatever deep thoughts had her captivated. "Let's get going."

We left the pool and walked through the empty hall to the biology classroom. She was back to normal as she explained our tasks for the afternoon. "I need to move my salt water tank across the hall and into Mr. Graham's lab. They've been with me for eight years. He had better keep those fish alive until I return." She had a bit of concern in her voice. Mr. Graham was a chemist, not a biologist. He usually wore a thick black apron and safety goggles. It was difficult to think Ms. Z's fish would be at the top of his "to-do" list. I reasoned that her job must have been very far if it meant she couldn't take her fish. Again, it upset me.

"Are you ready to help?" She asked.

"I guess," I answered.

"There are jars filled with salt water from the tank. I want you to grab one fish at a time and place them into the jars. Then we can drain the water from the tank into buckets, carry it across the hall and fill it back up. These little ones haven't been moved in 4 years, so we want to be very gentle. I don't like to use a net to catch them. It's so cruel. When I move them I use my hands, like this." She cupped her hands together and lowered them through the surface of the water, not a ripple was made.

The fish swam around her hands, inspecting and tickling with their fins. She giggled. "Not all at once, let's do this one at a time."

All but one of the fish backed away, like they heard her command. A black, white and yellow fish with a pointy snout made its way to her hands and waited as if it was in an elevator. She lifted and not a single drop of water fell to the ground. She walked with ease as the fish floated comfortably.

"Let's go Mr. Moore." She whispered to him.

"How are you doing that?" I asked. Still no drops of water fell.

"It's based on trust. He can sense that I mean him no harm." She held the fish over a jar and with a splash he jumped out of her hands and directly into the water.

"Incredible!" I squealed. "Mr. Moore?"

"Oh now Ms. Shedd, don't go feeding his ego. I don't know if calling him 'Incredible Mr. Moore' is going to help his already pompous attitude towards the other fish. They are all quite incredible once you get to know them." She was already loading another passenger into her hands. "Would you like to try?"

"No, I meant what you did was incredible. I mean, Mr. Moore was incredible too but the situation as a whole…well, I don't think I can do that Ms. Z. I would feel awful if I dropped a fish."

"Oh nonsense, I think you'll be fine. Now, bring yourself over here."

I could already feel my hands sweating. I cupped them together just like she instructed and lowered them into the tank. Ripples spread across the surface of the water and the fish scattered, hiding behind their little ceramic ship wreck and treasure chest.

"Now, give Ms. Shedd a chance. If you get up close, you will find that she is a very good friend." Ms. Z spoke like the fish could hear her every word and, oddly enough, the fish responded.

The smallest of three clown fish wiggled its way into my hands. I didn't know how but I understood that it was scared. First it bumped the side of my hand with its tail and then tickled the inside of my finger with its fin. It looked up at me and I glanced over to Ms. Z, she was smiling.

"I would like you to meet Penelope. She is one of the sweetest little clown fish I have ever had the pleasure of caring for."

"Uh, it's nice to meet you Penelope," laughing nervously.

"She likes you. She's ready to go when you are. Carefully lift her straight up—a little slower. Yes, just like that." Ms. Z cheered me on with more excitement than I expected.

Penelope felt bizarre in my hands. I could sense a little of her anxiety, or maybe I was imagining it. My hands were cupped and my fingers tight. Very little water dropped and, surprisingly, Penelope knew exactly what to do. She jumped right into a salt water filled mason jar.

We moved the rest of the fish into the jars, one at a time. Then we emptied the water from the tank into several large buckets. Ms. Z talked to the fish like they were her best friends; she explained each one of their personalities in detail.

After we emptied most of the water into the buckets, she and I brought the tank across the hallway into Mr. Graham's classroom. Together we carried the heavy buckets of salt water, pouring them into the tank. When it came time to return the fish, we put each jar into the water. I found it disappointing that we were not going to carry them by hand back to the tank. She explained that they needed to ease into the water slowly, at their own pace. So we put the jars in and waited. I watched as one at a time, starting with Mr. Moore, the fish swam out of their jars and into the open water of the tank. We sat, studying the fish for a while, giggling as they swam up to the sides of the tank to inspect the new classroom.

That afternoon had been so much fun and for the first time I realized how much I was going to miss school. School, along with Ms. Z, was the only constants in my life and I grew scared thinking about how uncertain my future was.

TWO

"Aunt Doreh, where are you?" A voice came from across the hall.

"I'm in here. You're a little late." Ms. Z shouted.

His voice grew louder and more excited before he appeared in the doorway. "You will never believe it, I did a dive on the Southern shore and guess who I—", a young man walked into Mr. Graham's room. His shoulders were back, his face held a look of enthusiasm. When he noticed me, all passion drained from his voice. "Uh—I'll have to tell you about it later."

I kept my eyes down and twiddled my fingers.

"Seraphin Shedd, I would like you to meet my nephew," she paused for a moment like she had forgotten his name. "Joseph Merrick."

"Nice to meet you," glancing at him. To my horror, he met my eyes. I stared back, waiting for a greeting. His eyes, ice blue, quickly changed to navy. I blinked—questioning the color shift that occurred.

Finally, he looked at Ms. Z and did something quite unexpected—he left the room. Turning the corner into the hallway, he mumbled to himself, "Why would she do that?"

Ms. Z shrugged her shoulders and smiled an unconvincing smile. "He's a little shy I guess. I'll be right back. Can you stack the buckets while I'm gone and put the top on the tank? I think we're about done here." She walked out and the sound of their footsteps moved further down the hall.

I did what Ms. Z asked then decided it was time to leave. I wrote a short note explaining how much I appreciated her as a teacher and thanked her for the fun afternoon. The thought of not seeing her daily was becoming too much to bear. I knew I had to be careful to not dwell on those emotions though or my mind would go into shut down mode.

Just as I was about to leave, she came back with Joseph and I did my best to dispel signs of weakness. For some reason, I did not want to show any fault in front of him.

He walked into the room with a sour look on his face. I ignored him and went to Ms. Z. "I should be leaving. I left a note for you on your desk." I was trying my best to avoid Joseph. However he made that difficult by picking up the note I left for Ms. Z and reading it. "That is not for you." Anger crept its way into my voice, which was surprising.

"Well, I know you must have lots of things to do this afternoon Ms. Shedd, but I would love to buy you lunch. Besides, you can think of it as a small payment for all your hard work today. I don't know what I would have done without you. Joseph was supposed to help me but he was temporarily detained." Ms. Z walked over to Joseph and took the note away from him. Not once did she take her attention off of me.

"Oh, that's alright, you don't have to repay me. I'm sure I'll be around, maybe we can do lunch another day?" I was uncomfortable around Joseph; he gave off a weird vibe. I felt as if he hated me from the moment we met, which was only about 12 minutes prior.

"Actually, I won't be around. My new job is taking me far from the coasts of Maine. Please let me take you to lunch." She pleaded. My fear of Ms. Z no longer being close was confirmed and I felt my expression fall. Heat surged through my body and I tried desperately to blink back the tears associated.

My eyes met Joseph's. "Don't worry, I'm not going," as if he could read my mind.

"I guess that will be fine then," relieved. "Should we walk over to the diner?"

"Yes," she smiled and found her purse. "Joseph, please finish taking those boxes out to my car."

"Sure." He sighed.

※

Ms. Z and I walked to the diner across the street from the high school. The food was never great and I always felt like they had way too many tables for such a little space. The service was always horrible too, but it was close and within walking distance. It was a frequent spot for students to hang out. Ethan and his group of friends were always at the diner; I hardly ever had a reason to eat there.

"Ms. Z, what's wrong with Joseph? I mean—I don't know him but—well, I get the feeling he hates me."

"Joseph is a very sweet young man—"

I cut her off. "I'm sorry. I shouldn't have said anything."

"You didn't let me finish. He's a very sweet young man *but* he lives a complicated life. It's hard for him to meet people. I'm sure he'll warm up to you, once he gets to know you."

"Oh, I'm not planning on spending much time with him. I mean, I doubt we'll even see each other again."

Ms. Z shrugged, "You never know who will end up in your life."

As we approached the diner a few families were leaving after celebrating with their recent graduates. Some former students stopped to talk to Ms. Z. I didn't know them, of course. No one said a word to me. I watched as the mother of a girl put her arm around her daughter. The girl reached up and placed her hand on top of her mother's hand. It was a simple gesture that represented so much. Out of everything missing in my life, sometimes the thing I missed the most is the one thing I never had.

Ms. Z continued talking outside while I went in to get a table. The diner was full of families and if it struck anyone odd that I was alone, no one showed it. There was only one empty booth so I sat in it. The waiter immediately came over to take my drink order but I told him to come back because someone else would be joining me.

About 10 minutes passed before I started to get a little annoyed at how long Ms. Z was taking. After 15 minutes the waiter came back and asked if I knew what time my guest would be arriving. I told him she was standing outside talking. We both looked up when we heard the ding of the diner door but instead of Ms. Z walking in it was a tall thin middle-aged woman with white hair in a braid that hung down past her waist. She was wearing a long black leather jacket and tall black boots. She was as overdressed as she could possibly be considering the temperature that day. We watched as the woman walked around all the tables in the diner and then left. The waiter asked if that was my guest. I shook my head.

I reasoned that Ms. Z might have been stuck in one of those situations where the person wouldn't stop talking and there was no way to end the conversation politely. I thought about several different ways to get her into the diner. Deciding that if I went outside and politely told her that I had already gotten us a table it might help her out of whatever talk-a-holic had trapped her. So, after 20 minutes of waiting, I went to rescue her. To my surprise, there was no one. I walked around; circling the perimeter of the diner, but Ms. Z was nowhere to be found. I came back inside, thinking that perhaps somehow we had missed each other. I checked both the men's and the women's restrooms along with the kitchen and still could not find her.

The white noise of the diner started to sound like the ocean and as I stood in the middle of the room I found myself fighting a blackout. *Stay here,* I told myself. I rushed out the door. I was still struggling to keep my mind in the present tense when my car pulled up; the roar of the engine shook me. In the driver's seat was Joseph, Ms. Z's nephew. He reached across the car and opened the passenger door.

"Get in." He demanded.

"What is going on?" I stood next to my car, not sure whether to obey or not.

"Just get in." He looked nervous as he glanced in the rear-view mirror. "Listen, I'm trying to help here. You need to get in the car. I don't know if they saw you with my aunt or not." He was yelling and people were coming out of the diner behind me. I got in the car, against my better judgment, because I didn't want to cause a scene.

For some time, we were both silent, I was afraid to ask what happened to Ms. Z. I can't explain how I knew; maybe it was because I expect things to go wrong. Something on his face told me that there was a problem. He glanced at me a few times, expecting me to say something but I couldn't come up with any words.

Finally he spoke. "You can't go back to the school, so where should I take you?"

"I don't know you and I'm not exactly fond of you…" I paused, thinking of whether or not I should finish the sentence, "driving my car."

"This is your car? Lucky guess, huh?"

"Yes it's my car!" I raised my voice.

"Good, so I'm in no danger of being called a thief…" he paused, "…again."

I was angry and confused; finally, all I wanted to do was get to my house. "Take me to wherever Ms. Z went, so I can drop you off and go home."

"I can't take you to my aunt. She's gone."

"She's gone? Oh, that makes perfect sense. The woman asks me out to lunch and then leaves. She must have had better plans." I said sarcastically.

"No. She's just gone." He sounded troubled. "This doesn't concern you. Where do you want me to take you?"

"Doesn't concern me? You have got to be kidding. One minute I was waiting to have lunch with my teacher, now, all of the sudden she is gone with no explanation. Then you pull up, *in my car* and tell me that you're going to drop me off somewhere." My voice grew louder. "How about you drop me off somewhere between 20 to 30 minutes ago so I can figure out what happened? Oh and you can leave my car and walk back to the present. Does that sound like a plan?"

"Trust me; you don't want to be a part of this so just tell me where I can bring you. I don't need your car. I could have just left you at the diner but I thought my aunt would want me to make sure you were okay. I'm trying to be nice here."

There was a long awkward silence. Joseph pulled over in an empty parking lot, reached under the dashboard and turned the car off. "Can I have your keys?"

I realized that I had been holding my keys the entire time. "Did you hotwire my car?" It occurred to me that I was alone with a complete stranger who knew how to hotwire a car and it scared me a little. I trusted Ms. Z and I didn't think she would intentionally put me in harms way, but there was something about Joseph that was unsettling.

"I needed to come and get you. Besides, I didn't know it was your car so, don't take it personally. It won't damage anything. I do this all the time." He said.

"That's what worries me. Can I just drop you off somewhere instead? Honestly, I'm fine. I just want to get home." I said nervously.

"I'll take you home," he demanded.

"NO," I refused.

"Really, I should. My aunt would want me to." He insisted.

Trying to convince him, "You understand that I just met you, right?"

"Yes. You understand that the woman you were about to have lunch with is my aunt and she just disappeared in a matter of minutes, right? You understand that perhaps there is more going on here than you could possibly comprehend, right? You understand that I am trying to get you home safe, right?" His blue eyes pierced me and my body felt numb.

I did understand. I handed him my keys. "My house is at 504 Briarwood Court."

"Thank you." He said and started the car.

Joseph knew his way around Bar Harbor. No words were spoken for the remaining 10-minute drive. He kept his eyes on the road while I stared out the window as we passed the familiar neighborhoods. Spring had been generous with rain; the grass was lush and green. When we turned down Briarwood Court my heart skipped. I was terrified but excited. The street was lined with dogwood trees in full bloom; white petals filled the branches that swayed in the summer breeze.

For a moment, nothing else mattered; not Ms. Z or the stranger who was driving. The only thing that mattered was my home, ahead in the distance. I could see the butter-cream yellow, cedar shingles and the large white columns on the front porch. The house was beautiful; an east coast treasure is how my father used to refer to it. For a moment, my grandmother was driving the car and I was beside her. For a moment, my father was driving the car and I was beside him. For a moment I was happy again.

He pulled the car into the driveway of my house—it was weird to think of it as mine, but it was. Grandma left the house to me.

Joseph turned the ignition off and we sat in silence. It didn't take long for dread to overtake my brief moment of happiness.

My house should have been filled with my family but all of them were gone, all of them were dead.

Joseph was speaking but I couldn't understand him. The last things I saw were his brilliant sapphire eyes.

I blacked out.

THREE

When I woke, I was lying on my couch. The sun had gone down and only the glow from the streetlight illuminated the living room. A breeze blew from an open window next to my father's old leather chair. The salty ocean air was refreshing. I was unsure of the time or how long my mind had been in the past. The flashback was more intense— I could hear my father's voice so clearly that even after I woke; it remained with me.

White sheets covered most of the furnishings in the house. Spiders had begun to make themselves at home with webs that hung from the crown moldings and fireplace sconces. The air was musky and a thin layer of dust lay atop every surface. On the wooden floor, one set of footprints remained in the dust. The prints lead to the couch and back out the front door. Joseph must have carried me in and then left. For the most part I was relieved that I didn't have to deal with him, but a fraction of me felt sad that I was truly alone.

I went to the back deck for some fresh air then made my way down towards the beach. The hill was overgrown with tall sea grass and the old path I used to run along with my father was buried under years of neglect. The only light was from the half crescent moon in the sky but I didn't need much more than that, I knew the way. The small patch of beach that belonged to the house was littered with branches and weeds, remnants of a harsh Maine winter. Sharp angles shot through the surface from broken glass bottles and the white shape of a Styrofoam container added a stark contrast against the darker wet sand.

The tide was low. It was something I was used to, something I grew up watching. When I was younger, I was able to predict the high and low tide cycles. Since I wasn't allowed in the ocean, low tide was my only chance to collect polished sea glass and shells. My charting of the tides proved to be useless once I stopped going down there. Usually the tide would pull further out in the morning and come back in the evening, filling in all the valleys and covering the rock paths that led into the water. That night, all the valleys and rock paths were exposed. It was unusual. I stared at the wet sand. The day my father died the tide was high, higher than usual. As I sat on the beach watching my friends play I remember feeling as though the ocean was closing in, creeping to grab me.

When my grandmother took me to a therapist after he died, I told him about the way the ocean crept up. He gave me a scientific explanation of that day having a Super Perigee Moon, which meant that the moon was closest to the Earth. He said that the tides were higher because of it.

I took off my sandals and wandered onto the fresh wet sand. It was smooth and cool. I could already feel the ocean pulling. That was another thing I told my therapist. Of course, he didn't believe it but it was true, water pulled at me like an invisible force. He gave me a psychological explanation though, instead of a scientific one. The theory was that I had a fascination with something that had been forbidden. At times, I thought he was the crazy one. I felt it in every inch of my body; the water was trying to pull me in. I resisted the urge.

Staring across the sand, I saw a tiny fin lift and fall. A fish had been stranded on the beach when the tide pulled out. It was something I would see often as a child. Usually I would run to get my father or grandmother, but there was no one to run to that night. It was gasping and dying and needed water, the air was killing it. The fish in Ms. Z's room came to mind; they were safe, away from the unpredictable ocean. The fish pounded at the sand with its fin, I felt it dying. Hurrying to the fish, I picked it up; its scales were rough and cut into my hands. It was a silver fish with yellow stripes. It needed the water but I froze, unable to go further. The fish lay in my hands, the gills lifting, reaching; I felt her hope vanish when she knew I couldn't save her. Her eye met mine and I started to scream.

"Help, she's dying." I called louder. "HELP, please someone, HELP her." I knelt down with the little fish in my hands, knowing she could not be saved, realizing that my fear was killing her. "I'm so sorry. I can't get any closer. I'm so sorry you have to die because of me."

Then I felt it, the tide began to come in; closer and closer with every wave, it rose. The ocean was answering my call for help but at what cost? Within seconds the water was surrounding, covering my legs; at my waist; up to my chest; then I was under and I felt the little fish swim away. The water was cold and hard against my skin. It pulled at me; deeper and deeper I sank. I screamed out to nothing.

Panic raced through my body, but before I could fall unconscious, my legs lifted from the sand and my head came out of the water. I cried loudly. The sand was hard on the backs of my legs as someone pulled me across the beach to safety.

"Will you stop screaming? You are going to wake up the world." Joseph Merrick was standing over me, his sandy blonde hair sticking up in every direction. Water dripped from his face and onto his bare chest. He was bent over, squeezing his shorts. Despite looking incredibly annoyed, I couldn't help but notice how striking he was. "What were you trying to do? It's a little late for surfing, don't you think?"

"The tide came up so fast and I didn't know what to do." I was panting and embarrassed. My shirt clung to me and my legs were covered with sand. I reached up to smooth my hair, only to find that a large twig was tangled in it.

"I don't know what's going on with the tide. I noticed it came up quick too. Though, did swimming ever occur to you? Or how about just standing up? Most people would have stood up and walked out of the water." He said sarcastically, smiling. Dimples dented his cheeks. "What is with you anyway? You pass out in the car, out cold. Then I find you screaming in the ocean for no good reason."

"There was a reason." I said defensively, still trying to untangle the twig from my long knotted hair. "There was a dying fish. It needed my help."

"A dying fish? That's it? That's what all the screaming was about?" He chuckled, and then with a big sigh plopped down onto the sand next to me. He playfully spread himself out as if he were making snow angels. "SO WHAT! Let it die next time and eat it for dinner. Isn't that what your kind does?"

Not understanding what he meant, "My kind?"

"Carnivores," his eyes were wide. "You nearly gave me a heart attack. I thought something had happened to you."

He was wrong. "I'm a vegetarian, so eating her was out of the question. And, something did happen to me. I am deathly afraid of water because of something that happened to me as a child. Please don't mock me." I was irritated with his teasing and even though he had quite possibly saved my life, I wasn't at all flattered by his concern for my safety. "What are you still doing here?"

"I'm still here because, against my better judgment, I wasn't going to leave a helpless young lady passed out in her driveway." He had a smirk across his face. "Usually when a hero rescues a damsel in distress, he gets a thank you. Next time you're having a panic attack in 4 feet of water, I will be sure to just let you drown."

I stood, brushing the wet sand from my legs. "I'm sorry to inconvenience you with my helplessness."

Joseph continued lying on the sand. "Hey, apology accepted. Don't you worry about it; I won't waste another minute helping someone so ungrateful. As a matter of fact, I can't fathom why my aunt wasted so much time on *you*." He mumbled, just barely loud enough for me to hear.

"What is that supposed to mean?" I had started to walk back to the hill but stopped and turned around. His words cut through me.

"It means, her time would have been better spent, elsewhere. For some reason she wanted to be at *that* school, with *you*." He sat up, staring at the water.

Maybe it stung because it was the truth? Ms. Z did spend an inordinate amount of time with me and maybe I took advantage of it. I went to her with every concern or complaint I had and she was always willing to give me her full attention. She never mentioned Joseph and conceivably that had something to do with our one-sided conversations. I knew very little about her and up until that moment didn't seem to mind. Suddenly, I wanted to know everything about her.

"Speaking of Ms. Z, shouldn't you be looking for her? Or maybe reporting her lost? Perhaps your time could be better spent?" My words were rude.

"I'm sure it could, besides, she's not lost. I know exactly where she is. I just don't know how to get to her." He put his head down, resting his forehead on his knees. His voice was distant and softer when he spoke again. "You know Seraphin; you're not the only one in this world with problems. Most people I know have something in their past that haunts them, that makes them want to forget who they are. But they move on, they keep going so it won't catch up to them and overwhelm *their* every waking moment, like it seems to do with *you*."

"I know people have problems—I mean I don't let…it's not like that at all." My fists tightened.

"I'm just stating my observations. Maybe you're not like that but it sure seems like you've got something deep that you're not willing to let go of. I'm no shrink but I have spent plenty of time with troubled people to know when I'm in the presence of one." Lifting his head and clenching his jaw—a stern look crossed his face.

The temperature dropped and the wind began to blow in from the water. Wet hair lifted gently off my shoulders—caught in the passing gusts.

I was speechless—which was a good thing because if I spoke my voice would have fractured with pain. How could someone I barely know cut me so profoundly with words? Joseph was angry, but at who? It couldn't have been at me, we had just met.

He rose turning his back to me.

My head wanted to argue but my heart was too tired. Struggling to maintain composure, I chose my words carefully. "You're right, it consumes me. Grief wraps itself around me so tight at times I can't breathe. How does it feel to be right? Do you feel better about the way you hide from your problems?" I knew it was bold and as I said it I felt a swell of adrenaline climb.

His response didn't matter, so I didn't wait for it. I decided that I needed no help feeling miserable. The reason I let Ms. Z into my life was because she never once made me feel the way that perfect stranger had. There are plenty of people that can make me suffer, I lived with one for 5 months. Mara Cottington was ruthless in her opinion but I knew she was hurting so I accepted it. Joseph was doing the same but he was a stranger and I only owed him a few words.

"Thank you for helping me." I whispered, walking away and I meant it.

He started to speak but I continued up the hill, I didn't want to know what he was saying. I was through with that conversation.

FOUR

I sat on the back deck with a cup of warm tea. Part of me expected to see Joseph still lying on the beach. I replayed our conversation in my head and was grateful to have remained conscious despite my building anger.

He *was* complicated, Ms. Z had been correct.

My stomach was growling. I hadn't eaten anything in almost 24 hours. Luckily, Keyes Market was only a few blocks down the street. The morning was beautiful and inviting. My bike was in the shed. The tires were deflated so I inflated them with the foot pump. I secured a basket to the handlebars for carrying groceries. As I passed through the ivy arch that separated my front walk from the back yard the sun seemed to shine brighter and the noise from the neighborhood's bustling occupants was more intense. It was energizing to be home.

The market was busy and filled with familiar faces. When I walked in Alexander Keyes, the owner of the store, yelled down an aisle. "Seraphin, my dear! Is that really you?"

"Mr. Keyes, it's nice to be back in the neighborhood." And it was. I missed being home and if I had to be somewhere without my family, I suppose that was better than most. I loaded my arms with as much as the basket on my bike could carry. The checkout line was long and as I waited a few neighbors smiled, waved and welcomed me back home. Mr. Keyes stood beside me, talking for the duration of the wait.

"The store is celebrating its 20th anniversary in August. We're having an Anniversary Gala at the Beach Club and I'd love for you to come." He was a friendly man who wore a white apron over a yellow Keyes Market t-shirt; the same outfit he'd been wearing for 20 years. "Shall I put you down for one or two?"

I questioned, "One or two, what?"

"Surely you'll want to bring a date; there will be dinner and dancing," he moved his shoulders to imaginary music.

"Just one," I assured him.

"I'll mark you down for two, just in case. A lovely young lady like you will surely find a nice gentleman in the next few months." He smiled and nudged me with his elbow.

I didn't argue further. At the mention of 'a nice gentleman', Joseph entered my thoughts but I quickly dismissed the idea.

"What do you have planned for the summer?" He asked.

"I'm not too sure. I just graduated yesterday but I am probably going to have to pick up a summer job and then maybe think about college in the fall." I said.

"You can't be old enough to graduate already, I remember you as a toddler coming in here with Sam. He would have bought you the whole candy stand if he had enough money in his wallet." At the mention of my father I felt sad. I dropped my eyes, hoping Mr. Keyes couldn't read my expression but it was too late, he caught on. He put his arm around me. "Seraphin, I miss him too. Your father was a wonderful man and it's alright to remember him that way. It's healthy to talk about him once in a while."

"I know." I swallowed hard. The entire neighborhood knew my father and loved him, which made it a perfect place to live. He used to say 'it takes a tribe to raise a child' and I guess those people were my tribe. In a way, they did help to raise me. He was working a lot and as I rode my bike up and down their driveways and ran across their front yards, they influenced me more than I knew. I didn't have any aunts, uncles or cousins. I only had my neighbors.

"If you're interested, my wife is looking to fill cleaning positions on the CORE campus where she works. Would you be interested in chatting with her?" He moved the conversation away from my father and I was grateful.

When I returned home I found that clearing my head was a difficult feat. I worried about Ms. Z. The day before was a blur. After pondering it, I decided to drive back to the school to take a look around.

The parking lot was empty except for Ms. Z's car, still loaded with books and boxes. My stomach dropped. She was missing. I thought about calling the police but I didn't know how to explain what happened. Joseph seemed to be genuinely concerned for her and he was after all, her family. *Perhaps he had already gone to the police?* Though, I doubted it. He seemed like the type to take matters into his own hands.

I walked the perimeter of the building and found nothing unusual. As I came from behind the school a black SUV pulled in and parked next to my car. Hiding behind the building, I immediately wished I hadn't gone there. A large man with no hair and a tattoo across his cheek climbed out of the vehicle. He wore a black leather vest with black pants and boots. Right away, I thought of the woman at the diner. *Was it a new fashion trend; black leather in the middle of summer?* Around his neck was a key hanging from a chain. It struck me as an odd thing to wear. He got into Ms. Z's car. Both vehicles pulled away leaving mine alone in the lot. A few minutes passed before it felt safe to come out. I ran to my car and quickly left, unsure of what I had just witnessed.

While driving home I glanced in the rearview mirror every few seconds. At a stoplight I thought I saw the SUV behind me, which took my attention off the car in front of me. With only a second to spare, I slammed on the brakes, stopping just inches away from a collision. Turns out, there was no SUV. Knowing I had to calm down and wanting to get home, I drove faster than the speed limit. If I got pulled over, at least it would have given me a reason to report Ms. Z's disappearance. I arrived home without incident, which just proves there's never a police officer around when you *want* to be caught.

As evening fell, I caught myself peering through the windows, looking down the street. Every time a car door slammed, I would check. Worried it would be the man from the school and hoping it was Joseph. At least, if he appeared, I could tell him about the man in Ms. Z's car.

To occupy my mind, I began cleaning and organizing the house. I knew that my father's room would be a challenge so I avoided it, cleaning the rest of the rooms first. My bedroom was how I left it; neat and organized. I wiped the dust from my dresser and cleaned the mirror on the vanity. As I caught my reflection in the mirror it was obvious that life was beginning to take a toll. A good night's rest was a foreign luxury and under my eyes, dark circles had started to form. No longer was I the little girl my father left behind. I often wondered if he could see me from wherever he was or if he'd recognize me if ever we met again.

My eyes are big and shades of gray, they are set wide apart, like a fish. When I was young my father said my eyes were fierce but calm, like the delicate forewarning of an approaching storm. In other words, I was a walking storm cloud.

When I actually did something with my hair, it was nice. Mostly, it was tied in a knotted mess on the top of my head. I rarely ever wore it down though that was how my father preferred it. Grandma used to braid it or pull it back and my father would let it down first chance he had.

Taking the hair tie out, I let it fall, shaking it with my fingers. It touched the middle of my back. I began brushing through it, my head jerked as I tried to smooth the tangles. Not only did the house need cleaning up, I did too; I had been neglecting myself for 8 years. When I thought about seeing Joseph the day before, looking that tired and worn out, I was a little embarrassed. He struck me as handsome and if he wasn't so annoying and rude—*maybe if I looked better, he might have*—I didn't allow myself to finish the thought.

Finally, I summoned enough emotional stability to go into my father's bedroom. After his death, I had trouble going into his room; all of his belongings still remained. My grandmother refused to get rid of any of his things, she felt like one day he would come home.

For a while, I sat, afraid to touch anything. Slowly, I began perusing the room. On the dresser, a half-empty bottle of cologne, I opened it and took a deep breath, closing my eyes. Chills went through me, the scent of his cologne made me remember and long for him.

Inside the top drawer was a neatly rolled pile of white socks, I took a pair out and put them on my feet. It was something I used to do as a child during the long Maine winter nights. My father would laugh when I pulled them up past my knees. They still were too large and I giggled at the two inches of extra fabric that extended past my toes.

It was hard to believe he was gone. Perhaps if I had attended a funeral it would have seemed real. His body was never found but the men who were on the ship gave first hand accounts of what happened. They all agreed he could have never survived the wave that washed him overboard, but I couldn't believe that he was lost forever. It was Grandma's problem as well. My therapist told me that I had to believe or I would never escape my flashbacks. I didn't know what the better way of living was. Both seemed pretty lousy.

In his closet hung a row of shirts and jackets, untouched for 8 years. I shuffled, still wearing the socks. Taking one of the jackets off the hanger, I put it on. It may have been my imagination but I think it still carried a little of his scent. Dressing in his oversized clothing, oddly enough, made me feel like his arms were again wrapped around me. Lying back, I slid my hands into the pockets of the jacket. In the right pocket, a crumpled ferry ticket from Northeast Harbor and assorted candy wrappers; from the last time we went to Great Cranberry Island. I smiled a little at the memory. In the left pocket, I found a crumpled piece of paper. Neatly written with my father's hand, a poem spread across the page; I read it out loud.

Where the land lay low,
the seeds best grow;
let die the life I hide from you.
Protect you as a father must,
into that world you'll not be thrust.

As to the meaning of the words, I did not know. I folded the paper carefully, placing it on a shelf, under a framed photo of the two of us.

༶

For the next few days sleeping seemed to be a battle and when I did doze, I had the same disturbing dream—I was in a tunnel, worried and confused. A man was there. I didn't want to leave him. We were in danger.

It stormed frequently that week. Thunder repeatedly shook me from a slumber. One night after lying in bed for hours, unable to sleep, I wandered onto the deck for fresh air. Down on the beach I saw a silhouette; it looked like Joseph but when I called out, there was no one.

FIVE

I interviewed with Mr. Keyes' wife, Tabitha Keyes, and she hired me. My new job was working for the Coastal Oceanic Research Expeditions or CORE, as a cleaning person. CORE employed the largest collection of marine biologists on the east coast. The company was known for the millions they donated each year to clean up pollution and preserve marine life in the Atlantic Ocean.

Mrs. Keyes was the Superintendent of Living Environments or the SOLE, which was a fancy way of saying she was head housekeeper. My official title was, Maintainer of Living Environments, or a MOLE, which was an annoying way of saying I was a maid. Apparently, CORE loved using acronyms.

I was given the option to commute or live on campus; I chose to commute since it was dreadful to think of living anywhere other than my house. There was a small problem. The only way to get to the CORE campus, located on the Great Cranberry Island, happened to be via water ferry from Northeast Harbor. It had been over 8 years since I had been on that trip. It was going to be hard to find the courage to travel over water everyday. I kept promising myself that it would be no big deal.

The first day of work, when I arrived at Northeast Harbor, people were already boarding the ferry. As they climbed on board, it rocked back and forth and I wondered how everyone was keeping their balance. Waves slammed into the bow, splashing water onto the deck.

The ferry was old and the paint on the side was chipping and faded. I didn't want to disappoint Mrs. Keyes, by not showing up for work, but I began to doubt my ability to set foot on the ferry, let alone ride it all the way across the Gulf. And then there was the return ride I'd have to face later. The water was visible through the wood boards of the pier and I found myself staring, feeling nervous and confused.

"Phin," someone was beside me. It was a welcomed distraction. I glanced up to see Ethan Cottington looking down at the wood boards of the pier. "See anything interesting down there?"

"Ethan! What are you doing here? I thought you would be on your way to Michigan by now." I welcomed the distraction. Of course, I would have welcomed a swamp monster if it had helped to take my mind off of the rickety ferry.

"Ms. Z convinced my Mom to let me join the summer research program at CORE." He was wearing a backpack and he had two suitcases. "My parents usually send me away every summer so they can go on a Mediterranean cruise. It was easy for them to let me do this. I'll be out of their hair."

"That's why you were looking for her?"

"Yeah! Ms. Z is the best. She said that if I did well this summer, maybe CORE would sponsor me like they do for exchange students. That way I could finish my senior year here in Maine." At our mention of Ms. Z my stomach knotted.

"So you found her at the school, after graduation?"

"No. I couldn't find her. I was totally starting to panic and I needed to stall. So, I made my mom take me to the diner for lunch. It was a shot in the dark but I was hoping Ms. Z would be there. Luckily when we pulled in the parking lot, she was standing outside. It was awesome; she arranged the whole thing from my Mom's cell phone. It took her 5 minutes to get me a spot on the team—called this dude named Jay Mason." Ethan was beaming with excitement. I, on the other hand was terrified. He was one of the last people to see her.

"I was in the diner waiting to have lunch with her." I said in disbelief wanting to tell him the truth about her disappearance but instead holding back the information.

"No way, cool! She didn't tell you about how she hooked me up?"

"No." I said quietly. "Was anyone around when you were talking to her?"

"I don't think so," he tried to recall.

"I didn't see you. I went outside looking—to get Ms. Z," I caught myself before I revealed too much.

"My Mom wanted to get me checked into a hotel so she could get on the road. I've been staying at the Harbor Inn downtown the past few days. That place rocks. Did you know they have a pool that is part inside and part outside? Plus a free breakfast buffet every morning?"

"Oh yeah? I heard that place was nice. So…" trying to direct the conversation back to Ms. Z. "You didn't see anyone?"

"No one was with her—but there was a creepy biker looking chick in all black with white hair. She walked past us in the parking lot. My Mom yelled at me for making fun of how ridiculous she looked wearing leather from head to toe on such a hot day."

That was it! Maybe the woman in all black was connected to Ms. Z's disappearance. I wondered if Joseph had gotten far with his investigation. I wished I could contact him so I could tell him what I knew. "I saw her too. She came into the diner and left without eating. She did look ridiculous."

"Right? I know! My Mom is such a bummer sometimes." He was going to say something else but stopped and instead glanced around the dock. "You didn't answer my question. Are you in the research program too?"

"I'm not." I said, feeling slightly ashamed to tell him I was part of the cleaning crew. "I take it you're staying on campus?"

"They have rooms for us on land but most of the summer we're going to be on the research vessels, out at sea. It's going to be awesome! I think a bunch of my friends are signed up too, though I don't see anyone I know, besides you."

"Out at sea, for how long?"

"Jay, the guy who got me in, said we could be out there for up to three weeks." Ethan said excitedly.

I couldn't imagine being at sea, surrounded by nothing but water, what a nightmare.

A loud clank came from the ferry and with a big plume of smoke the engine started. Ethan picked up his suitcases. "Let's go before they take off without us."

"Uh, Ethan, I don't mean to be clingy but boats—well, anything that has to do with water makes me really uneasy. Can I sit by you? And can we make those seats as far away from the edge as possible?"

"Sure, I don't care." He stepped onto the ferry, put his suitcases down and held his hand for me to grab. I literally had to step over the edge and into the boat. "How are you going to work for CORE if you're scared of water?"

"I guess I'll just stay on land." Of course, that would be easier said than done.

We took our seats in the center of the ferry. I was terrified of the water, but even more so, I was terrified of blacking out and having another flashback. Ethan put his headphones on and was no help.

I tried to distract myself from the unsettling water with happy memories of my father. The last time I was on the ferry, it was with my father. He and I would ride to Great Cranberry Island when I was young. We would spend the day picking low-bush cranberries. I had a basket that my grandmother gave me and we wouldn't leave until it was full. Dad always knew where to look for the best cranberries. The plant itself was only about an inch tall and the berries were quite small.

I had become very familiar with the group of islands during my childhood. There were five islands, but only two were inhabited year round. The largest of the islands was Great Cranberry, which is where CORE set up headquarters. It was no more than two miles long and only a mile wide.

When we reached the island, I breathed a sigh of relief. Ethan took off as soon as he spotted one of his friends. I wasn't surprised. I checked in for my cleaning job and was assigned a locker along with a stack of uniforms. The standard issue, as a MOLE, was a plain green shirt. The embroidered emblem in the corner top left of the shirt read "CORE MOLE."

The CORE campus covered most of the island. A few weeks prior to graduation, I heard Mara Cottington gossiping with her neighbors about how the company had taken over the entire island—she was right. Most of the locals moved and their properties were demolished to make room for more campus housing and bike trails.

The eastern coastline of the island was lined with docks where large research vessels were anchored. Some of the vessels were a few stories high and one even had a swimming pool on deck. We toured all 6 of CORE's vessels. They were magnificent with full laboratories for the biologists. The two largest ships, named *George Washington* and *Theodore Roosevelt*, were even equipped with water filtration systems that turned salt water into fresh water for drinking. Those two ships were used for the extended research expeditions with big crews. They were so large, in fact, that I wasn't as nervous as I thought I would be touring them. For the most part it felt like I was still on land and not on a ship.

The ferry ride back to Northeast Harbor was a different story, I was nervous. Only a few people were on board, since most were living on campus. I blacked out halfway through the ride but the Captain didn't realize it until we docked. Everyone else thought I had fallen asleep. It didn't last very long and when I came to I was laying on the wooden pier with strangers surrounding me, perched over like they were looking down a hole in the ground. Actually, falling down a hole in the ground would have been much less embarrassing. It was horrible and after assuring everyone that I didn't need an ambulance, I went home.

My house was a sight for sore eyes. I was glad to be home; so glad in fact that I feared I was turning into a hermit. After a hot shower and a warm bowl of noodles, I went straight to bed. The day's events were slightly exhausting and I slept great.

SIX

The sun was just beginning to rise over the Atlantic and the June air wasn't unbearable, yet. My alarm still had an hour before it would sound but I was wide-awake. Instead of staying in bed, I went for a jog before work.

There was a trail that ran between the neighborhoods but when I reached it, it was overcrowded with people walking their dogs and pushing their children in strollers. Wanting something less crowded, I opted for a more remote trail that my father and I used to walk. It followed the coastline just a half-mile south of the neighborhood. It took me a while to find it but when I did, it was exactly how I remembered it. The tree branches stretched out like a canopy over head. Lush green ferns lined the way. The ground was damp from the dew and more than once I slipped on the mud. Once I had gone about a quarter mile my muscles warmed up and I was more confident in my stride. The waves below pounded at the rocky coast. It was very peaceful to hear nothing but the water, the birds singing and my heart beating.

I felt strong, like I could run forever. As I rounded a bend in the trail, something in the water below caught my eye. Just a few feet under the surface was the silhouette of a large fish. I slowed to a walk, focusing on the shape. My curiosity got the better of me and I left the trail for a new one heading down hill to the shore. The new trail was damp and slightly overgrown. I was focused on the surface of the water; I didn't notice the large tree root that was sticking out of the ground. My toe caught the root and I fell.

It was fascinating to watch the clear, colorless waves of energy wash over my face. I could hear soft tones—or is it a melody? Whatever the sounds were, they were beautiful and captivating.

"Please wake up. Open your eyes." Joseph Merrick was whispering in my ear, then talking to himself. "Great, why does this girl keep passing out?"

"Joseph?" I was flat on my back. The damp ground soaked through my clothing. The temperature had dropped 10 degrees and the wind was blowing hard. Goose bumps rose on my arms.

I repeated myself. "Joseph?"

"Yes," saying with a hint of disgust.

"Is Ms. Z back yet?" She was all that concerned me.

"No." Answering with even more disgust in his voice, he looked away.

"I saw people." I started to say but knew I wasn't making any sense. His hand was between my head and the ground.

He looked around. "You saw people on the trail?"

"No, I saw people at the school and at the diner."

"You're worse off than I thought." Feeling my head like a doctor would, he put pressure on it with his fingertips. "Does this hurt?"

"When Ms. Z—your aunt disappeared. I saw a woman at the diner. Then a few days ago I went to the school and saw a man take her car."

His face filled with concern but he ignored my findings. "Seraphin, does it hurt when I apply pressure to your head?"

"Do you think they have her? Can we find her?" I was surprised at my enthusiasm. I wanted to help him find the woman I so cherished but he only wanted to help me.

"SERAPHIN!" Trying to catch my attention, he put his face directly in front of mine.

"WHAT?" I shouted back, angry that he was avoiding my questions.

"You fell and hit your head." He stated the obvious.

"I know." Reaching up, I found my hair to be coated with mud. Every time I saw him it seemed there was something stuck in my hair. He must have thought me repulsive. "I don't care about my head, I care about Ms. Z. I'm fine, she's not."

Pausing, he let out a puff of air. Then the lecture began. "You shouldn't be jogging by yourself. What if I didn't hear you? I doubt anyone would have found you. You could have a concussion."

"Stop changing the subject—wait, what are *you* doing here? Were you following me?" I said, trying to straighten my hair.

"Don't flatter yourself. Why would I follow you?" He snapped. "It was just a lucky coincidence that I was on my way to work and I heard you call for help—AGAIN. And again, it seems I have to ask for a thank you. Obviously you still don't appreciate a helping hand."

In the distance, thunder rumbled. Anger swelled in me. I tried to calm myself, knowing that if I didn't my body would do it for me. Our eyes connected for several minutes. His eyes changed to a deep blue. I gasped and broke free, glancing at my watch. Almost 30 minutes had passed. "I need to finish my run so I can get ready for work."

"You can't be serious, Seraphin?" Joseph raised his voice and when he said my name I gave him my full attention. "We're going back your house. You need to get cleaned up. You have blood in your hair and mud all over your face."

"I have blood in my hair?" Touching, I realized that what I thought was mud, was actually blood mixed with dirt.

"Let's go." He commanded. When he reached to help me up, I stubbornly ignored his hand. I turned, pressing my palms into the mud. He leaned back and folded his arms across his chest, watching me with a look of amusement. As my hands sunk down into the soil my body lifted, I dug my heel into the ground but my shoe slipped and I landed on my rear end.

Joseph let out a chuckle and before I could be upset with him, his hands wrapped around my elbows. Like a child, my arms bent out in front of my body and my shoulders lifted to my ears. His hands were warm and soft against my skin and I immediately regretted not regularly exfoliating my elbows. Glancing at his arms I noticed his muscles tightening as he lifted.

"Thanks." I conceded.

"There it is." He said, acknowledging my thanks in a way that made me want to punch out his perfect smile.

"Don't walk me home. I'm fine." Scornful, I passed him.

"And there it goes." He mumbled.

The thunder moved closer. Strong winds began to blow. Footsteps were close behind me. He was following even though I told him not to. "What is wrong with you? Can't you take a hint?" I spoke loud, keeping my eyes ahead.

"What? Did you seriously just ask that question?" He stopped abruptly, grabbing my arm and forcing me to stop as well. With a quick motion I was facing him. Standing at least a foot taller, he looked down, still gripping my arm. "What is wrong with ME? Don't you mean, what is wrong with you? You are out, on a remote trail, jogging by yourself. Why didn't you go on the trail in your neighborhood?"

"That trail was too crowed." I started to explain but he interrupted.

"Too crowded? You sure are careless for a girl who lives alone and has no one to look out for her."

Those words hurt. I had no one. I hid my pain with anger; shouting back. "Wait a minute, answer my question. What were you doing over here anyway? You're alone."

"I WAS ON MY WAY TO WORK. I already told you that." He shouted but continued ahead. I watched him catch his toe on a root that was sticking out of the ground. He stumbled forward, regaining his balance. "Besides, I'm a guy. Guys are supposed to be on remote trails, it's what we do. We explore on our own. Women shouldn't be on their own, defenseless."

Pushing past him, I felt the mud fall from my knees. I dreaded looking in the mirror when I finally did get home. "I'm far from defenseless and I don't need you looking out for me; you can leave now."

"Oh, you are something else, Seraphin!" His voice grew louder. "Next time, I'll just ignore your calls for help when I hear them. Obviously, you don't need rescuing."

"Why do you keep insisting I called for help? Oh wait, now I remember what I said. 'Joseph, please save me!' Right before I knocked myself out." Keeping my eyes forward, I was not going to give him the satisfaction of seeing any tears. Trying to clear my head before I lost all emotional control and blacked out, I focused on the sky above. Dark storm clouds moved in quickly.

Joseph was not far behind. We continued in silence. Occasionally, he would let out a sarcastic, "Unbelievable!"

I fought blacking-out harder than I ever had. Unintentionally, I slowed down as my head began to grow lighter.

He noticed something was wrong and his voice was calmer. "Seraphin, are you feeling alright? Maybe you should sit down again. You did just smack your head against the ground."

"I'm fine!" I was stubborn, as I straightened my back and continued tromping up the hill. He followed close behind.

When we reached the top of the hill, I heard his footsteps slow and on impulse stopped to look. He was staring at the sky nervously. In only a few steps he was beside me. "Let's get back to your house. There is a bad storm coming."

Grabbing my hand he led me away from the patch of trees. I had to run to keep him from pulling me. The sky over the water from where we had just come had turned a dark greenish-gray and there was a low rumble of thunder. The wind was violent. My hair slapped at my shoulders.

I was still angry. My pace quickened and I passed Joseph with ease. We were almost to Briarwood Court when it started to rain. The drops were heavy and painful when they landed on my skin. We sprinted the last quarter-mile. When we reached the trail that earlier had been packed with people, I slipped on the wet pavement. Without hesitation, Joseph threw his arms out, catching me before I could fall. My anger dissipated and I muttered a thank you.

We took shelter on my front porch and I doubled over, panting from the dash and soaked from the rain. Joseph started pacing back and forth in front of me mumbling. "I shouldn't have done that. Now what? What am I supposed to do now?"

"Joseph, are you alright?" I was still panting, although, surprisingly, I felt great after such an exhilarating run. Within minutes the clouds cleared and the sun started shining again. It would take only 10 minutes before the water on the streets evaporated; leaving no indication of the storm that had just blown in from nowhere.

He didn't answer, so I tried foolishly to lighten the mood. "That was kind of fun, don't you think? It's been a long time since I ran in the rain."

"FUN? You think that was fun? Have you no idea how much danger we were in?" His voice panicked.

Obviously my attempt didn't work. I wondered if the only thing he could do was make me feel bad about myself.

"It's a storm. I guess we could have gotten struck by lightning, but we're fine. Calm down." Right away, I knew it was going to upset him.

"Calm down? She wants me to calm down." He was mumbling, angry.

"Joseph, maybe we should go inside?" I interrupted.

"Great idea. You should get inside." A bit calmer, he took his hand and gently guided me to the front door. "Go on."

My house key was in my shoe. As I took my shoe off, he gave a crooked smile when he saw what I was doing but held back any comments. I appreciated his reserved judgment.

"Do you want to come in? I cleaned the house; it's not nearly as creepy as it was last time you were here."

He shook himself off like a dog and his mood seemed to lighten, "Oh, your house wasn't that creepy. I've been to some caverns that would make…" He stopped himself.

"That would make what?" I asked.

"Nothing. Forget it." He pushed at me to get in the house.

I stepped inside and the screen door shut between us. "Wait, I still want to talk to you about Ms.—your Aunt Doreh."

He ignored me, "I have to get to work. I'll see you around."

"Sure. Yeah. See you around." I said, disappointed. Evidently, he was not going to discuss her. As he walked away I wondered what he was hiding.

Later that morning, I took the ferry to Great Cranberry Island with no incident. There were a handful of familiar faces from the day before. Keeping myself busy with a few tabloids I bought from Keyes Market, I was able to distract myself with the ludicrous articles and the nostalgic thoughts that came along with them. Grandma used to read them all the time. I would laugh the older I got but she would defend the crazy stories, telling me that they reported on the *real* news.

That month's headlines read, Dolphin leads Scientists to Lost City of Atlantis; Man Abducted 30 Years Ago Found Wandering along Beach Has Not Aged a Day; and the one that caught my attention was Next Super Perigee Moon to Bring Apocalypse. Of course, none of those actually occurred or would occur. However, they were fun to read and besides, the day my father died there was a Super Perigee Moon; it brought my own personal apocalypse. I reasoned that it would benefit to know when the next one was scheduled to rise. They were predicting an early cycle. According to the tabloid, I had four years before the worlds end—I laughed at the absurdity.

When I clocked in for my shift, I had to pass by Mrs. Keyes office. The door was open and a man dressed in a full captain's uniform was speaking with her. I overheard part of their conversation.

"Mrs. Keyes, with all due respect, it is *your* job to provide the vessel with a capable staff that will serve for each mission. Now, we are leaving this evening on the *John F. Kennedy* for an overnight and I expect two MOLEs to be waiting at 3:00 sharp." The Captain said with authority.

"But I haven't even had a chance to train the new hires. Usually the first mission isn't for two weeks into the summer program." Mrs. Keyes sounded upset.

"Things changed this year. I don't know why, I just drive the boat." He turned and placed his hat on his head. "3:00 SHARP!"

Mrs. Keyes followed the Captain out of her office; I turned and pretended to be looking in my locker. I didn't want them to think I had overheard.

After he left, she approached me. "Seraphin, I need you to work tonight. I know you haven't officially been trained on the vessels but two of my more seasoned MOLEs are sick. You and I are the only people left to work."

"Mrs. Keyes, I can say, with utmost of confidence, that bringing me on a vessel overnight is a terrible idea. I am terrified of water."

"No problem. You won't be in the water. You'll be on a boat; a perfectly safe boat. Plus, you'll earn overnight pay, which is double your hourly rate. Follow me and I'll give you a crash course in cleaning a vessel."

"Alright," I sighed.

The ship I was assigned to was one of the smallest in the fleet, the *John F. Kennedy*. It was used for day trips and occasional overnight outings. My instructions were straight forward, *"keep the ship clean and stay out of the way."* Mrs. Keyes repeated that phrase during the hour it took for her to train me. It seemed simple enough.

When we were finished, she said I could go home as long as I returned for 3:00 crew call. I decided to hang out on campus instead of going back and forth on the ferry. My nerves where shot as it was. Mrs. Keyes gave me a free cafeteria pass for being such a cooperative employee. It was better than nothing.

The dining room was nearly empty when I arrived for lunch. There were about half-a-dozen people scattered across the room and it was silent except for the clattering of pans in the kitchen.

Taking a few slices of veggie pizza and a salad, I sat at an empty table near the television. World News Daily Worldwide, WNDW was on and I starred blankly at the screen while I ate. The volume was down and closed captioning transcribed. There was a breaking news story, an oversized block of text slammed across the screen; BREAKING NEWS ALERT. Red graphics flashed to reveal a WNDW reporter on location. The story was about a vessel that capsized in the Pacific Ocean, off the coast of California. Seeing the news report was, of course, not helping to calm my nerves regarding the *John F. Kennedy* trip. Usually, the Coast Guard could get to the ship and airlift the crew to safety. Although, that time they lost one crewman. The bottom of the screen read that a 24-year-old man by the name of Nicholas Trite was presumed to go down with the ship.

"Was that a vessel from Pacific Coastal Research?" A voice asked.

I turned to see Ethan standing with a tray of food.

"They haven't announced a company name yet." Someone answered.

I knew the voice that answered Ethan's question. The voice belonged to Joseph Merrick. He sat in a corner booth, with a baseball cap on, by himself. His eyes were glued to the television and didn't bother to turn when he spoke to Ethan, of which I was grateful.

What is he doing here? I thought he was going to…WORK. He must work here. For as much as I had seen Joseph that past week, I knew very little about him.

"Hey Jay, are you going on the *John F. Kennedy* with us?" Ethan walked past me to the booth where Joseph sat.

I eavesdropped.

"Not this time I'm afraid. I have some other business to tend to. You will be with Dr. Radski for this research mission. It's cool that they're taking a group of you, usually the summer researchers don't go out for the first two weeks. It must be important." Joseph continued watching the television.

A sense of relief washed over me knowing that Ethan would be on the *John F. Kennedy* and Joseph would not. Even though I knew deep down that he wouldn't be of any help if I blacked out.

So, Joseph is Jay? Now it makes sense that Ms. Z was able to get Ethan into the program with only a moment's notice. She called in a favor from her nephew. Now, what's with the alias?

Not wanting any awkwardness, I purposely hurried through the rest of my pizza. It wouldn't be good if Joseph realized I was there. I was nervous enough and the last thing I needed was another argument with him.

Ethan spotted me and shouted across the dining room. "Hey Phin."

No Ethan, NO! Please don't draw attention to me. I didn't speak but instead put my hand up and waved. I glanced at Joseph; he was still enamored with the television. *That's right! He knows me as Seraphin. Only Ethan calls me Phin.* Maybe I was safe? My plate was already folded in half and I started to get up to throw the rest of my lunch away when Ethan approached the table.

"I forgot to ask you on the ferry, did you move back into your grandma's house on Briarwood Court?" Ethan said innocently.

"Yes," answering, knowing that his question would bring unwanted attention. And, I was right. Joseph took his eyes off the television only to meet mine with a look of horror.

He immediately stood and walked to my table. Calm and polite he spoke, "Seraphin, I'm surprised to see you here."

"I bet." I said casually, avoiding his eyes.

He turned to Ethan. "Am I interrupting?"

"No." Ethan looked confused. "You two know each other?"

His question went unanswered as Joseph turned to me. "Can I have a word with you?"

"No. I was just about to leave." I didn't want to talk to him.

"I'm leaving too." He insisted.

"But it looks to me like you haven't finished your lunch." I pointed to the booth where his salad remained untouched.

"I'm not hungry all of the sudden." His voice was intense, almost pleading. "Please can we talk?"

I turned to Ethan. "I'll be on the *John F. Kennedy* with you tonight. I'll see you at crew call."

"Super." He mumbled, chewing half a sandwich.

Without saying another word, Joseph walked past and I followed out of the dining room and into the hallway. He glanced over his shoulder several times; I assume to be sure I was still there. When I passed, I considered escaping into the ladies restroom, but I resisted. We arrived at an office with a nameplate on the door that read Jay Mason, Marine Research. He closed the door behind us. An empty leather chair was in front of a desk, he gestured for me to sit but I refused to make myself comfortable.

His arms spread wide and his shoulders shrugged, on his face was a look of disbelief. "What is going on? Why are you here?"

Ignoring his questions, I had my own. "So, do you work here? Jay? Mason?"

"NO. I mean, yes. You can't know about this. You can't. Why are you here?" A touch of panic was in his voice.

"I work here Joseph, I'm a…"

Grabbing my shoulders, he whispered in my ear. "You can't call me Joseph. I'm Jay." He walked to the other side of the office, mumbling. "After I save you Aunt Doreh, I am going to kill you."

"Alright, JAY. I'll call you JAY. What's the big deal?"

"Seraphin, you can't be here. You can't work here. How did you even get a job here?"

"Wow." Slowly taking a few steps back, feeling confused and a bit angry. "First of all, I'd rather not call you anything because I wish we had never met. However, since that's not possible, I'll call you whatever you want."

"Good, so you need to…"

I interrupted. "Second, I don't know why you feel the need to tell me where I can and cannot work. I don't even know you, JAY. AND, you barely know me, so do me a favor and stop coming to my rescue if the only thing you're going to do is make me out to be a hindrance." I had my hand on the doorknob, ready to leave.

He stepped closer, his voice low. "You don't belong here Seraphin."

"I don't belong here? The last time I checked it didn't take a PhD in Marine Biology to scrub toilets on research ships!" I shouted. "It's refreshing to know how you really feel."

"How I really feel? What does that mean?" He asked.

"The fact that you feel I'm too dumb to work here," I was being a little dramatic.

"That's not what I was saying." He paced around the office, his fists were clenched and his jaw tight.

"Why do you…" I paused and with a deep breath finished, "…hate me so much?"

His shoulders slouched at my words. Several moments passed before answering. "I don't hate you Seraphin. I hate." Stopping, as he chose his words carefully. "I hate the way we met."

Slowly, he leaned against the desk; he looked overpowered for the first time. My accusations seemed to make him sad and unexpectedly, I wanted to comfort him.

He moved to be closer when I sat down in the leather chair. Using his arms he effortlessly hoisted himself so he was sitting on his desk just a few feet from me. His hands were folded in his lap. He glanced at his hands, then at me and finally through the glass window and into the hallway. "I think you've got a visitor. We can talk later. Just please remember that I'm Jay here."

Turning to see Ethan standing behind the frosted glass of the office door, I was disappointed. Waving awkwardly, the shape of his head looked even rectangular through the patterned glass.

"Right. Got it, I'll call you Jay." I assured Joseph.

"Thanks." He said.

When I opened the door, Ethan knew he was interrupting and seemed uncomfortable to be doing so. "I'm sorry, Dr. Radski sent me. She's looking for you, Jay."

"Not a problem, we're done here." Assuring Ethan, I left.

Ethan caught up; we walked back to the cafeteria together. He asked how I knew Jay. "Ethan, I don't know him that well. Ms. Z introduced us after the graduation ceremony and we've seen each other around since then."

From the sound of it, he thought very highly of Jay Mason. "Phin, he is the top researcher here at CORE. He's written countless essays. The most recent was published last month in Sea Life Magazine about the adaptations of phytoplankton to sunlight."

"Super—good for him." Finding out that he was accomplished annoyed me.

"Did he get you the job here?" Ethan asked.

"NO!" a little put off, though I wasn't sure why. It was a reasonable assumption. "I got myself the job here."

"Okay." Ethan held up his hands. "Relax. He's not a bad guy. I don't know what you're all worked up about but he's super cool once you get to know him."

"Ethan, you have been here for one day. You think you know him?"

"Why? You just said you didn't know him that well." He responded, but did not continue to argue. "I'll see you at crew call, Phin."

We parted ways.

SEVEN

The crew call for the *John F. Kennedy* was at 3:00. The vessel was scheduled to leave port at 3:30. I was so nervous. I was shaking. To make matters worse, Joseph met me at the dock.

"Seraphin, wait." He yelled. "You can't go on this mission. It's dangerous for you."

I did not stop. "You have made it clear that you don't think I should work here. However, my supervisor told me that I had to go on this mission. Believe me; I'd rather not."

"But, it's dangerous for you." He repeated.

"You think? Anyway, it doesn't matter. I'm going to be swabbing the deck, not swimming with sharks. Jo—I mean, Jay, I'm the cleaning lady. How much danger can I really be in?"

Joseph followed me onto the deck; the Captain was waiting to welcome his crew. Mrs. Keyes had not arrived.

"We push off at 3:30." The Captain announced.

"Sir, can I have a word with you?" Joseph asked the Captain.

"Sure Mr. Mason. Good to see you. I'm pressed for time though, so make it quick."

"I'd like to join your team today." Joseph said.

I could not believe what I was hearing. Joseph was putting himself on the mission.

"Absolutely not," the Captain said. "You'll have to sign up for the next one."

Oh, thank goodness.

Joseph seemed genuinely surprised. "Captain, I have to be on *this* one."

"I know you're not new to this place so I don't understand why you are questioning the safety procedures, Mr. Mason. Just for fun, I'll explain them to you again." The Captain had a touch of a southern drawl, which made his words seem more relaxed than his face indicated. "There are only enough life vests and cabins for eight crew members and if I allow you to travel with us, we would have nine. That's one too many."

"I don't need a vest or a cabin. However, I do need to be on this boat when it leaves the port. Please understand it's a matter of safety." Joseph, seeming both anxious and agitated, was oblivious to my standing only a few feet behind him.

The Captain tipped his hat and said with authority, "Mr. Mason, I think we are done here."

Joseph, throwing his arms in the air with a sense of defeat, turned around abruptly, knocking into me. I tried to prevent myself from falling but the weight of his clumsy body was too great and we both slammed down onto the hard wooden deck of the *John F. Kennedy*. Just as I was about to hit, his hand slipped against the back of my head protecting it. As he lay on top of me, the look on his face was puzzling. Anger grew inside of me.

"Your eyes are beautiful." He whispered then smiled.

I pushed him off and refused his hand when he held it out. Everyone had stopped what they were doing to watch us. I was infuriated with his clumsiness and confused by his compliment. "For goodness sakes, watch where you're going. How can you possibly think we would all be safer having you on our vessel?"

Joseph's smile dropped and he uncomfortably shifted his weight. Then, he hurried off the deck without the slightest indication of an apology for knocking me down.

After about twenty minutes, I started to worry. Mrs. Keyes was nowhere to be found. I paced along the deck, watching the boardwalk, hoping I would see her sprinting to make it in time. I knew she went home for a while. *Perhaps she was running late?* The Captain came to warn me that we would be leaving the port at 3:30, with or without Mrs. Keyes.

At 3:29 the crew started to pull up the anchor, just as Joseph came running down the dock. "Captain, do you have room for me yet?"

"Why Mr. Mason, I suppose we do. I hope you like cleaning toilets." The Captain said with a smirk. "It seems we are one MOLE short. Ms. Shedd will show you to your cabin."

"No Captain, you can't possibly be considering—"

The Captain interrupted me. "Ms. Shedd, I know this is your first time on a ship so I will give you fair warning. You never question an order from the Captain. Please take Mr. Mason to his cabin." He turned and shouted to no one in particular. "Let's get this ship to sea."

As the *John F. Kennedy* set out into the Atlantic Ocean for an overnight journey, my stomach was in tangles. I was the most experienced maintenance person on board; with only a few hours of training. However, that wasn't the worst part. What was most upsetting was that I had to train Joseph Merrick.

Joseph kept pace as I hurried through the belly of the ship to our maintenance cabin. He brought nothing, no overnight bag or change of clothing. Trying desperately to control my temper, I showed the utility closet where all our supplies were housed. Stumbling through my words, I tried to remember everything Mrs. Keyes showed me but I knew I'd forgotten most of it. I did remember one thing though.

"So basically," I said with false authority. "Stay out of the way and keep the ship clean."

"That sounds easy enough. Where do I get one of those snazzy green shirts from?" He tugged at the corner of my shirt.

"I have an extra in our cabin." It was my only extra shirt. I wasn't going to have a clean one to change into the next morning, thanks to him.

We walked together through the narrow halls. I tried to speed up or slow down so that he wasn't next to me but he stayed by my side, silently claiming his spot. Some of the halls were so constricting that our shoulders touched. When that happened I pressed my other shoulder against the wall allowing an extra inch between us.

I lead him down below to our overnight cabin, horrified that we had to share sleeping quarters. They should have been called overnight closets because they were so small. Honestly, it consisted of two cots that were more like shelves and a bathroom that I struggled to turn around in.

There was one drawer in which I had already put my things. I took the green shirt out, reluctantly, I handed it to him. Instead of changing in the bathroom, he took his shirt off in the cramped cabin. It brushed my cheek as he pulled it over his head and he apologized for hitting me but failed to step further away.

It embarrassed me and when I caught a glimpse of myself in the mirror, I was even more humiliated to see my cheeks were flushed. The shirt was too tight on him and he pulled at it, trying to stretch it out. "I look ridiculous, don't I?"

I knew what he meant but I skewed the meaning when I answered. "Think you're too good to wear one of those?"

He didn't respond, instead he seemed to be searching for the right thing to say. We were close, very close. He was almost a foot taller and made me feel small, which I did not like. Feeling inferior to Joseph, in any manner, irritated me. It was impossible to move because he was in the way. My eyes shifted to the door a few times, hinting that it was time to go but he stood his ground. I could smell him, his scent like a fresh ocean breeze. I, on the other hand, had started to perspire and was suddenly aware of how hot it had become in the tiny room.

"I meant what I said, you're eyes are amazing. They're like the delicate forewarning of an approaching storm."

A breath escaped. I hadn't heard those words in years and it hurt me more than it flattered. "Don't ever say that again."

"Why? It means I like your eyes."

That was the very thing my father used to tell me. My pulse quickened with anger. "Why did you say that?"

"Because that's what they remind me of. It means that they are calm and captivating but when one looks deeper a furious storm is on the horizon. I've seen plenty of terrible storms in my life, lately more than ever, and the most beautiful moments are those before the sky erupts."

"They're just gray, like an overcast day." I looked down, unable to meet his eyes.

Lifting my chin, he forced our eyes to connect. "Why are you angry?"

"I'm not." I lied.

"You are. Your eyes give you away. You know they change? They are so many shades of gray. When you're fuming they're darker, more intense." His voice lowered. "Just like a story my mom used to tell when I was a kid."

Never had I stared back at my angry reflection. I turned and looked into the mirror. My eyes were nearly charcoal gray. They changed as my mood turned to confusion, lightening like storm clouds subsiding.

Joseph moved, sitting on an overnight cot, a hand ran through his hair. A confused expression crossed his face.

"What story?" I was suddenly interested.

"An old fable told through the years about a girl who was blessed with the ability to create great storms." He explained.

"I'd say that is more of a curse than a blessing. Why would anyone want to be as powerful as a storm? Only destruction can come of that." I reasoned.

"Storms aren't necessarily only destructive. They do great things for our environment." Answering with science, his expression still puzzled me.

"Spoken like a true oceanographer. So how did the story end? Did she knock down power lines and flood valleys for fun?" I teased.

"Nah, the girl ends up drowning in her own tears." Standing, his voice was more casual than a few seconds prior. "Sorry, it's not really a happy ending."

The first time I saw Joseph, his eyes shifted color as well. Maybe it was more common than I thought. "You're eyes are the captivating ones." I instantly wished I hadn't said it.

He smiled wide and I could have been imagining it but I think his cheeks flushed. The room was pretty warm too, so he could have just been hot. The color of his eyes lightened to a clear sapphire. "Oh, you think so, do you?"

I quickly took the compliment back. "Don't flatter yourself. I just mean that they are very curious shades of blue and at times they remind me of the sky on a summer day. No clouds to be seen, no storms approaching…" I drifted in thought as I spoke.

"So you like my eyes?" He harassed.

I grimaced. "Don't let it go to your head, Joseph."

"Jay, my name is Jay. Get it right," he said, stern.

"Of course, how could I forget? So, answer me this while we're alone, who are you really? Are you Joseph Merrick or are you Jay Mason?"

"To you, on this boat, I'm Jay Mason—"

I cut him off. "Yes. I know. What is your *real* name? Or is there a third name that I might soon discover? My guess is Joseph because that's how your Aunt Doreh, whom I assume knows your real name, introduced you. Although, she did know about your alter ego—it is definitely a mystery."

Disbelief overtook him. "How do you know that?"

"Ethan Cottington told me that she called Jay Mason to get him into the research program. So, why did she introduce you to Ethan as Jay but to me as Joseph?"

Suddenly, he seemed flustered. He was hiding from something and Ms. Z knew what it was. "We should go."

"NO! I don't want to go; I want you to tell me where Ms. Z is!" I shouted.

He threw his hands up, trying to calm me. "Please don't shout."

"Fine, but will you just talk to me about her?" I lowered my voice to a whisper. "You've been avoiding my questions and believe it or not, I miss her. I care about your aunt and I want her to be safe. How do I know she's still alive?"

He sighed. "I know you do. I miss her too. She's still alive, I promise."

"We need to find her." Sorrow filled me. "You said you knew where she was, right?"

"It's more complicated than that—you've got to let this go." Pain crossed his face. "Seraphin—"

His head hung low and his fingers gripped the back of his own neck—struggling to speak he let out a deep sigh.

I waited. "Joseph?"

"There's so much I need to say. I don't know where to begin—I don't know why this is all happening." As he released, blood filled the skin's surface—8 red finger marks ran side-by-side on the nape of his neck. Directly below the fingerprints a faint tattoo caught my eye. His head shot up before I could comprehend its design. "Do you trust me?"

"I don't know," I confessed.

"That's not an answer," he was surprised by my honesty.

"You've helped me—and I don't know why. You're here—for no reason that I can think of. At times you're nice but other times you're cruel; the fact is, I don't know you. You don't know me. It's hard to trust a stranger."

"It's hard to trust people you've known for a lifetime as well." He muttered

My face was pleading. "I can't give you an answer."

"Fair enough," he accepted.

The Captain's voice rang over the intercom. "MOLE NEEDED ON DECK"

"I'll go" I said. "If you promise we'll pick back up with this conversation tonight?"

"If I have a choice, I'd rather not involve you." He admitted.

"You don't have a choice. Besides, I have a feeling Ms. Z involved me the minute she introduced you as Joseph Merrick." I reasoned.

"You're probably right." He agreed.

When I arrived on the deck it was a chaotic scene. The *John F. Kennedy* had come across a kill of some kind. The remains of a large dead animal floated along side the boat. I was nearly sick to my stomach. The smell of the rotting carcass permeated the air. Seagulls were flying overhead, squawking high pitches. A warm wave of anxiety washed through me. I was going to black out. Joseph came running up behind me; putting his arm around my shoulders he guided me to the other side of the deck, far away from the carcass.

"I'm going to black out." Sliding down one of the exterior walls, I said weakly.

"Try to focus on something else," giving his best advice.

The Captain came over the loud speaker again. "SECOND CALL: MOLE NEEDED ON DECK."

Angry, I shouted. "Oh my goodness, we're on the deck. What do they need? Do they want us to clean up that rotting animal?"

"Its fine, I'm used to seeing dead floating animals. Try to hang on to consciousness and I'll go see what they need." He disappeared around a railing.

About 15 minutes later he came back, looking sicker than I was. Sliding down the wall next to me he put his head between his knees.

"Well, what did they need?" I asked.

"Apparently you weren't the only one sickened by the smell. One of the new guys vomited all over the deck." His voice was shaky.

"Oh no."

"Oh yes."

"And you had to clean it up?"

"Oh yes."

"Why would the Captain stop the boat just to look at a dead floating animal? That's absolutely repulsive," sounding disgusted.

"It's research Seraphin. Dr. Radski needed to take photos and coordinates so they can later be logged. She'll have to analyze bite marks and distress patterns to determine what killed the animal."

"How can she possibly make any sense out of that tangled flesh?" I couldn't begin to guess what it might be.

"We think it's a seal."

"You mean it *was* a seal."

He laughed. "Right—*was*."

"Why is it important to log the coordinates of where a dead animal floats?"

"Marine species regularly migrate and it's hard to keep track of where they currently take up residence. There are only a few species that we follow regularly, the most deadly, of course. We have to keep track of where the predators reside. We do it to protect the innocent. CORE regularly releases stat sheets to help protect humans from wandering into kill-zones."

"And, what killed that most unfortunate seal?" I asked, and then added—"Obviously not a very hungry animal."

"What makes you say that?" His eyes were curious.

"There's so much of the seal left. It would seem that a creature killing out of hunger would have devoured the carcass, leaving little to the waves. However, this seems like it might have been a recreational kill—maybe even territorial?"

"You're insightful Seraphin. This type of kill is rare but very serious. Sometimes when a cool current travels too far north or south, things can come with it that are not welcome. It seems that this 'most unfortunate seal' may have encountered an animal that is unwanted so close to the shores of the United States—an animal that doesn't just kill out of necessity." Joseph then went on to explain ocean currents and the animals that travel them for various reasons.

When he spoke he was professional and knowledgeable. It was the first time he discussed anything that related to his occupation and I could see what Ethan saw. He was a big deal. I instantly felt awful that he had to clean-up vomit and promised he wouldn't have to do my job again. He assured me that he didn't mind.

We sat for a few moments before the engine of the boat roared to life. "Oh thank goodness we're leaving. My head is pounding."

"You have a headache?" He was worried.

"Yes. Do you think it could be from when I hit my head?"

Sounding even more concerned, "That could be the cause, though I was certain you were fine. May I?"

"May you what?"

"I think I can help." He said, moving in closer.

"Are you a doctor as well as an oceanographer?" I joked.

"Seraphin, can I try to help you?" He asked, more serious.

"Okay." Reluctantly, I agreed.

He placed his hands on either side of my head and closed his eyes. After about 30 seconds he let my head go and opened his eyes. My headache was gone.

Shocked, I asked the obvious. "How did you do that?"

Like it was no big deal, he answered. "Pressure points, of course. Haven't you ever heard of reflexology?"

"I have, but you didn't use any pressure," at least I didn't feel any.

"I'm just good, I guess." He said mysteriously then changed the subject. "The researchers wanted me to check out a new bacterium they found in the water. Do you mind if I go?"

"Sure," I was lost in disbelief. The pain from the headache was completely gone.

He hesitated, started to get up but then sat down. "I'll stay. You might need my help."

"Don't worry. I'm fine."

"Great. I'll catch up with you at dinner." He winked and left.

When he walked away I replayed every moment we had spent together in my head. Out of everything that he had said and done, only one thing bothered me. The way he commented on my eyes and when he spoke about the story of the girl who drowned in her own tears. It was that moment when I realized how long it had been since tears poured from my eyes.

Later that evening, the crew gathered for dinner in the cafeteria. I avoided the main table where the researchers sat. They ignored me and kept to their conversation. However, when Joseph entered the room they fell silent; a short woman pushed her chair back, standing up. She was as round as she was tall and the white lab coat she wore didn't flatter her in the least. Her hair was pulled tight into a bun on the top of her head and her eyeglasses were thick and dark. When she spoke, her voice was raspy and masculine.

"Jay Mason, what are you doing in that green shirt? Why has my top researcher been assigned to toilet duty?" She scowled.

"Dr. Radski, it's great to see you." He said in the friendliest of tones. "I'm just getting a few overtime hours in."

"I have loads of work you can do. Get out of that green shirt and into the lab coat you were meant to wear," she was absolutely the most unpleasant woman I had ever seen.

Joseph spoke, nonchalant. "Sorry Doctor, I can't do that, Captain's orders." He shrugged his shoulders as if nothing could be done.

"We'll see about that." She grumbled, leaving the cafeteria.

All eyes were on Joseph as he grabbed a cheese sandwich, a can of Coke and headed for my table.

"Can I sit with you?" He asked.

My mouth was full. I shrugged.

"I'm going to take that as a yes, since you didn't outwardly protest." He sounded too confident and it was slightly irritating.

When he sat down in the chair next to me, I wondered why. There were 4 other chairs, three directly across the table. Our backs were to the researchers and we were facing the cafeteria door.

He opened the can of Coke, taking a sip. "So, what's first on the agenda for us this evening?"

I continued to chew and shrugged my shoulders again. Ethan came into the cafeteria and waved. I smiled at him. When he sat with the other researchers, no one acknowledged him. I watched one researcher completely disregarded him when he said 'hello'. Compassion filled me and my expression must have changed.

"Huh?" Joseph said as he watched. "Your boyfriend seems like a nice kid."

Swallowing hard, I responded in a higher pitch than usual. "Excuse me? My boyfriend?"

"Yes." Joseph said, nodding his head to Ethan, who was behind us.

"Ethan isn't my boyfriend. He's just a…" I stopped because I didn't know what Ethan was to me. Even though we lived together, we barely spoke. If anything he was more like a distant acquaintance that was forced to feel some sort of loyalty to greet me.

An accusing smile crossed his face. "He's just a what? You two haven't quite established things yet? Is he too shy to ask you out?"

"Ethan, SHY? Not even close. That guy is far from introverted. He's just someone I know, that's all. We're not really friends but we know each other and I lived with his family for a while."

"Well, it's obvious that he's crazy about you."

Turning to catch a glimpse of Ethan, I laughed out loud then lowered my voice to a whisper. "There is no way that Ethan Cottington thinks of me like that. There is no way anyone thinks of me like that. Besides, what makes you such an expert on love?"

"I'm no expert, just prone to state the obvious. He couldn't take his eyes off of you back at the dock during crew call." Joseph said with confidence. "What makes you think no one would think of you that way? Aside from your constant blacking out, you're not that bad of a catch Seraphin."

It wasn't clear whether he was complimenting or making jokes at my expense so I ignored his latter comment. "Perhaps that's due to *you* making a spectacle of us both with your clumsiness?"

His hand flew up in the air and his face held a look of disbelief. It seemed as though he was forming an argument— I quickly cut him off.

"You STILL haven't apologized for knocking me down." I added a bit more fuel to the fire.

A chuckle escaped him. "I can't believe I forgot. Was it my infliction of emotional or physical distress that I should be apologizing for?"

"I don't know what you mean," I was confused.

"Let me explain. I know that you were not hurt when we fell, I made sure that didn't happen," confident when he spoke.

I remembered his hand on the back of my head, protecting it from the ground. He went on. "Perhaps you were emotionally distressed? Was it embarrassing for you to fall in front of a group of people? I don't think that's the case, considering you tend to drop out of consciousness, all on your own with almost no warning to others. I imagine you are used to it by now.

"So, this leaves my comment about your eyes. Should I apologize for this? Perhaps it made you uncomfortable and squeamish?" Acting like he was contemplating an impossible mathematical calculation, he put his hand to his chin and gazed off to nowhere in particular.

An apology was not going to come out of his mouth.

"Oh honestly Joseph" I said loud, then immediately realized my mistake. Looking over my shoulder I noticed a girl with coal black hair from the research group raise her head curiously. She had large brown eyes that were lost in her dark features. Avoiding my eyes, she seemed to be waiting for him to respond.

Joseph didn't move, he continued to stare off at nothing, far away.

I fumbled for a way to fix it but couldn't think of anything.

Finally he spoke. "No, I don't think that was his name. Robin Hood's Merry Man was named 'Honest John'." He spoke loud and clear, so everyone could hear.

Ethan turned from a conversation he was having with a guy next to him. "Jay, you're wrong, his name was 'Little John'."

Joseph spoke enthusiastically. "Yeah, that's it. Thanks man!"

He looked at me, scolding. "Seraphin, it seems you are really bad with names."

I sank down into my chair. "It seems I am."

"I think this makes us square on the apologies, don't you?"

"Sure." I agreed, wishing I could bury my head in the sand.

It was then that I realized I didn't like disappointing Joseph.

He leaned in, speaking low, "Thank goodness your boyfriend bailed you out of that one."

"Again, Ethan is not my boyfriend."

"Well, you sure are the center of his attention."

"If he is showing me any extra notice, it's because I'm one of only a few people here he knows." I rationalized. "I think he was expecting more of his friends. He's used to being followed around by drones of uninteresting people. Maybe there is a shortage of dull people on this boat."

Joseph smiled and nudged into me with his shoulder, "Sure thing."

Mumbling under my breath, just loud enough for him to hear, I shifted in my seat. "I'm so very sorry I made that horrible mistake. Please stop teasing about Ethan. I don't want him to hear."

My hand was flat on the table; he placed his on top of mine. It was warm and smooth but strong. Chills went through me as our eyes locked. His expression was unfamiliar and his eyes a brighter shade of blue, less soft than before but far from worried. The cafeteria seemed to disappear around us; he gripped my hand, lifting it slightly off the table. "So does this mean you're not interested in him?"

Where was Joseph going with this line of questioning? I honestly hadn't considered the idea of dating Ethan. Sure, he seemed nice and interested me, but not in a serious way. He was more like a potential friend. As difficult as it was, I pulled my eyes away from Joseph and glanced at Ethan. His shoulders were broad and strong, his smile welcoming and polite, however, he looked too much like his mother and that detail alone was the one thing I could never get past.

Before I turned to Joseph, I noticed the same curious girl raising her head to look in our direction.

I answered him truthfully. "I am excited that he's here. Plus, I'm interested in seeing if we can actually develop a friendship outside of the domestic weirdness we just came from."

Joseph's face seemed to sadden.

"With that said, he and I could never date. I don't feel that way about him and know I never could. He's like family, in a weird distant kind of way."

"Good." Letting go of my hand, he focused on his food again.

We finished eating. The cafeteria cleared and we were the only people remaining in the room. Voices echoed down the hallway and I was suddenly very aware of the silence between us. It didn't seem to bother Joseph; he appeared relaxed with one elbow on the table. He had a slight lean towards me, which I was not opposed to. Uncomfortable with myself, I continually shifted my weight from side to side. Finally, I stood up and brought my tray to the trashcan.

"We should start cleaning up." I said.

Devouring the rest of his sandwich in only two bites, he agreed and began picking up trays that the others had left behind.

I made an attempt at small talk while we cleaned. "You're kind of young to be a top researcher." The words came out wrong and I regretted saying it.

"I'm not that young, already 22—an old man compared to you. Are you 18 yet?"

It made me feel like a kid. "Yes."

"I wish I was 18 again, I'd do a lot of things differently." He mumbled, barely loud enough for me to hear.

"What does being a top researcher mean?" Wanting to know more about Joseph, I kept the questions coming.

He thought then shrugged his shoulders. "It means they give me more work than everyone else. Or, it means I have no life outside of work so I'm able to do more."

"I have a feeling it's a little more than that. Ethan told me that one of your articles was just published, something about radioactive plankton."

Joseph laughed. "That sounds familiar."

"This seems like a great company to work for, I mean, there's job security. I heard Ethan's mom talking about how CORE was founded by a billionaire investor in Europe who wants to clean up the ocean. Is that true?"

"Yes, it's true. There is a guy, though he's not as great as you make him sound. He dumps his endless pile of money into this company with the understanding that he remains anonymous."

"You sound like you're complaining. I mean, he gives you a paycheck, right? He can't be too bad."

Then he turned serious and his voice dropped to a whisper. "Seraphin, there is more to my job than the money. Protecting the ocean and the lives that depend on it is what I was born to do. Remember that little fish you tried to save back at the beach?"

"Sure. And just so you know, I did save her—right before you had to save me." I trailed off, slightly embarrassed when I thought back to myself screaming, soaking wet with a twig tangled in my hair. What a sight I must have been. Without thinking I reached up and smoothed a few wild strands down.

"Right, of course." Sarcasm seeped through his voice. "Anyway, you felt like you *had* to save her. It came from deep inside you, am I right?"

I thought about how I needed to rescue her and how I had no choice. My life was second to that little fish's life. "Yes."

"That's how I feel all the time, for everyone, even people I don't like. I feel the need to heal them, protect them. The urge is unfathomable to most. It's so strong at times I have to suppress all my instincts. Maybe it is impossible to imagine?"

Shame flooded my memories as I recalled the many times he came to my rescue. He was *just* doing his duty. It was instinctual and I understood because while some people are able disregard all compassion, I let it consume me. My father's life ending haunted me because I continually looked for a way to help him. Joseph and I were very much alike and that new realization terrified me—though I wasn't sure why.

He was intense with his delivery and he didn't leave much in the way of explanations. I got the impression he wanted to tell me more—hoping it could be leading to an account of where Ms. Z might be. Unfortunately, Dr. Radski walked in and shattered my hopes of digging deeper.

She interrupted. Her face was red and by the looks of it, the Captain didn't heed to her demands. Again, she gave orders for Joseph to abandon his green MOLE shirt for a lab coat.

"Mason, you have three minutes to get out of that ridiculous shirt and into your lab coat. There are some radiolarians slides that need classified. Get on it." She demanded. "Your time can be used more efficiently."

She left.

Surprisingly, he didn't respond to her hassle. It was as if she had not walked into the room. He seemed deep in thought while sweeping the floor and remained not at all affected.

I was surprised at his insolence. "Aren't you going to classify the radioactive slides?" I provoked.

"Nothing we do here is radioactive, you know that." His tone was mocking.

"Sure. Yeah, I know." I laughed. I waited a few minutes before entering into my next line of questions. My approach was straight; I wanted to know what he was feeling and thinking. "Don't you think this work is a little beneath you?"

"Yes."

"I knew it. You think you're too good to be on the cleaning crew here." Part of me felt validated, like it was a new development that had been uncovered.

"What is wrong with that?" He asked.

I shrugged not ready for such a response.

Explaining, he stopped sweeping and our eyes met. "I think that most people are too good to have to clean up after someone else and that includes you. You shouldn't have to mop up after these slobs. People should pick up after themselves, but sadly, they don't. That's why this planet is dying off one species at a time."

He was right. Most people felt they were statistically higher than someone on a cleaning crew, but sadly, sometimes it was the only job a person could get. Not everyone has a PhD in Micro Biology. Ms. Radski was right though; Joseph's talents could be used more effectively.

"You should go. I can handle this on my own. If you stay, you might jeopardize your job and for some reason I feel like it's my fault you're here."

"Seraphin, I was given a job to do by the Captain of the *John F. Kennedy*. The worst thing a man at sea can do is disregard orders from his Captain. Until the Captain tells me otherwise, I will continue to carry out the job that I was told to do. You have no effect on my contempt for Dr. Radski."

"But I have something to do with your being here. Don't try to hide it. You're protecting me from something, aren't you?" Looking away it was difficult to not yell.

"I protect lots of people from lots of things. I told you before, it's my duty."

His elusive behavior bothered me because I wanted to know more. About him or about the situation, I wasn't sure. "Why won't you just be honest with me? I can tell you're hiding something."

He met my eyes again. "Seraphin, solitude is where I'm most comfortable and I don't confide in people so it's hard. I know you think I'm odd but it's the truth."

How could I argue with this? It's the same way I felt. I wasn't ready to open my life to him so why should I have expected him to do the same?

Sensing some tension on the subject, I decided to shift the conversation to something a little less intense. "Have you been on all the research vessels? Some of those are amazing. I toured the *George Washington* and *Theodore Roosevelt*. They're more like cruise ships."

"Every one of them!" He said proud, relieved at the change of topic. "I helped design the labs for the *George Washington*, they're spectacular. We took a whale tagging crew up to Alaska last October. It has all the comforts of home. State of the art everything; you could live on those two ships. They're like floating cities."

We continued talking casually about the ships and the CORE facility. When he spoke I listened attentively, he was quite intelligent and even though I carried a 4.0 grade point average, all through high school, his knowledge intimidated me.

When we finished in the cafeteria we were called to the main deck to clean bird droppings from the railings. The work was demeaning. If Joseph felt ashamed, he didn't show it. His spirits were high and he talked almost non-stop. Most of the conversation revolved around his classes at the University of Maine. Earlier that spring he had finished his Bachelor of Science degree in Marine Science. In the fall he was entering into the first year of the Master of Science, Oceanography program. When he asked where I would be going to college, I shrugged my shoulders.

"You should have picked a school by now. What are your choices?" Concerned he stopped working and gave me his full attention.

The truth, I hadn't sent any college applications in. When my grandmother died earlier that year, so did my ambition. The attorney said I had a trust fund that my father arranged. I could use the money for college but it didn't appeal to me.

"I don't have any choices," sheepishly admitting. "I never actually applied to any schools."

"Seraphin, please forgive me if I'm overstepping any conversation boundaries but the least you could do is try. My aunt said your grades were fantastic and that you graduated top of your class. Why would you want all that hard work to go to waste?" Forcing me to look at him he moved around my body each time I turned to avoid him.

The point was valid. Knowing that my actions were irresponsible, I admitted fault. "Joseph, I know."

He made quite a few attempts to speak but retracted his thoughts before vocalizing. Instead, he simply offered to help. "Well, if you need anything, let me know. I'd be happy to help."

His sincerity took me by surprise.

The curious girl from the cafeteria interrupted us. "Jay, we could use your help for about an hour. Could you manage to take a break from this? Dr. Radski is analyzing the photos of the carcass and some of our new recruits still don't know lab protocol. They're—how can I put this lightly, unsatisfactory?"

"Perrine Canard, I'd like you to meet Seraphin Shedd." She greeted me with her intense brown eyes. They were the color of milk chocolate. She was quite stunning and as I shook her hand and politely met her acquaintance, jealousy was stirring inside.

"Seraphin, that's an interesting name." Not a nice name, I noted. I wondered what thoughts she was not speaking. No response came to mind so I remained silent.

The three of us stood awkwardly, awaiting Joseph's answer. It seemed like it took him longer than it should have. He finally spoke. "Can I go?"

"Go where you're needed." Without as much as a 'thanks' they took off for the lab discussing particle samples and carbon levels. Ethan passed Joseph and Perrine. Joseph's head turned a little as he passed and I met his eyes from across the deck. The corner of his mouth turned up slightly just barely cracking a smile as he rounded the bend and disappeared.

The more I grew to know Joseph, the more Ms. Z echoed in my head. *You never know who might end up in your life.* I found it peculiar how right she was.

I slumped down to take a break. My back was sore and the skin on my hands felt raw from the cleaning solution. My having a dislike for showing any weakness in front of Joseph had been standing in the way of my physical comfort. It was a welcomed interlude.

Showing fault in front of Ethan didn't matter, he had seen me at my most vulnerable moments. He never tried to console me with meaningless words, which in itself came as a comfort. After the death of my grandmother words would not have made anything better, though they did seem to make things worse. I didn't want to move in with the Cottington family and Mara made it clear that she didn't want me there. Hiding in my room became the norm and one night while Mara was on the phone complaining about how I had to live with them until June, Ethan knocked at my door. Reluctantly, I answered. He handed me a warm cup of tea. That action said more than any word could convey. Then I knew, as far as he was concerned, I was welcome in his home. It might have just been my imagination but I also took it to mean that he understood how impossible his mother could be. At times I felt sorry for him. He and his mother had almost no relationship.

When Ethan sat down beside me he let out a defeated sigh. We stayed shoulder to shoulder. I gave him the same courtesy he gave me many months ago and asked him nothing. Instead I leaned my head against his shoulder and felt his headrest on the top of mine. Together we sat for nearly half an hour. I realized that somehow Ethan Cottington had come to represent family. He was, after all, the closest thing I had to a relative. I didn't know how he felt about me and would never ask, instead I was content with the way I felt about him and assumed his feelings were similar.

After watching sea gulls defecate all over the once clean deck, I went back to work. The rest of the day I didn't see Joseph. Ethan came to chat often throughout the late evening and into the night. A few times he even helped when I was barely holding on to consciousness. It seemed like every time the *John F. Kennedy* hit a wave I had to fight blacking out. It helped that he knew I was frightened and in his own quiet, unemotional way, he took my mind off of the fact I was standing on the deck of a ship out in the open sea. At one point he even gave me his headphones and I listened to his play list. The music held my attention, redirecting it from the looming waves.

I returned to our cabin around midnight. Exhaustion inhabited my body and my mind. Expecting to see Joseph sleeping, I was careful not to make any loud noise, though once in the cabin, I realized he wasn't on his cot. It made me curious that I hadn't seen him, considering the

John F. Kennedy was rather small. Earlier in the evening, when I went to the lab for a spill clean-up, he wasn't there either.

I stripped down to my tank top and shorts. My clothes were filthy and I was hot and sticky with sweat. The skin on my fingertips felt like it was on fire from having my hands in cleaning solution. My thighs hurt from squatting down to clean the deck and my lower back hurt because I was lifting buckets of water with my back and not my legs, contrary to what the illustration on the side of the bucket so clearly told me to do. The worst part about it was that in a few hours, I was going to have to wake up and do it again.

When I finally put my head to the pillow and started to drift to sleep, footsteps and muted voices outside the cabin door pulled me awake. The knob on the door turned but it was locked. It made me realize that I never gave him a key.

Then there was a gentle knock.

"Seraphin, let me in." Joseph whispered.

Crawling out from under the thin covering, I moved slowly. It was warm in the cabin and the cool cotton of the sheet felt nice. It was a bit aggravating to move my body since it had found such comfort. After unlocking the latch and opening the door, I waited for him to step in. Thrown over his arm was the green MOLE shirt and he wore only his shorts. No shoes were on his feet. Goose bumps covered his skin and his hair was dripping wet.

A big smile crossed his face. "I hope you didn't wait up for me."

"I didn't." I hurried back to the cot, my body trying desperately to be content again. "Where have you been? Did you fall in?"

He didn't answer. With his back to me he took a towel from the shelf and began to dry off. I tried to make sense of the tattoo on the nape of his neck but could not. Before I could ask about it he began his own line of questions.

"How did your evening go?" Asking in a hushed voice though I wasn't sure why. "Did you and Ethan have a nice time?"

"A nice time? This evening was exhausting." I didn't lie. "Ethan was a huge help though. He kept my mind off of things."

Turning to face me and leaning against the wall, he folded his arms. "By what means did he use, *to keep your mind off of things*?" His voice was almost mocking.

Though I wasn't certain, I sensed a tinge of jealousy. Or perhaps it was just an endearing tease but regardless; I wasn't in the mood to entertain either. "If you'll hit the light when you're through, I'd like to get some rest before breakfast."

Before he could respond I turned over in the cot, facing away from his curious gaze.

"Alright." Mumbling, the light turned off and the room went black. "Sleep well Seraphin."

"Mmhmm," I mumbled back. "G'night, Joseph."

The cot shook as he jumped up onto the top bunk. He was quiet for some time and I had begun to doze when he whispered. "Are you sleeping?"

My mind was slipping quickly into a restful state so I didn't answer him.

He waited a few moments and then asked a second time, "Seraphin, are you sleeping?"

Again, I didn't answer.

Climbing off of his cot, I felt him standing beside me. He drew the air in deep, letting out an almost painful sigh. Barely audible he spoke. "I wish I could stay."

Then he mysteriously left.

Resisting the urge to follow him, I knew I had to focus on sleep. The boat gently rocked and soon I drifted into a deep slumber.

My mind attacked with a horrible nightmare. One I had before.

His voice was soothing but his words were alarming. He repeated himself, "Seraphin, you have to go. They are coming, they know we're here." Everything was black except for a small light at the end of the tunnel. I held Joseph tight as he pleaded. "You have to go. Please go."

I was too afraid to cry and too stubborn to let him face the oncoming danger alone. Something horrible was approaching, or was it someone? Loud sirens began sounding and the closer they came the louder they were. The light was moving toward us. At first the noises were slow and dreadful but they grew faster and out of control. The light twisted into quick flashes of color spinning.

Joseph yelled to leave but I wouldn't. I knew we had to face this together.

EIGHT

*T*error ripped through my body and it escaped my lips in the form of a scream.

I woke. Red lights were blinking and sirens were sounding on the *John F. Kennedy*. Someone was pounding at my door and shouting. "PHIN, WAKE UP. YOU HAVE TO GET OUT OF THERE." It was Ethan.

Opening the cabin door, I found him wearing a life vest. Water dripped from his face. His white t-shirt was so wet that the skin on his arms showed through.

I wanted to shut the door and crawl back into the cot. The nightmare I was having seemed like a fairy tale compared to what reality was presenting.

The gentle rocking ship had turned into a violent carnival ride. The floor began to tilt. Ethan wrapped one arm around me, holding onto the hallway rail with the other. The panic in his eyes was unforgettable.

The walls seemed to shift around us; reminiscent of the children's crooked fun house at the Bar Harbor annual fair. Ethan held me close as we slowly crept through the creaking hall. Our bodies moved from side to side as the boat churned. Each step was a fight for balance. When I lost mine and was thrown into a wall, Ethan did his best to shield me from the impact.

The sirens were too loud. I had trouble comprehending what he was saying. He had to yell several times before I understood. "YOU NEED A LIFE VEST. THEY ARE IN THE MAIN CABIN."

Why did I need a life vest? Was it naivety or just denial? I wasn't sure, but the thought of the *John F. Kennedy* sinking didn't enter my mind until that moment. It took seconds for the magnitude of the circumstances to consume me. My head grew lighter and, according to Ethan, all the blood drained from my cheeks. Seeing my face turn completely white caused him to panic.

Violently shaking me was the only thing he could think to do. "FOCUS! I CAN'T HELP YOU IF YOU BLACK OUT."

It was true what he said. There was not a lot he could do for me once my body went limp and my mind escaped to the past. I needed to help him, help me.

Ethan continued shouting. "PHIN, FOCUS! FIGHT IT!"

My eyes locked with his, they were Mara's eyes and I hated them. Anger swelled inside me and I focused, but not on the boat or the ocean. Instead I focused on Mara Cottington and how she would blame me if anything happened to Ethan.

I had to save him. I could almost hear Mara's voice telling me I was weak.

"I am not weak." I said but the sirens were so loud, Ethan couldn't hear me. All that mattered was that I heard and believed myself.

We wrapped our arms together and continued fighting forward. As we approached the stairs leading to the deck I could feel the cause of our distress. An enormous squall was overhead. My thoughts turned to the girl Joseph spoke of. He said storms were not always bad. That didn't seem possible. There was no way to put a positive spin on the storm that hovered over the *John F. Kennedy*. My mood grew increasingly angry. I was angry with Joseph for not being there to save me, though I wasn't sure why. I was angry with Mrs. Keyes for not showing up for crew call and forcing me on a sinking ship. I was angry with Mara Cottington for the blame she would place on me if anything happened to Ethan.

Pure and simple, I was angrier than ever before. However, I was also more aware of my existence and the possibility that those moments could very well be my last. And, I was conscious. For the fist time in many years, my mind stayed on.

Rain pelted our faces. Water was pouring over the railings with each wave that hit but I fought. Pushing in front of Ethan, I became his protector. He yelled but I ignored. Finally, he lined his body behind mine, allowing me to take the lead.

As we emerged from the stairway, an enormous tidal wave emerged from the ocean. The *John F. Kennedy* was under its crest.

"HANG ON." I screamed to Ethan, pointing at the wall of water. We wrapped ourselves around the railing. The powerful wave crashed. Water surrounded us and panic showed itself. I quickly blocked my thoughts, instead recalling my new purpose. I focused on Ethan who looked to be struggling. The life vest was too thick, preventing him from gripping. His arms slipped down the wet slick metal. Letting go, I shot across the stairway just in time to grab the fabric handle on the back of his life vest. His body skimmed the surface of the water as it washed down the hallway below us. I held onto Ethan tighter than I knew possible.

The ship cleared the rest of the wave, allowing us a small window of calm. We stepped onto the main deck but instead of moving upright, we moved on our hands and knees. Thunder crashed as lightening flashed across the night sky. The door to the main cabin was with in sights. Ethan pointed. I responded with a nod of my head, letting him know I understood. Inch by inch we crawled across the deck. The wood was wet and slippery; sheets of water ran across my knees and wrists. The closer we came to the main cabin, the nearer to the side of the boat we were. Ethan pointed to the ocean. Again I nodded, letting him know I understood we were dangerously close. The door was only about 6 feet from us. I tried to keep my focus on our destination but when a large crate full of equipment began sliding, I had to turn away. It was headed straight for Ethan.

My pace quickened. Ethan turned in time to see me position myself in front of the crate. It hit me full force. It hurt so badly.

"SERAPHIN, NO!" Ethan screamed.

The weight of the crate was too much and the deck was excessively slick. It threw me against the guardrail. My back slammed into it, and the crate trapped my feet. Trying to hold on, my fingers were too small to wrap around the thick railing. My eyes met Ethan's; he was so close to the door. Knowing what he was thinking, I shook my head and pointed to the main cabin.

He shook his head and began to rise off of his knees. Balance would not let him attempt a rescue though. The water pulled back, the stern of the *John F. Kennedy* followed. Ethan was thrown onto his rear end, sliding through the open door to safety.

Relief flowed through me knowing that my original purpose was fulfilled. Ethan was unharmed.

I, on the other hand, was in quite a predicament. Trying to wiggle my feet free was not possible. The crate was too heavy. Thankful that my legs were numb but concerned with how much damage had been done to them, I made the mistake of bending forward to see. My center of gravity was lost and as the vessel righted itself, momentum was gained.

The crate slid away from my feet. No longer pinned, my legs were free. I righted myself but with nothing holding me in place and nothing to grab, I was exposed to the whims of the ocean.

Another wave, like a gigantic hand, pulled itself high above the boat.

The *John F. Kennedy* tipped forward again.

Foot above head, I flipped over the railing. In the blink of an eye, I was washed into the raging sea.

Screaming.

Screaming.

Gasping.

I sank under the water and had to fight to the surface. Only seconds later I was pushed under. Again, I had to fight to the surface.

The sirens of the *John F. Kennedy* were softer.

Ethan was leaning over the railing.

NO!

Someone came and pulled him back. Relief filled me. Ethan would not be diving in. He would get home safe.

Would I get home safe?

Screaming; all I could do was scream. Raising my arms in the air seemed futile, but I did it anyway.

The waves seemed to carry me further away from safety; from life.

A helicopter hovered over the *John F. Kennedy*. They looked like toys rising and falling with the waves.

There was movement on the opposite side of the boat. Someone dove into the water.

Maybe it was the rescue swimmer? No. The bright white strobe light, attached to the rescue swimmers jumpsuit, flashed on deck. *Did they know I was in danger?* I continued to scream, still fighting.

The night grew dark. Lights from the rescue helicopter moved further away. I was alone.

My legs, as well as my arms held no feeling. With a raw throat, I held back the useless screams. After so many years of trying, the water finally had me. Grabbing at the surface with my frozen fingers, it offered me nothing to cling to. With little hope for life, I took one last breath.

A furious wave, like the bully it was, pushed me under. Even if I had the strength to swim, I didn't know where the surface was.

It was dark.

It was quiet.

It was an uneven match.

I prayed. *Please God, let me be with my father. I miss him dearly. Amen.* Closing my eyes, there was no difference in the darkness. Warmth filled me. It was peaceful. The most peace I have ever felt.

I let the air go from my lungs. Bubbles tickled as they left. *Goodbye air.*

Something brought me back. My ears rang loud. Then a voice called to me. *Seraphin, stay with me.*

The ice cold of the water returned and I longed for the warmth of giving up.

The voice, again, Seraphin, do not breathe.

My lungs longed for oxygen. The involuntary impulse of needing to breathe took over. If a person can live their life never knowing such a desire they should consider themselves blessed. No longer could I resist. Gasping, I flooded my lungs.

Burning. Vehement burning. The pain was harsh. I wanted death. Only death would stop the pain. Suddenly, I could feel my legs. Though, I wished I could not. They were smoldering with ache.

Panic struck. My legs were stuck in something slimy and warm. The sea was black. I could see nothing. Or could I? Someone was swimming but it was too late, death grabbed me before he could.

NINE

As the dog panted there was whispering telling it to control its breathing. The dog would not listen. The whispering was kind but the panting was angry. Agreeing with the whispering voice, I wanted the dog to stop panting too. It was painful to hear. *Someone stop the panting.*

"Breathe slowly. Try to take deep breaths." Joseph whispered.

I felt the warmth of his lips by my ear. The awareness pulled me conscious. The realization that Joseph was giving me instructions on how I should breathe sank in. I was the panting dog—rather, I sounded like one.

The memory of drowning had me gasping for air again.

He urged. "Seraphin, please try to be calm."

Was Joseph all I had? Am I in a hospital; recovering or dying?

He assured. "You are safe."

I could see only black and I could not speak. As I tried to move, pain snapped.

Joseph still close to my cheek began to hum. Fingers ran across my forehead, down my face and back around; repeatedly.

Focusing on the soft sensation, I fell asleep.

The dream was peaceful and calming. Clear, colorless waves washed overhead. They continued moving in a stream like sea currents and as I wiggled my fingers, they shimmered. A powerful flow of energy passed over my body. An iridescent glow moved to tranquil tones.

A woman was singing. When I opened my eyes, she stopped. Before they could focus, I closed them, hoping she would begin again.

She spoke. "Welcome Seraphin, is my song helping?"

Yes, though, I wasn't certain how. I nodded my head—unsure where the voice was coming from.

Pain was no longer my companion. Able to move again, I turned my head—trying to make sense of everything—looking for the voice.

Perrine Canard crossed into view. The contrast between the woman and the environment where she stood was extreme. So extreme, that I thought it was a dream. She was lovely. The space was dreary and cave-like.

"Am I dead?" My voice was rough. Only three syllables and my throat burned. Obviously, I was not fully healed.

Perrine giggled. "No. Please, try not to move or speak. Your lungs are still functioning at 60% and your leg muscles are only 70% adapted which is usual for a first time transformation."

What did that mean? Shouldn't I be in a hospital?

"Joseph will be here momentarily." She said, sensing my irritation. "You must have many questions. He will explain everything." We were quiet for several minutes before her attention turned to a dark opening in the corner of the room.

Joseph announced, "Good morning."

His voice was pleasant and familiar. The feelings caught me off guard.

"Thank you Nasani." He politely said to Perrine.

Perrine smiled at Joseph and gave him a warning, "She's still very weak."

Who is Nasani?

He answered my silent question. "Seraphin, you know how I'm both Jay and Joseph? Well, Perrine's name is actually Nasani Caro."

"Nice to meet you—again," she smiled.

For a second, I wondered what I would change my name to if given the chance—then realized an alias is an indication that someone is in hiding. And I had no one to hide from.

I tried to speak but sharp pains raced through my throat.

Nasani whispered. "Seraphin, you need to rest." She gracefully left the room.

Joseph gave me his attention. With an expression full of concern he approached. "I don't want you to speak; I'll do all the talking. I recognize that might be hard for you." Winking he let a massive smile take over his face.

I let a little smile escape. *Did he save me?* I recalled someone diving off of the *John F. Kennedy* and the voice before I drowned. It was Joseph who warned me not to breathe and while it didn't seem like it at the time, it turned out to be a very valuable message. *How did he find me?*

"Nasani, doesn't sense you're in good enough health for in-depth explanations. You need rest. We have plenty of time to talk about the things that have happened. Healing is your most important task." He was formal in the way he addressed me and I recognized that his concern was very real.

Is Ethan safe? Shifting—I could only rest knowing he was safe. "Eee—" Was the only sound I let escape.

"The Coast Guard airlifted Ethan and the rest of the crew to safety. Nasani even went for a ride. Only because she had never been on a helicopter, though, it did help to bring down their losses. You and I were the only ones who didn't go with the Guard. We, uh—went our own way. Falling in the ocean wasn't the best thing to do Seraphin."

My shoulders relaxed. Ethan was safe.

A playful smile crossed Joseph's face as he brushed a piece of hair away from my eye. "That's interesting. Out of all the questions I thought you'd ask, I didn't think Ethan's wellbeing would have been the first."

Is Nasani your girlfriend?

Unexpectedly was the second question that came to mind but I didn't attempt to ask. It mattered little at the time.

"Anything else you need to know before you rest?" Everything—although to my amazement, I didn't want to hear it right then. I reasoned that it couldn't have been great news that I was laying in a cave instead of on a hospital bed. Perhaps Nasani was right? I wasn't ready to hear in depth explanations.

Oddly enough, I also felt out of harm's way and even though I barely knew Joseph, the clear peaceful blue of his eyes made me trust.

He let his eyes wander down my body. Whispering as his affectionate hands wrapped around mine. "You should sleep, I will go."

I shook my head, not wanting to be left alone in the eerie cave.

"I can stay. But, only if you want." With surprise in his voice he suggested.

Smiling, I nodded my head. It was nice to smile.

Joseph sat beside me. I drifted to sleep.

It wasn't a dream. Currents of energy washed over my body. It was the same as before, yet more powerful. The colorless waves were stronger and flowed faster. Areas of iridescent waves clustered around my throat, lungs and legs. There was more focus.

My eyes were closed but I was awake.

A man was singing. I focused on the song, but couldn't make out any words. It was composed from a series of striking tones. "Seraphin?" The singing stopped.

When I opened my eyes Joseph was still beside me though appeared pale with dark circles under his eyes. Immediately, I felt bad for asking him to stay.

"Joseph? What was I seeing?" The roughness and pain in my voice was no more.

Joseph smiled. He sat on the bed, fussing with the pillows behind my head. Pulling me forward; I noticed his hands were cold and his skin rough.

Taking his hand, I voiced my concern. "You're hands, they're like ice."

"Sorry." He pulled away. "It's cold down here."

It wasn't cold; the air was damp and warm. "Something's wrong."

"I'm fine Seraphin, or at least, I will be after I get some rest." Unconvincingly, he tried to assure me.

"You should rest now." I worried.

"No, what I need to do is talk." Speaking seemed to exhaust him and his eyes were a sickly shade of bluish gray. The color was disheartening.

Though I disagreed, I held out my hand, signaling for him to begin talking.

He obliged. "The currents are healing waves created through sound—from the sea. Nasani and I are able to use this power. It's an ancient form of healing that some of us have been gifted with. We healed you."

As he spoke, I gazed around the room. The bed I was lying in was stunning. Purple velvet blankets covered my legs. Lavender trimmed pillows stitched with elaborate embroidery supported my body. The bed was large and the Victorian inspired bed frame held wrought iron interwoven wisteria branches with blooms.

"Thank you." I mumbled. *They healed me?*

Bragging, he continued. "I was able to go for one full moon orbit this last time."

"Moon orbit?" I asked, wondering if aliens had abducted me. Before asking, I convinced myself that aliens would not have such nice bedding.

"The time it takes for the moon to orbit the earth. Approximately 27 days." He spoke nonchalantly.

"I've been asleep for a month?" Pain moved through my throat as my voice grew louder and I sat up.

Joseph placed his hands on my shoulders, gently guiding me back to the pillow. "Seraphin, don't undo all my hard work. I'm exhausted and I don't think I have anything left in me to fix you again."

"I'm sorry. It's just that—how is all this possible? I remember the falling into the ocean and drowning. What happened after that?"

"Actually, you *almost* drowned, which should be impossible. You took a lot of water in, even though I specifically told you not to breathe. Next time don't suck water into your lungs. It makes things worse." As if what he said was common knowledge, people drown all the time. He made no sense.

"Why are we here then—why didn't you take me to a hospital?" The obvious place for healing, I asked.

"Because I knew I could heal you." He tiptoed around the question. "You told me that you didn't want me to leave, so I stayed. Then, I couldn't bring myself to stop until you were healed. The energy was different. Like when…" his voice trailed off, "Forget it. I don't quite know how to explain."

"I'm sorry I kept you here. I had no idea. When I said I wanted you to stay…I shouldn't have…well, you can go now. You need to rest." I urged. "We can talk later. Unless—is there a possibility that I might fall asleep for another month?"

"No. Your body is healed, weak, but healed." A sense of satisfaction washed over him. "Truth be told, I've surprised myself."

"Really, I mean it. Thank you for whatever you've done. I feel like I'm healed." I sensed no pain in my body. He was right though; I did feel a bit weak.

"If you are comfortable with it, I'd like to take a little nap and maybe get a bite to eat. I won't be long. In the meantime, Nasani can bring you something to eat so your energy level will be restored."

"Yes. Of course I'm comfortable with you resting. I'm close to demanding it. You've done so much. The least I can do is let you rest.

We can talk later." Assuring him, my voice was positive and encouraging.

Placing his hand on mine he smiled with his tired eyes. "Thanks Seraphin. I'll send Nasani in."

Before he left, I had to know one minor detail. "Joseph is Nasani—you know…I mean, who is she?" Squirming a little with embarrassment, I wanted to ask if she was his girlfriend but I stopped short.

"Nasani and I have been friends for a very long time. I trust her with my life and you should too. She's amazing. The two of you will get along wonderfully," he left.

A tinge of jealousy ran through me. "Yeah, she seems great," I muttered.

The room was large and for the most part, it was empty. There was, of course, the bed. However, besides that, only two antique wooden chairs and a side table filled the dreary space. Atop the table sat a gold urn, which held a floral arrangement. The flowers were a mixture of aqua blue petals, green blooms, and deep red foliage. I wondered where they were indigenous, perhaps the rainforest. Even though I had never been outside of Maine, the dampness of the room and the strange moss covering the rock walls had me guessing we were far away from my house on Briarwood Court.

Nasani entered the room carrying a silver-serving tray. Her brown eyes were friendly and her hair was arranged like a Greek goddess—ringlets fell far down her back. Thin ribbons were braided in, serving as a headband. The threads of the colored ribbons fell to one side of her face. A long robe crossed her thin body and was held tight by pink satin sash. She moved with the grace of a ballerina.

"Seraphin," saying as if she were starting out a song, "Joseph tells me your appetite might be back. I have prepared warm tomato bisque and you have to try this tea. It's my favorite. I just finished drying the leaves, which is a difficult feat down here."

She unfolded little legs from the tray and placed it over my lap. The serving set could have been from the Queen of England's personal collection. She moved over to the flower arrangement and began to rearrange the stems—pulling out a few withered leaves.

I took a spoonful of the bisque, my stomach roared with hunger. I remembered that my last meal had been on the *John F. Kennedy* with Joseph. Finishing too fast to be considered ladylike, I began sipping the tea.

"Is that not divine?" Nasani said, referring to the tea. She finished arranging the flowers and sat on the edge of the bed where Joseph had been. "Did you like the bisque?"

"It was delicious. Thank you." I said, trying to slow my drinking. I wasn't sure if it was her elegant presence or the silver serving pieces, but I felt like I had very little etiquette and almost no manners.

"I'm glad Joseph is resting. I've been worried. He's been channeling his gifts more than usual and I could tell he was beginning to wear down. His determination to get you back is something I would not have thought him capable of." She gazed into my eyes. "Although, I can see the appeal, you are quite remarkable. Aren't you?"

"I'm not sure I know what you mean Nasani." Feeling quite uncomfortable locked in her gaze. "Why would he be determined to save me? I'm no one special."

"Do you feel like going for a walk, Seraphin?" She ignored my question.

"YES." The idea of getting fresh air was exciting. It wasn't until I stood that I noticed I was no longer wearing the tank top and shorts I fell off the *John F. Kennedy* in. A blue silk robe, of which, I had never seen before was draped over my body.

As I began taking steps, my legs were wobbly. Nasani helped to stabilize. Against the rough rocky floor, my feet were bare. They were decorated with little silver toe rings and beaded bands, just like Nasani's.

"Are you alright Seraphin?" She asked, concerned.

"Just getting my footing, my feet feel so heavy and hard to lift." Taking steps was a struggle.

"That's something we have problems with down here. You'll get used to it. The source of gravity is stronger because we are closer." She made little sense.

"Down where, exactly?" We entered into a large open chamber with candles burning along the walls. Stacked in random piles were planks of weathered wood and broken pieces of what looked to be antique chairs and tables. There was a waterfall that poured down. Growing from the ceiling was a maze of vines with blooms of blue and green; the same kind that were in the golden urn.

"We are no longer by the coast of Maine. After the attack, it was too dangerous to stay in the Atlantic area, so he brought you here to heal. I know, deep down, you understand that you are different. He couldn't just take you to the corner clinic. Do you know he saved your life?" She continued a few steps ahead.

"I do know that." I answered.

She was right. I could tell that home was far. I knew Joseph saved my life. Did I understand I was different? That depended on what part of my life she was referring to. I wanted specifics. "You said Joseph brought me here for a reason? Forgive me if I sound a little reluctant to sing his praises. I'd like to know that reason before I abandon all skepticism."

"I won't speak to his reason; you'll have to ask him why. I can show you where we are but I doubt you'd believe me. So, I'll just show you something spectacular." She continued along a narrow dark path—there was a glow at the end.

The path opened into a massive cavern, the space was comparable to the size of a football field. Blue stalagmites and stalactites covered the entire ceiling and most of the floor. A few hung so low that we had to duck under. Weaving in between the tall formations, I wondered where Joseph had taken me. Never had I seen nature in such a raw form.

The light from her candle lit the space but outside of the candle's protective circle, the air was a dark glow of greenish-blue. "Seraphin, we are in the crust of the Ionian Sea—right between Italy and Greece."

"Italy and Greece!" I squealed. At least, we were still on the planet Earth.

"Yes." She said, seeming bored with my excitement. "We only come here when it's time to lay low. Think of it as a summer home."

She confirmed my suspicion. They were hiding from something. "What do you mean 'the crust'? And why are we hiding in a cave?"

"Like I said, this is a very dangerous time. The *John F. Kennedy* was attacked."

"Nasani, the *John F. Kennedy* was in a storm—unless you consider it an attack launched by Mother Nature."

"That's what they want you to think Seraphin." She dismissed sarcasm. "Do you want to go for a swim?"

"You cannot be serious," laughing.

"Oh, I'm perfectly serious. Follow me." Her voice was commanding as it echoed around me.

We entered a grotto. Crystal speleothems decorated the space. Stone arches sprawled over two pools. A soft cloud of steam rose from the water.

"Welcome to Cosa Identica grotto. This is the most amazing puddle on the planet." Nasani untied the pink sash that held her robe together, letting all her coverings fall to the floor. Wearing a tank top and bikini bottoms, she kicked her leg and with a hop, dove head first into the farthest pool.

Even the smell of it was frightening. My lungs began to ache as I could feel the salty air filling them.

She popped her head out of the water and shouted. "Seraphin, are you coming in?"

"Oh, Nasani—no, I don't…"

She cut me off. "You have a suit on, you know? It's under your robe. I let you borrow one."

"I do?" Sure enough, under the blue silk was a tank top and bikini bottoms—just like Nasani wore. Folding the robe back over myself, I tried to explain again. "This is all so thoughtful of you, but really, I'm not a swimmer."

She swam to the side. "Oh, I see. Can you put your feet in at least? The water is smooth and warm. No pollutants can enter this far down. This is probably one of the only times you'll experience such purity."

Sitting down on the edge of the pool, I clung to the rocky arch.

She reached out her hand to assist.

I eased my feet into the warm water, letting them soak.

"That's a start." She smiled then dove away, leaving me with a splash.

For a long time, I simply watched her swim. No part of me wanted to join her in the water.

The room was quiet and the gentle splashing was calming. The water was a cloudy blue and even though my feet were not visible under the surface, I was not worried. For the first time in a long time, I felt at ease being near it. The air was thick and steamy and I closed my eyes to rest.

Within a few seconds Nasani popped her head out of the other side of the pool. "Are you feeling well?" She asked.

"I was just relaxing. You were right; this pool is like nothing I have ever experienced. The texture of the water is different. It calms me." For a second I closed my eyes again.

In that short time, Nasani was in front of me, bringing her head and shoulders up onto the rock. "Seraphin, look at the other pool."

Listening to her command, I turned to see an image of Nasani in the opposite pool, waving her arms.

The copy confused me. "How are you doing that?

"It's a twin, an identical illusion of the pool and everything in it. Go and see for yourself. Try to put your toes in the other pool, though I warn you, do it slowly. Joseph will eradicate me if I let you wound yourself."

I walked to the other arch to see for myself. There was no pool. It was a solid wall, made from stone, with the illusion superimposed.

Then a face emerged from the mirage. "Joseph?"

"I heard my name. Why am I going to eradicate you Nasani?" He asked with a smile.

"No reason. Seems there's no need. She's still in one piece." She teased.

I reached out to touch him, only to run my knuckles against the rough stone.

"Seraphin, it's good to see you walking around again." His voice came from behind, sounding more energetic than before.

A mirrored reflection of the pool still seemed impossible. "This isn't real. This can't be real." My fingers moved over the image as my brain tried to process what I was seeing.

Staring into my eyes as he spoke through his reflection on the wall, I wondered if he could see my confused expression though I was not facing him. "You're absolutely right. This is the real pool—over here. That's just a fake one to confuse intruders."

"Intruders?" I went back to the real pool to see if I could see myself—or a mirage of myself. But I couldn't. "What kind of intruders?"

Joseph swam to the edge. "The unwelcome and careless, I suppose. Think of how easy it would be to dive into the first pool by mistake."

"Easy for me? No. That would not happen. However, I can see how the image of a realistic pool onto a stone wall could be life threatening for others." Again I tried to make myself appear in the mirage.

Joseph caught on to what I was doing. "The only way you'll show up in that pool, is if you get into this one."

When I turned around, his hand was outstretched. I felt the urge to jump in. The pull was strong and I wasn't sure if it was coming from Joseph or the water.

"Thanks, but you already know how I feel about water. I'll just hang here on the rock, where it's safe." Again, I sat with my feet dangling in the water.

Joseph was beside my leg, his head and shoulders above the surface. While treading, several times he brushed against my calf as his arms moved back and forth.

Nasani was across the pool, swimming. She was flipping, turning and giggling like a child and it made me smile.

Joseph turned to watch her while I watched him.

The dark rings that were under his eyes had vanished. His skin held more color than it did earlier. A little bit of rest worked wonders on him. Again, I noticed a small tattoo on the nape of his neck. It was slightly darker than his skin tone and not very noticeable. The design was a simple geometric figure, consisting of two curves opposite one another with a perfect circle on the tail of each. It reminded me of the letter 'S' but with a break in the middle.

Before I could ask him what it was, he spoke. "You'll be good for her. I'm all she has and that's just not enough. She seems more relaxed since I brought you here and it's been years since I have seen her playful. She's like a dolphin out there." Then he closed his eyes, held out his arm and hollered "MARCO" to which Nasani laughed out "POLO."

He swam away to search for her.

Envy swelled inside as I watched them play like children. He was calling out—eyes closed—free of all inhibitions. Nasani laughed and dodged away from him. The water pulled stronger but I resisted, taking my feet out and pulling my knees up. I rested my chin on top of them.

Not sure of where the jealousy was directed, I found myself wishing I could play the game and giggle with Nasani. When Joseph finally located her position, he wrapped his arms around her. I found myself wishing it was me he held close. It was silly to be jealous, she was sweet and it shamed me to feel that way.

They both got out of the pool. Nasani was still smiling as she pulled the robe around her body, tying it tight with the pink sash. Joseph stood next to me and shook off like a dog, throwing water everywhere. "If you won't get in I'll bring the water to you. You have to feel it somehow, it's invigorating."

I held my arms over my head and laughed. The warm water felt good and so did his attention.

"I have to be going. Joseph, don't keep her out too late. She still needs rest." Nasani looked back and smiled, winking at him. "Behave."

"Yes, Dr. Caro." He laughed.

Nasani left but before she did, she shot Joseph a horrible glance and muttered. "Do not call me that."

Joseph ignored her.

We were both quiet. I knew we should have immediately begun discussing the 'whys' and the 'hows', but neither of us knew where to start.

Questions ran through my mind. Why did you bring me here? When am I going home? How does Nasani swim so fast? Why do you both have alias'? Where is Ms. Z?

Joseph broke the silence. "So, what do you want to do Seraphin?"

My answer was ridiculous. "Well, since Nasani tells me we're in the neighborhood, I'd like to start by seeing Rome. Probably grab an authentic Pizza Marguerite and maybe ride around on a Vespa."

With a big smile, he shot my plans down. "We probably won't be able to do that. You have to stay here. It's for your own safety."

"No offense Joseph but the last time you tried to keep me safe, the boat sank." I smiled even though I was quite serious.

"No offense taken. Sadly, I'm unable to control the weather, that's not my special gift. However, I did heal you. So, that has got to count for something, right?" He looked over shyly with a silly grin.

"I suppose that counts for something." Smiling too but then remembering what Nasani said. "I heard it wasn't a storm that sank the *John F. Kennedy* but rather an attack."

"Oh yeah? Who did you hear that from?" His sarcasm was thick, as was mine.

"The Director of the United States Coast Guard called me this morning—they're investigating." I said then glanced towards the hallway where Nasani had just made her exit. "Who do you think told me?"

He laughed—I waited for an explanation. It wasn't going to come easily. "Well? What happened? Why do you believe we were attacked?"

With a sigh he caved. "I don't exactly know. One minute Nasani and I were swimming—we had only left the boat for half-an-hour—then, a swell came from nowhere. Next thing we knew the boat was getting tossed around like a toy."

"I don't follow. It was a storm, not an attack. Perhaps the sounds of the cannon blasts were lost amongst the thunder?"

"We were attacked with the storm. This was a centrally located storm that only had a diameter of a quarter mile. It was only above the *John F. Kennedy*," he was trying to convince me of the illogical.

"So God attacked the boat? Mother Nature? The North Wind?"

"No—I don't know." Growing frustrated with my questioning, he shifted his weight.

"Joseph, you realize how crazy you sound, right?" I said in all seriousness.

He only shrugged his shoulders and changed the subject. "Do you want to learn how to swim?"

I laughed loud. Why would he suggest such a thing?

"I can teach you. I'm a *VERY* good swimmer! I was NCAA Men's Swimming Division 1 Champion last year in Freestyle!" He held his shoulders proudly and offered me his hand. "No better time to learn than now."

"Wow, congratulations, that sounds like quite the accomplishment. I can see that you are a good swimmer and I don't doubt you'd be a great teacher. This might come as a surprise to you, but I can already swim. I just prefer not to. Thanks anyway."

"But, do you know how to swim, the way you were meant to swim? Besides, might be helpful, seeing as though right now we're under approximately 13,000 feet of water."

Before I could react he jumped into the pool and sent a large splash, soaking me completely. The silk from the robe stuck to my arms. *What did he mean we were 13,000 feet under water? Almost everything I've experienced today was unfathomable.*

Joseph healing me was still at the top of my list of unbelievable feats but a part of me already knew he had such abilities. It finally occurred to me that when I fell jogging, the waves of healing energy appeared right before he whispered for me to wake up. In addition, on the *John F. Kennedy* he took care of my headache with just a touch.

Could it be that all this was a dream? Was I actually in a coma, lying on a hospital bed at the University of Maine Medical Center? I pinched myself, just to make sure. It hurt.

I watched the surface of the pool closely, waiting for Joseph to emerge, but the water stayed still. The ripples created by his cannon-ball style jump settled and there was no movement.

Where was he? I sat on the side of the pool and put my feet in the water; my ears began to ring and then, I heard him.

Seraphin, don't freak out. I'm fine. I'm at the bottom of the pool. His voice rang through my mind, as clear as if he was standing next to me talking. I was reminded of him speaking to me as I was drowning. *I need you to continue touching the water so you can hear me. If you don't, I won't be able to communicate with you. I want to show you something.* Again, he was doing something that was rationally impossible.

I spoke out to an empty room. "Alright—I guess." Feeling like *Alice in Wonderland*, I reasoned it was possible that Joseph would emerge as a giant multi-colored cat.

His face came out of the water first and he smiled.

I smiled. "Ok, why would I freak out? You can talk to me through water. It's a little odd, but cool."

Holding my gaze, he looked deep into my eyes. The blue of his eyes was impressive; I was trapped in them. Staying silent, he winked at me then dove down, head first.

Then, a large fin with silver and blue scales came out of the water where Joseph's feet should have been. I pulled my feet out of the water and scurried back. I wondered if it was another illusion from the crazy pool. I waited before moving to the side, very slowly, I put one foot in.

I thought I scared you away. His voice was calm and gentle. *I'm going to resurface when you're ready to talk and I'll explain everything. Put your other foot in when you want me to come up.*

I waited, carefully deliberating, taking into consideration how he put my safety at the top of his priority list. He had been there, pulling me out of high tide and shipwrecks. I thought about Ms. Z, his aunt, and how she seemed to talk to fish. Joseph growing a fish tail made sense, in an anomalous way. Oddly enough, I wasn't scared; it didn't make sense to be frightened. He wouldn't have saved my life so many times just to put me in more danger.

My toe barely touched the water. With a force more powerful than humanly possible, Joseph shot through the surface; half-man and half-fish. His upper body was perfectly normal but just below his hips began the fascinating sheath of texture that housed his lower extremities. And, though they were joined, the curves of his thighs, knees and calves remained but his feet were spread thin, stretched to create a caudal fin.

The silver scales were not, in my opinion, beautiful but they were remarkable. A stretch of blue that matched the color of his eyes ran down either side of the covering. Not a costume, it appeared too organic; so, what was it? It seemed to make him powerful. Nearly 20 feet above the pool, he twisted his body, bending over the stone arch and returning to the water without a splash.

Joseph caught my attention with a gentle tug on my foot. *Are you freaked out?* There was a touch of worry to his voice.

"A little," I answered him honestly, speaking loud, hoping he could hear me under the water. "More so, I am curious as to what just happened."

Reluctantly, he peeked above the water and tried to gauge my expression. Knowing what it felt like to be labeled a freak, I gave him a friendly smile and he seemed to relax. A smooth, soft tickle ran up my calf. The wide flat fin floated to the surface of the water. As I touched it with my finger tips it changed, shrinking back into two bare feet.

He laughed and pulled himself out of the water, sitting beside me with two absolutely normal legs stretching out from his swim shorts. "I know you don't like the water. But you need to give it another chance, it's where you belong."

"Joseph. I can't—did you just turn into…?" Facing him I didn't meet his eyes but rather focused on his legs, waiting for them to change again.

"Yeah," he leaned into me and nudged with his shoulder. "It's pretty cool, huh?"

"Is it the pool?"

"No, it's me." Moving closer, he was inches from my face. For a moment, I thought he was going to kiss me but instead, he whispered in my ear. "Seraphin Shedd, you are a mermaid."

I began laughing. There must have been something in the air. The pool was creating another illusion or Joseph was playing pranks. Taking my feet out of the water and standing up I noticed that he was not laughing, but instead, he looked offended. "You are very funny Joseph. Have you gone to such great lengths to get me into the water? Suppose I dive in now, will a magical tail just appear?"

Still very serious, he answered. "No magic, just nature and if you give me a chance I'll show you how to make your scales materialize."

Pulling the robe tight around me; I left Joseph alone by the side of the pool. "Make my scales materialize? Yeah right. Why are you playing games with me? I haven't a clue where I am, why I'm here and who you are. If you don't mind, or even if you do mind, I'd like to go home now." My head was cluttered with thoughts and I found it hard to breathe. I continued laughing because if I didn't, I would have cried.

"Seraphin, I'm not playing games. Please trust me, I can show you." Joseph pleaded.

Nothing made sense but at the same time everything made sense. It had been so long, I almost forgot what was happening. He reached me just in time to stop my head from hitting the stone floor. His eyes met mine before everything went black.

My flashback was lucid. The details remained the same. I defied my father, my friends were horrible to pressure, I was weak to give into their demands but when I saw my father on the ship at sea, things were different. I watched in horror as he was pulled into the sea. What I remember as a giant wave was no longer that but instead a massive black creature emerged from the violent water, wrapping its self around the ship. Tentacles slithered the deck—capturing him. The other men huddled together, screamed in terror. As he was pulled to his death, he spoke his last words. *"Seraphin, get out of the water."*

Wrapped in purple blankets and still shaking from what my mind showed me, I was afraid to move. It was the first time I had seen a vision of him being swept away. The creature was confusing. I was alone and thankful for it. Stepping down onto the cool rock, I noticed how much better I was feeling. My legs were no longer difficult to lift and my lungs were functioning better than before.

The waterfall was pouring down in the cavern adjacent to my room and as I passed by, I thought I saw a small shadow emerge from the steady stream. When I turned to take a closer look, Joseph walked in behind me.

"Seraphin, you have to stop passing out all the time." He placed his hand on my shoulder. "How are you feeling? I know it's a lot to digest."

The shadow faded into the waterfall when Joseph came near. Touching the water and pushing my hand through, I felt nothing unusual. I did not respond to his questioning but remained silent. Truth be told, I was angry at him and confused by my reluctance.

With a soft voice he continued. "Nasani found these things for you to wear. If you would like to get cleaned up and change, I'll take you to the spring."

Nodding my head, I obliged.

Joseph led the way down a narrow pathway. We curved around a stone wall and into a majestic room that held a trickling fall and a shallow pool.

"It's only 2 feet deep, so no need to panic." He laid the clothing on a rock. "Nasani has some soap over there. I'll wait just beyond the stone wall."

"Thanks." I said. What I really wanted was my shower at the house on Briarwood Court, along with my clothing. I missed home, even if it was empty.

With a soft voice he spoke with meaning. "Seraphin, I'm sorry that I had to be the one to reveal such an unbelievable reality. I can't begin to understand why your parents would hide such a thing from you. All I ask is that you don't hate me for being the only person in your life to tell you the truth."

When I turned to respond, he was already gone.

The pool was warm. More than once I closed my eyes and tried to imagine lying in the bathtub at home, but the rough rocky floor made it impossible to picture. I washed with an oversized block of lavender scented soap. It left my skin soft and silky. The clothing that Nasani supplied me with was unlike anything I would usually wear. The black leggings reminded me of yoga pants but fit too tight and were cropped right under the knees. The tank top was also black and made from the same stretchy material as the leggings. She also left me with a pile of ribbons, just like the ones that ran through her hair. I tried to braid them in to mine but with only my reflection in the water to rely on, it proved impossible. Finally, I gave up and tied a thick black ribbon around my head to serve as a headband. It would have to do.

When I came around the wall, Joseph was waiting, as promised. Standing up slowly, he glanced at the leggings.

I felt uncomfortable with the attention and began tugging—pulling them away from my body. "I think these are too tight. Does she have a larger pair?"

"I doubt she does, besides, I think…" he trailed off, "…they look great on you."

Together we walked to the main cavern. He was quiet and I felt bad for being angry. "Joseph, I don't mean to come off as difficult, it's just that I long for my life before the *John F. Kennedy*. Ethan, the Keyes and my neighbors are probably so worried; they need to know that I'm alive. It's really cool that you are what you say you are, but I'm just a girl who misses her life back home."

"Seraphin, I should have talked to you about this sooner but I didn't know what to say." As he grabbed my hand, chills went through my body. He directed me over to a pile of wooden boards and gestured for me to sit. Then, with a match, he lit two candles that hung on the rocky wall. The flames danced as he walked past to join me on the wooden board where I sat.

"You remember when we met at the school, right?" He asked awkwardly.

"Of course," I was sarcastic. "You were so warm and friendly."

"Right, so you do remember." Joking back, my sarcasm seemed to ease his nervousness. "I hope you understand now why I was such a jerk. When my aunt introduced us—it was a bit of a surprise. You're the first person she's ever introduced me to, using my real name. I thought she had lost her mind but when she pulled me into the hallway, she explained that you were worth meeting. I probably could have handled it better."

"I understand—and yes, you could have." I agreed with him.

"After that day, even though I tried, I couldn't get you out of my mind."

That took me by surprise. "Sorry?"

"Never had a girl captured me like—" He stopped, shifting awkwardly. "It's just that, you had a way about you. Something I've not—and when you spoke to me on the beach, you were so—"

I remained silent as he stood up and began to pace the room.

"I couldn't help but think that my aunt brought us together for a reason, so I started to watch you."

"You *were* following me."

"No, just observing."

"Isn't that essentially the same thing?" I didn't know whether to be unsettled or flattered.

"No. It's not the same thing. I wanted to keep my distance but you made that impossible." He smiled. "I just wanted to find out why my aunt thought you were so special. The moment I started healing you, the day you fell—I could feel it."

"You could feel what?"

"I could feel—YOU. Your essence—life; whatever you want to call it. I could feel that you were—like me; like us, Nasani and I—oh and my aunt too."

"Ms. Z is…" I couldn't finish the sentence.

"In all the years you knew my aunt, she never once spoke with you about being a mermaid?"

The corners of my mouth dropped as I cringed at the absurd word—still not convinced Joseph wasn't playing a trick. I searched my mind for the answer to his question. "Only once, the day I met you. We cut through the pool area and looked at the mosaic at the bottom of the pool. She was acting strange."

"What did she say?"

"Only that the female and the male featured in the mosaic were powerful—that they were protectors. To be honest, I was too nervous to ask questions." I admitted.

"The Guardians?" He stopped pacing and stared at me.

"Yes, they were Guardians, not protectors—sorry."

"Huh?" He muttered to himself and began pacing again. "She didn't say anything else?"

"No." I had a few questions of my own. "Joseph, when you said that you could feel that I was…well, like you, what did you mean?"

"The best way to explain it is like when you're alone, say in a room and then even though you don't see the person walk in, you can feel that you're no longer alone. It is kind of like that. When I placed my hands on your head to heal, I was no longer alone. It was strange—I've never felt like that before." Lost in his own thoughts for a moment he paused then continued. "Though, I think I made a big mistake by healing you like that."

Confused by his statement I defended my behavior that day. "I wasn't expecting you to show up like that and I know I can be stubborn at times but you have to know I was grateful for whatever you did to help me heal."

He laughed. "That's not what I'm saying. It's not that I regret healing you. I believe the storm that day was an attack. There was something in the air—it wasn't right. The same thing happened the night the *John F. Kennedy* went down. Remember I told you about the girl who could manipulate the weather? Well I couldn't help but think that someone was using the weather against us."

"I remember the story—but you said she had the power of a storm you didn't say anything about her being able to control all aspects of the weather." Suddenly I wanted to hear the tale.

"The storm was her demise, so I guess that's the part that everyone remembers but she could create snow in the desert or make the sun hot enough to melt glaciers in the arctic."

"Was she real or was she a merperson?"

"Are you saying that merpeople aren't real?" He didn't give me a chance to answer. "We are real Seraphin."

"I didn't mean—"

Cutting me off, he continued explaining. "There are many stories; some true and some are meant to teach a lesson. I don't know if she actually walked this earth at one point in time. Up until recently I didn't think it possible for someone to manipulate the weather. Merpeople have always been labeled with such abilities—being blamed for great storms that destroyed enormous ships."

"Why do you and Nasani think the *John F. Kennedy* was attacked?"

"Because I sensed the threat—it's another gift I have. I can sense when someone means to do harm, whether it is directed at me or the people around me."

"Is that why you thought I was in danger? Why you forced yourself on board?"

He sighed. "Not entirely."

"Then why did you throw such a fit—telling me it was dangerous? Obviously you knew something was going to happen."

His hands met his forehead then his fingers moved through his hair. "I didn't know—well, I didn't know for sure, I suspected something. More so, I worried that I put you in danger the day I healed you. It's possible that they know you were with me."

"Who?"

"The people who don't like me, let's just leave it at that for now." With dark eyes he moved across the cavern.

Sensing the tension, I shifted the conversation. "Where did you go when you left me in the cabin on the *John F. Kennedy*?"

"I met up with Nasani. We took a dive so we could talk without anyone overhearing. When we noticed the storm begin, Nasani went back to the boat to help the rest of the crew. I waited in the water in case someone fell in." His eyes lightened and he seemed to relax. A smile crossed his face as he continued. "Then, of all the people on the boat, you had to fall in."

With a tilt of my head I raised my eyebrows and shrugged my shoulders.

"At first I thought you knew what you were. So I didn't go after you right away, instead I climbed aboard and tried calming Ethan down. He was hysterical and nearly dove in to save you. I had to promise him I would save you before he would get into the rescue basket."

Tears swelled when I heard that Ethan almost risked his life to save mine. Quietly I mouthed his name and sighed. "Ethan."

Joseph went on to explain how he dove into the water to be sure I was safe. "You still hadn't transformed. Then I realized, you didn't know you could transform; you didn't know what you were."

"All I know is that I was dead. The rest is just a theory." Making sure he understood that I remained skeptical.

He ignored me. "I didn't want to get too close, I had transformed. Looking back, I should have saved you sooner but I was scared."

"Of what?"

"Of your reaction—that you would think I was a freak."

"You *are* a freak." I assured him, in a joking manner.

We laughed.

"I'm so sorry. I should have told you sooner."

"Well, if it's any comfort, I wouldn't have believed you. As a matter of fact, I have my doubts."

"How could you have doubts? You're alive—which should have been impossible for an ordinary human being. You're in a cavern under the Ionian Sea. AND, you just saw the lower half of my body turn into a fish tail. What other proof do you need?" His arms raised into the air in disbelief.

"You saved me. As far as I can tell, *you* have amazing abilities—to heal with magical waves of energy—to swim at impossible depths; but just because *you're* a mermaid, that doesn't make me one."

"First of all…" Obviously flustered, "…I AM NOT a mermaid. I am a merman."

I laughed. "Oh, forgive—"

He cut me off. "SECOND, you transformed right in front of me Seraphin. When I found you after the *John F. Kennedy*, you were in full-on mermaid-form; fish tail and all! So don't act like I don't know what I'm talking about."

I didn't want to argue with him so I stood and quietly began to walk away. As I passed the waterfall, he caught me, grabbing my arm.

"Please wait. I'm sorry I raised my voice." He stood behind me. "You have to trust me, it's so dangerous for you right now and it's not your fault. It's my fault. Anyone who gets near me—"

"Joseph?" I turned around just as a black shadow hand came through the waterfall next to us. It reached for me but Joseph shoved me against the wall. He grabbed a large wooden plank from the pile of debris, swinging at the shadow hand. It went instead for him, gripping his leg and pulling him into the waterfall.

I screamed for Nasani but she didn't hear.

Then, without thinking, I jumped into the waterfall and found myself floating in pitch-black water, 13,000 feet under the Ionian Sea.

TEN

Now what?

There was so much pressure. It was impossible to swim. The water was ice cold and dark. It encased me. Panic was close by and a feeling of claustrophobia set in—trapped. The opening to the waterfall was no longer visible. If I didn't get my mind and body to cooperate, the chances of survival were slim.

Please God. If Joseph was telling the truth and this is not a strange dream, now is the time for something magnificent to occur.

The weight of the ocean was too much. Breath escaped and air bubbles tickled past my nose. Joseph had warned about the dangers of allowing salt water to enter my lungs. He was certain there would be no chance of recovery if it happened a second time. Already knowing the pain and suffering involved, I resisted—though I found it near impossible to fight my body's instinct to draw breath. I floated in limbo, waiting for anything.

For so long, there was only black—too deep for any light. Theoretically or scientifically speaking; I shouldn't have been alive. The pressure at that depth was insurmountable. It alone should have killed me.

After a while, shadowy shapes began to form in the distance. The contrast between my light skin and the black pants I wore showed itself. Much like being in a dark room, my eyes dilated to their fullest, allowing the slightest variations in darkness to register.

Still, no gills appeared; my legs remained unchanged.

The cold crept through, numbing my fingers and toes first. My forearms and calves were next—I wondered if the sea could claim me. Joseph said it was near impossible to drown but surely there would be no surviving when the cold reached into my chest and slowed my heart to a stop.

With only an ounce of fight remaining, I began to kick my unfeeling legs. At first, the sinking continued. Anger surged inside—Ms. Z was missing—Joseph was now missing—am I missing too? Would I ever see my home again? My lovely house in Maine—would I see Ethan again? He probably thinks I'm dead—but I'm not dead, am I? I am very much alive.

Perhaps this was the end? It sure didn't feel that way though, if felt like the beginning of something. The beginning of my life with unbelievable possibilities—it must be real and why not? If this were all a lie, surely death would have captured me by now. Yet, still I remain.

Staring into the darkness, twinkling lights began to flash. Lines of brightness, like a child's glow toy, began forming and pushing through the distant water. Neon colors of blue, purple and pinks formed tiny umbrella shapes as they came near. Jelly fish! They moved gracefully and the bioluminescence coming from within their bodies was enchanting. Hundreds of them lit the immediate area—yet they kept their distance forming a ring.

Were they curious? What did they want?

I could do them no harm; surely they knew that the upper hand was not mine.

Slowly they began to spiral into a cone, surrounding me. The pressure of the water decreased. Were they helping me—somehow able to reduce the weight of the water?

I reached with my arms, grabbing. My legs kicked harder and faster until they began to burn with ache. Still the jelly fish swarmed like bees protecting their queen. The water began to pass. I was going up.

Then I wanted it. I yearned for a tail—a large glorious fin. My legs came together and with one deliberate kick, I was stronger than the ocean.

A thin layer of scales started at my ankles and slid up my legs—encasing them completely. My feet grew flat and long, like Joseph's had been; shaped like the caudal fin of a fish. Though, mine was much more ornate than his, with several layers that spread in the water, thin and beautiful like fabric floating. When I tried to wiggle my toes, the fin danced at my control. Running my hands down the smooth scales that covered my lower body, I could hardly believe it was so. On my hips, small gills had formed yet—I still had to resist the urge to breathe with my lungs.

The jelly fish exploded out of formation and faded into the darkness below.

The water rushed past my face as I swam faster than I could ever imagine possible. Senses were heightened—the sounds of the jelly fish below were joyous. The water tasted fresh and smooth and salt coated my body, protecting it from the cold.

Then I heard him calling to me and I followed.

Seraphin, you are doing it. I need your help. Follow my voice. Joseph's voice rang through my head and instantly I was able to determine how far he was and how fast I needed to swim to catch up. I also knew that he wasn't alone, someone was near him.

His voice led me to a coral reef, overcrowded with fish. I swam around; searching for him. The water rippled and someone came towards me—though I couldn't see anyone, I could feel. Somehow I knew it wasn't Joseph. It whipped past me so fast I spun around several times before regaining my bearings.

Still I searched; he gave off a distress signal. The signal was weaker and I could no longer hear his voice in my head. My senses brought me to a large overhang covered with sea mollusks and a vast, flat sea creature pressed firmly against the reef. It spun around and I met its face. I knew instantly it was harmless but could still sense Joseph underneath the creature's body.

How was I going to move a sea creature? I swam behind it; it had a long tail with a stinger on the end. I thought about pulling the tail but common sense kicked in and I decided that wasn't the best plan. After all, it seemed safe but even a puppy bites when its tail is pulled.

The creature lifted up the side of it's large thin body, it must have been nearly 12 feet wide, and slapped it down against the reef. A large push of water raced towards and knocked me head over fin. I swam back, giggling a little.

My best option was to use the water to move it, as it did to me. I folded in half, pulling my new lower body close. Then with all the energy I could conjure, I thrust my large fin against the rock. A push of water raised the creature and sent it floating wildly away from the reef.

A small tunnel was revealed and as I crept closer, I wondered what I had gotten myself into. It was dark and I couldn't see inside. I reached down and someone grabbed my hand, before I had time to react I was being pulled away by, to my surprise, Joseph.

I could hear him in my head again; he was amused—sounding like a mad man. *Seraphin, you were amazing!* He laughed, pulling me to his chest and hugging me tight. I loved the attention. Though, I was confused, he seemed so calm for having just been fish-napped. *Let's go to the surface, I'll explain what just happened.*

He signaled for me to follow. At times he raced ahead, showing off with flips and dives. For the most part though, he swam beside me; gesturing for me to imitate his movements. It was shocking how much energy flowed through my body, I felt like I could swim without ever growing weary.

After what seemed like a few miles, he reached out his hand for me. He placed his other hand in front of us and a protective water dome formed around our bodies. Like a torpedo we shot through the water, I couldn't begin to estimate how fast we were traveling.

We slowed down as we came near the surface. I could see the sunlight and feel the warm water surround my body. It had been over a month since the John F. Kennedy—I'd never been away from the sky for that long. The sun floated like a blurry orb above the surface. It was so intense that I had to squint.

You first. Follow my instructions carefully. Joseph pointed up. *Don't gasp for air. Let yourself adjust then when you feel your gills close, take a deep breath of oxygen. Your body will do the rest.* Nervous, I did exactly what he said and broke the surface of the water slowly. I wanted to gasp for air but resisted, paying close attention to my gills. They closed and I took a deep breath. My lungs came to life and my legs separated as the thin layer of scales slid back down and were absorbed into the bare flesh just above my ankles.

He broke the surface of the water laughing hysterically. "I told you."

I didn't feel much like laughing though. "Joseph, what is going on? I'm a mermaid. How is this possible?" I cringed as I said it, feeling embarrassed at the ridiculousness of the word.

"Your parents, who are they?"

"Who were they? Is more accurate a question. Samuel and Ester Shedd; though I never knew my mother." Curious as to why he was asking such a personal question.

"Well, they're merpeople. Or rather, they were merpeople."

"There is no way my father was a merman. He drowned, Joseph." Nearly admitting that I had visions of him being pulled into the ocean by a sea monster, but I stopped short.

"They both had to be; otherwise you'd be—well, a goonch," sneering a little as he said the word.

"A goonch?"

"If a merperson mates with an ordinary human," a little uneasy as he spoke, "their kids are deformed. They're like mutant fish-people. Some of them can't even swim."

I thought about what he was saying but, I would have known if my father was a fish…right? Then again, I didn't even know I was one.

Exhaustion was taking hold and I could barely draw a breath. "Can we call a water taxi or something?"

"Your legs tire faster when you're breathing air into your lungs. Since gills are capable of removing oxygen from water because of their feathery makeup, more gas exchange can occur—the whole process energizes your body differently." Sounding like a high school biology teacher, he added a sprinkle of humor to lighten the lesson. "That's why most people are fat. Oh and whales too, they are super fat. Although, this is more of an advantage since their blubber is less dense than water. Being fat helps their enormous bodies stay afloat—otherwise they'd sink like the Titanic."

"Dolphins aren't fat." I said.

"Well, that's because they watch what they eat." He teased. "Alright, hop on, I'll take us to shore. I doubt you'll be able to transform if you're not threatened with the idea of drowning."

"Sorry to say, you're probably right." I smiled.

He grabbed my arms and put them around his neck. *Hold on tight.* I heard his voice in my head.

I locked my legs around him like he was giving me a piggyback ride and he took off. It was by no means smooth and I had to bury my head in the back of his neck to avoid getting splattered in the face with water. I thought back to the 9th grade when Lucy Stevenson returned from Florida bragging about how she swam with dolphins. I was so jealous. *If she could only see me now, I'm hitching a ride from a hot merman. Beat that!*

I heard Joseph laugh in my head. "What's so funny?" I spoke in his ear.

Nothing, he replied.

When we were close to the shore, there were a few people wading in the water. Luckily they didn't notice anything unusual; after all, Joseph looked average from the waist up. I swam next to him the rest of the way. He transformed, kicking with his legs, but I still found it difficult to keep pace. It made perfect sense that he was the state swimming champion, what didn't make sense is the fact that he was an average, everyday college student. "You go to college? On land?"

"Yes. Like a real boy." His sense of humor was endearing.

"But you're not normal." I regretted the second it slipped out.

"Wow, thanks. Neither are you and that didn't stop you from going to high school...on land." It was very logical response.

"You have a point." It always felt like I didn't belong there. All of the sudden, my life seemed a lot more complicated—even if some things were beginning to make sense. I smiled as I realized my therapist was wrong, water DID pull at me. It wanted me to know what I was and that I belonged in it.

We reached the rocky coast and I made the mistake of standing up. Not only did my legs ache but the rocks on the bottom were sharp against my feet.

"Oh, you shouldn't stand on these if you can help it. They'll cut the bottoms of your feet; mess with your tail fin. You cut your foot—you cut your fin. The tail fin is the most delicate part after you transform but it is also the most important. Your feet essentially are your fin. They morph. It's where all your power and control comes from."

I had so much to learn. "What about my leg? If I cut it will my scales be cut too?"

"No, just your foot and your toes; your scales originate from just below your ankles. You must have felt them."

I did feel them but still found it hard to believe. They slithered right over the black pants I was wearing.

He was crawling with his hands, letting his legs float behind him. "This is how you get across sharp rocks. You can cut your hands all you want and it won't affect a thing."

"Good to know." We were in only 2 feet of water but I did what he said and crawled across the rocks with my hands.

The water was green with algae and seaweed. The jagged bottom was covered with a thin layer of slime. Joseph, again sounding like a biology teacher, went on to explain how it was good to see the growth along the coast because when the water was green it indicated a healthy environment where fish and other marine life could feed.

I was less enthusiastic about the growth. The seaweed was caught in my hair and the slick rocks made it impossible to keep my balance. More than once I fell under the surface when my hand slipped.

The water was deeper the closer we came to the side of a sprawling wall made of stone, and I wondered why we were there. Before diving under he glanced to be sure no one was watching and then instructed me to follow him. "Take a deep breath, though, it won't really matter if you don't." He said before he disappeared under the surface.

I, reluctantly, did as he instructed and followed. Nearly 10 feet down I could see him waving. It was difficult and I had to fight a current that wanted to pull me to the surface. Recognizing my struggle he floated up to assist. His hand grabbed my foot and he pulled me down and we met face to face. My hair swirled around us and for more than a few seconds we were caught in each other's gaze. With a smile, air bubbles escaped his mouth, which, for some reason, made me giggle. Air bubbles danced out of my mouth as well.

Then it hit me, I was having fun, which should have been impossible considering the fact that my life had just been turned upside down.

He wrapped his arm around my shoulder and guided me to an opening in the rock. Together we swam through.

On the other side, the surface appeared darker. To my amazement, we were inside of a grotto. When my face met the air, I gasped at the beauty. It was dark with the exception of a blue glow that made the wide-open space seem magical. The water was calmer than the waves that brought us there. The walls and ceiling seemed to hug the space with their gentle but strong arcs. A thick layer of salt deposits coated nearly everything while blue crystals jutted out of the walls like spikes.

He caught my expression and smiled wide. "I had a feeling you would love it here. This is my favorite place in the entire world. It's one of the only places on the surface where the water is deep enough and the ceiling high enough to really have some fun." He pointed to the naturally vaulted ceilings above us.

They were much higher than in the Cosa Identica grotto. Recalling how I was amazed at his ability to jump out of the water with such force. "Do you mean you can jump even higher than you did before?"

A smug look came over his face. "Uh, yeah. That was nothing—child's play. Even these ceilings are no match for me."

"But they have got to be nearly 50 feet at the highest point."

Then he sighed. "What I wouldn't give to be able to jump out in the open ocean."

"Impossible. Even a dolphin can't jump higher than 20 feet above the surface of the water." I doubted him.

"Seraphin, you saw how I travel, right? Imagine me going that fast but allowing myself to break the surface of the water. There's no telling how high I could go."

He was right. I couldn't begin to guess the speed in which he traveled. Miles meant nothing. I was certain he could cross an ocean in a day's time.

"How do you go so fast?" I wondered. "Is that one of your special gifts—like healing?"

"I bet you could go that fast too."

"I doubt that. I'm not really great at this whole mermaid thing."

He swam closer. "Don't feel bad. I've been doing this my whole life. You're just getting started and you're already better than most of the mermaids I've met."

"I doubt that too."

"I'm being truthful. It's who you are; besides, you're so good at it. Already your senses are extremely powerful. More accurate than most—not mine of course." At this he smirked and held his head high.

I did feel powerful for the first time in my life. My senses were amazingly precise—it was hard to believe I found Joseph so easily at the reef.

He continued. "What astonished me the most is how you caught my signal through Louie. Usually signals don't travel through other animals or coral reefs. I should have been completely hidden. I'm the only one who ought to be able to do that."

"Looks like you've met your match." I joked. When I said it, I got the feeling it meant something more to him. There was an uncomfortable moment between us—interrupted only when I realized I didn't know a Louie. "Who is Louie?"

"Louie is the manta-ray who was covering me in the tunnel, back at the reef." We swam together to the side of the grotto and climbed onto a large rock. He held out his arm to help me—pulling me out of the water.

"He has a name?"

He went on to explain that there are 'regulars'. Some marine animals he encounters more often than others—he's pretty sure they follow him around but he can't prove it. It's almost like having a stray dog that keeps showing up but won't quite claim you as its owner. He doesn't take care of them—he just names them and observes. I had a feeling maybe he was the one being observed though. Louie the manta-ray looked less out of place on a coral reef than Joseph did.

I held his hand and followed through a narrow passage—large stones served as steps and we climbed higher into the grotto. It was so dark that I lost confidence in my own feet. Joseph caught on to my slowing pace. He reached his free hand back to my other hand and pulled both of my arms around his waist.

"Hang on to me and try to mimic my steps. We're almost there."

The hanging on part wasn't going to be a problem. "We're almost where?"

"The top of the cliff; I want you to see the sunset from up there."

It was quiet as we moved together. The front of my body was against the back of his and I rested my forehead between his shoulder blades. I closed my eyes and concentrated on his motions—trusting, since I couldn't see in the darkness. My legs moved with his quite naturally, we were in sync. I felt this way when we swam beside each other as well. It was comfortable to be near him.

Light seeped through my eyelids as we climbed closer to an opening in the rock. I lifted my head, glancing around. An extremely narrow passage bursting with light held a steep incline with small notches that reminded me of a very poorly designed rock-climbing wall—only without harnesses.

"Joseph, is that the way out of here?"

"We could always go back the way we came but what fun would that be? I thought we could work on your dive once the sun goes down."

"My dive?"

"You'll see." He assured with an untrusting glance.

I let go of him. There was no chance we could fit through the steep passage together.

"I'll go first, watch where I step." Then he gripped two notches and pulled himself higher. When he was near the top I watched him turn his shoulders in order fit through the opening. His arms dangled down, waiting for mine.

I glanced back, reminding myself of the pitch-black passage that led to the breathtaking grotto. I almost turned—intimidated by the steep climb ahead. But then, I heard his voice coaxing—challenging me. "C'mon Seraphin, you can do it—don't be a soggy noodle."

"A soggy noodle?" I laughed. I felt like a soggy noodle and was certain, with my new lifestyle, that wasn't going to change. I wondered what I looked like and since I was clear of his line of vision I took the opportunity to run fingers through my water logged hair. It proved to be a good idea as I untangled two slimy strands of seaweed from the thick black ribbon that was still tied around my head.

"My arms are starting to fall asleep." Joseph shouted. They were still dangling, waiting impatiently to lift me through the narrow opening.

I grabbed the two notches, like he had done. It was difficult to lift myself higher and I used my feet more than Joseph had. I tried not to injure them—well aware that any injury would damage my fin. Stretching, my hand was barely able to make contact with his awaiting fingertips. He surprised me by taking hold and gently pulling. I was narrower than he was but still couldn't fit through the opening with my shoulders square—my body contorted as I shimmied through.

When I finally emerged we stood at least 100 feet above the Gulf of Taranto on a cliff. There was barely room for two and I leaned against the rock, afraid to look down. Then a thought occurred to me. "I am not diving off of this cliff."

He only laughed—not responding to the panic in my voice. "Have a seat. We've got time."

I slid my back down the hard stone, sitting as far away from the edge as possible; though it was still only a few feet. Joseph perched himself on the edge with his legs dangling over. I wondered how many times he sat up there and if he had ever brought Nasani to see the sunset. "Do you and Nasani come up here often?"

"I'm always trying to get her to come up—she says I'm crazy to even try. Diving isn't her idea of fun."

"I'm pretty certain it's not mine either." I said nervously.

"How do you know? You've never tried. I bet you're great at diving." A poor attempt at trying to flatter me into seeing it his way no doubt. "Besides, I'll be right beside you."

That thought held a little comfort but not nearly enough. "And you'll be able to put me back together again with your magic super healing powers when I bash my head off the jagged rocks below." I said with false enthusiasm.

He laughed again.

For a while we were silent, it seemed wrong to ruin such a spectacular sight with meaningless chitchat. Joseph moved beside me, away from the edge of the cliff. A breeze brought a chill across my damp skin, which resulted in goose bumps. He caught on and pulled me closer to his warm body—wrapping me in his arms. It surprised me how at ease I was—though his casual behavior nagged. I had nearly forgotten about what got us there in the first place. "Joseph, you don't seem the least bit concerned with what happened earlier."

Confusion crossed his face. "Concerned about what?"

"What was the shadow hand? How were you in danger?"

"OH!" He chuckled. "That was Nasani. We realized you wouldn't transform unless you were under extreme pressure to do so. We staged that whole thing." He shrugged his shoulders and tilted his head. "Please don't be upset. It was the only way—AND you were amazing! Thanks for coming after me, by the way. It's nice to know I could count on you to help if I was actually in trouble."

"That was a horrible trick." I tried to stand up, feeling foolish after falling for their ploy. "I'm not so sure I'd help again."

He put his hand on my shoulder. "Where could you possibly go Seraphin? We are on a cliff in Italy along the Gulf of Taranto. Please sit and watch the sun set with me."

I looked into his blue eyes and I knew I had no other choice. However, I didn't have to snuggle with him. I sat further away—and he noticed.

"You're upset with me?" he asked with sad eyes.

Before answering, I thought about it. It wasn't that I was upset with him. It was embarrassing that Joseph and Nasani had to go to such lengths to break through my stubbornness. "No. I'm not upset with you. I understand why you tricked me. Though, I was very worried about you and I didn't like feeling that way. Please don't do it again."

I stared at the setting sun disappearing behind the horizon—I didn't want to look at him and I wasn't sure why. In my peripheral vision I could see him staring at me with big eyes and a wide smile. He closed the gap between us and I felt the warmth of his body once more.

"Nasani will be relieved to know that you're not mad at us. For the record, she thought it was a horrible idea and didn't want any part but it was taking her too long to come up with an alternate plan so she had to give in."

"Good to know. Though, she could have let me in on your little secret when I got to the reef instead of just blowing past."

"What?" He looked concerned. "She wasn't at the reef."

"Are you sure? You know we weren't alone right? There was someone close to you the whole time I was following. It wasn't until I got to the reef that who ever it was left. And you said your senses were better than mine."

"Honest, I didn't know we were being followed. I was so focused on you that I disregarded our safety." He looked terrified and stood up, glancing at the water, then to me and back at the water again. "Seraphin, I have to go. I have to leave you here for a while. I'll be back, I promise."

"Joseph, you can't be serious. You're not leaving me on a cliff, alone. I don't know how to get back to the cavern. What if something happens?" I was in a strange place and he was all I had. No way would he leave me; for a moment I thought it was another trick. "If you think you can trick me into diving off this cliff, you're mistaken."

"This is no trick. I have to leave you behind because you can't keep up yet. I have to go. She's in trouble." He gave me one final glance; he took my face into his hand and gently brushed my cheek with his fingertips. "I promise I'll come back for you. I'm so sorry, I have to protect her."

He barely made a splash when dove into the water.

There I was, alone on a cliff over looking the setting sun and the Gulf of Taranto.

"Oh……no……." I whispered. My head felt light and I leaned against a large boulder for support. My vision grew blurry and my heart raced. Blacking out, I relived my father's death yet again though that time I could see the monster's familiar eyes. I felt like I trusted those eyes, like I had seen them before, like they would protect me but instead they were attached to a monster that was killing my father.

When I woke, I couldn't move. I was belted to a board with large foam padding surrounding my head and body. A man wearing a green jumpsuit and a white helmet stood next to me, sending hand signals to an awaiting helicopter, a spotlight shined down on us and he was shouting to me in a different language.

"Sei al sicuro." He yelled over the thumping of the helicopter blades. "Lo son il tenente Enzio, Italiano Guardia Costiera. Devo portarti in ospedale."

"I don't know what you're saying." I yelled back. "What are you doing? Let me go."

"Ah, you speak-a English. A little bit, I speak-a English." He shouted with a thick accent. "You safe now. My…eh…name-a Lieutenant Enzio, Eh…Italian Coast-a Guard."

"NO. NO. Don't take me anywhere. I'm waiting for my friend to come back." I tried to struggle but it was useless, I couldn't move. "I am safe here. Let me out of this thing."

"RELAX-a. ALL GOOD." He gave me a large white smile and thumbs up. "You go for ride to-a hospital."

There was no arguing with Lieutenant Enzio. I supposed it looked quite peculiar that a woman was passed out on the side of a cliff. I could see how he thought he was helping. He waved to the helicopter and a long cord with metal hooks came down—he grabbed it. He attached the hooks to the board I was strapped to and gave a tug and thumbs up.

As I was lifted into the air, I thought about Joseph and wondered where he was and if he reached Nasani in time to protect her from the invisible threat.

The board I was on reached the red and white helicopter and I could read the words GUARDIA COSTIERA in bold letters along the side. Another man was in the helicopter and pulled me in. He then unhooked the board so he could send the line back down to the Lieutenant waiting on the cliff. Once he was inside the helicopter, they slammed the door and we took off. Three men dressed in green jumpsuits and wearing white helmets, spoke to each other in Italian.

One man moved closer. His English was much better though he still had a thick accent. "How are you feeling, Miss? Do you feel any pain in your body?" He belted himself in next to me, took his helmet off and grabbed a clipboard. He began writing things; he looked at his wristwatch and shouted something to the other men. Lieutenant Enzio belted himself into a seat opposite me. He took his helmet off; his thick black hair was a mess of curls. He had blue eyes that squinted a little when he smiled.

"I'm fine." I said, irritated. "Can you please take some of these straps off?"

The two men glanced at each other then back to me. Together they refused. Then Lieutenant Enzio explained in his broken English that the shackles were for my own good, while the other man checked my pulse and blood pressure. He then promised to set me free, with a doctor's approval, as soon as we landed at the hospital.

"I'll hold you to that promise." I assured him then laughed at his use of the word shackles.

He gave a gentle laugh as well. "My English need-a help. No? I help-a you, now you help-a me. Maybe you teach-a me good English?"

I couldn't help but blush a little with embarrassment. "Sure."

"So you-a promise." He winked.

The other man had finished taking my temperature. While he was recording the vitals on his clipboard, he asked for my full name and country of residence.

"Seraphin Olivia Shedd, United States of America." I answered.

"Siete sdraiati?" He said in Italian.

"What?" I asked.

"Sorry. Are you lying?" He looked up from his clipboard and stopped writing to stare at me. Then he gestured for Lieutenant Enzio to bring him a different clipboard with a thick stack of paper attached to it. He flipped through the pages; each had a large photo. He stopped at one. "Non posso credere! Ella è la ragazza mancanti dall'America."

Lieutenant Enzio glanced several times from the clipboard to me then casually said, "She is-a missing no more."

He held the clipboard over me so I could see it clearly. "Is this you?" It was my employee photo from CORE with a single red word printed above it SCOMPARSA.

"Yes." I cringed as I stared back at the worst photo I had ever taken.

"You are the missing girl everyone has been looking for. We all assumed you were dead. How did you end up on the side of a cliff?" He went back to writing on his clipboard; Lieutenant Enzio got on the radio and called someone. I could understand my name and America as he spoke to the person on the other end.

I was internationally known as a missing person? It was so embarrassing. How was I going to explain being under the sea floor with a couple of merpeople for a month? "I don't know." I suppose it wasn't lying. I still didn't know how my life had taken that strange turn.

"You don't know?" He questioned back. "How is it that you don't know?"

I repeated myself. "I don't know. I just want to go home. Can you take me home?"

"We will get you home-a Miss." Lieutenant Enzio was calmer and placed his hand on mine.

I realized that despite the unfortunate situation I had fell into, it was probably going to end with me being back on Briarwood Court. I let out a small smile and sighed a bit of relief. Above all else, I just wanted to go back to Maine.

The Guardia Costiera men took me to a hospital in Taranto, Italy where they established that I was in amazingly good health. Thanks to Joseph, I thought. Lieutenant Enzio kept his promise and freed me from the safety board as soon as he had the doctor's clearance. Since the hospital wanted to keep me for a few days—he asked if he could stop in and see me the next afternoon for an English lesson. I told him I didn't mind.

It wasn't long before I became an international sensation. After just a few hours, guards were placed at my hospital room door to keep the media out and I was no longer permitted to walk freely around the hallway. Apparently, everyone wanted to know 'the story' of how a girl survived a shipwreck and 30 days at sea.

The following afternoon Lieutenant Enzio showed up at my door, flashing his Guardia Costiera identification badge to the guards outside the room. I almost didn't recognize him without his uniform. He was dressed in a simple light-blue button-down shirt that was not tucked into his relaxed jeans. In his hands be held a bright bouquet of wild flowers—a peculiar mix that I had never seen before. The most interesting was a tulip shaped bloom with pointed petals and a red velvety leaf.

For an hour we exchanged words in our respective languages. He brought a list of words and phrases he wanted translated. Since I didn't know how to speak or read Italian, it was difficult to communicate with him. He would stand up and act out a scene or draw a picture to help—when he did this, we both laughed freely at the silliness of the situation.

"How you say 'sirena' in-a English?" He turned serious and sat beside me on the bed.

"Do you mean 'sirens' like an emergency vehicle? An ambulance?" I asked.

"No. I mean 'sirena'. I show you." He leaned over my legs—tucking the white sheet that covered me under them.

I tried to guess what he was doing. "Are you tucking me in?"

He put his finger up. "Un minuto."

Then he moved closer to my upper thighs and I grew uncomfortable. "Excuse me!" I put my hands on his and he simply smiled and moved back down to my calves. When he got to my feet, he took a blanket off of the chair in the corner and began folding and shaping it. His body was in my way and I couldn't tell what he had done until he moved away from the bed. To my horror, he had fashioned a mermaid tail out of the blankets. A white tail encased my legs and feet.

"So—" He waited.

"So what?" I asked.

"Sirena?" He asked innocently.

It took several minutes for me to speak. Did he know what I was? Was this some kind of coincidence? I wanted to jump out of the hospital bed and run—but to where?

He waited patiently with a large smile across his face.

"Mermaid."

"Ah, YES. A mer-a-maida!"

"Why do you want to know that word?" The suspicion in my voice was hard to hide.

The large smile returned as he traced his hands down my legs.

"You're creeping me out Lieutenant."

"Creeping?"

"You're making me uncomfortable." I clarified, hoping he could translate that.

"Oh. So sorry." He withdrew his hands. "I know-a you; is what I say."

Was he saying that he knew I was a mermaid? I still cringed at the silliness of the word. I was fantasy; mermaids were not real. My mind was having a problem processing the fact that I was something that was considered daydream; make-believe; supernatural.

"You know me how?" The language barrier was proving troublesome.

"I know-a you—you are like me."

"I don't follow. How am I like you Lieutenant?"

"Seraphin, please—I am Gianni."

I shifted away from him, frightened of what he meant. Deep down I knew what he was saying and I searched my mind for any slip-up I might have made indicating that I was part fish. "How then, Gianni, are we alike?"

"I am a tritone." He said, low—glancing at the door as he did so.

"I don't know what that means." Though, it didn't take long for my mind to make the connection to the Mythological, conch shell carrying; son of Poseidon—Triton.

A simple smile crossed his face and he leaned into me. "You-a know."

I nodded my head. Yes, I knew the meaning. He was telling me that he was a merman, which was just as absurd as my being a mermaid. How many of us were there? "Lieut—Gianni, I'm new to this."

"I don't know what you say." He struggled to understand.

Pointing to the blanket tail that still surrounded my legs; I said the word 'new' again. Hoping he would recognize that I was not a veteran mermaid.

"Ah—I see. Bambino sirena."

I knew that bambino meant baby. I laughed and nodded my head again.

"How?" He asked with a look of concern on his face. "Your mamma and papa not tell-a you?"

"No mamma and papa." I looked away from his puzzling eyes.

"I see." Still concerned. "You-a have friend-a."

"You? Yes. We are friends, I suppose."

"No. You-a have friend-a. Missing friend-a—I read news—the man."

A smile crossed my face. He was talking about Joseph. "YES! My friend Jay Mason is still missing."

He frowned. "No. No Jay Mason—Joseph Merrick. He no tell-a you name?"

"I know his name. How do you know his name?"

"Joseph Merrick no friend-a Seraphin—no friend-a Gianni—only friend-a Joseph Merrick."

The language barrier was frustrating—though his message was quite clear.

I remained silent, only shaking my head—trying to process what he was saying. Obviously, he thought very little of my friend Joseph Merrick—should I as well? What made me think Joseph was my friend? He saved me—but why? Gianni saved me too, after Joseph left me stranded on a cliff.

Finally he spoke again. "I leave you to think."

"Okay." I wanted to be alone. "Gianni, thank you."

Bending down, he took my hand. "You-a nice girl. If you-a need me—find me. I'a easy to find—ask around."

ELEVEN

When the hospital discharged me, I was sent immediately to the American Embassy where a representative assured I would be on the next flight to Maine. However, before she could book a flight to the States, the Managing Director of Coastal Oceanic Research Expeditions called to say that they had chartered a private jet to bring me home. I felt uneasy about it but the Embassy representative persuaded me into accepting the ride due to the amount of media attention I was bound to receive on a public flight.

I was interviewed by two different representatives at the Embassy, a representative from CORE that flew with me on the Jet, three FBI agents before I could leave the airport in Maine and the cab driver on the ride home. I told them all the same story of how I got washed into the sea the night the storm hit the *John F. Kennedy*. I told them I didn't know how I got on the cliff in Italy. I told them I didn't know what I ate or where I slept or why I was so healthy. I lied to everyone and I felt lousy about it but I knew that if I told the truth, no one would believe me. The last thing I wanted was more psychological evaluations; I had quite enough of those in my life.

Finally after a full 72 hours from the time Joseph told me to wait for him on the cliff, the cab driver pulled into the driveway at 504 Briarwood Court. The Gran Torino was still parked in the driveway. A thick layer of dirt covered the usual shiny coat. I ran my finger down the side of it, wondering if anyone in the neighborhood knew what had happened.

My question was answered when I turned on the television. How could anyone NOT know what happened? Plastered all over the news was my CORE employee photo. Again, I cringed when I saw it. I looked half asleep with shadowy circles under my eyes; it was the image the world would remember. My 15 minutes of fame stunk. The anchors on the screen discussed me in the typical over-hyped news fashion. "MERMAID GIRL" was the headline that caught my attention on one of the national news channels. I listened as the anchor interviewed several medical specialists asking them the same questions, *"How did this girl survive?"* And *"Does she have amnesia?"*

For a moment I hated Joseph. It wasn't his fault I was a mermaid, but it was his fault that I was found on the side of a cliff nearly 5000 miles from home. Maybe Gianni was right.

The news anchors then went on to speculate the possibility that the other lost crewman, Jay Mason could be found alive. They reported that the Italian Guardia Costiera was patrolling the area in hopes of finding him. Then flashed Joseph's CORE employee photo, across the bottom of the screen—the caption read, 'STILL MISSING-Jay Mason'. My heart sank when I looked into those cobalt eyes on the screen. I finally turned it off when the tight-faced over-powdered news anchor made the joke, "Maybe she's a mermaid." A round of laughter ran through the news studio.

Good thing I didn't tell the truth.

That night I thought a great deal about Joseph and Gianni. Lost in the shock of what he said, I failed to ask Gianni how he knew Joseph.

Though, it would have been difficult for him to explain due to the language barrier. It seemed impossible that there were more of us—more fish people living normal lives. Hiding from society in plain sight—it didn't seem like the greatest way to live. Their lives cloaked by lies.

Regardless, I was delighted to be home—away from the questions and the doubting. I knew that eventually I would have to face a changed reality. However, at that moment, I wanted to feel protected by my ordinary existence and far away from Joseph's complicated life.

There was no denying my life was slightly more intricate. Questions about my family and the past swirled in my head. It was difficult to sort through. *Who was my mother? Did my father know she was a mermaid? Is that why she left us?* Nothing added up. He hid my life from me. I knew why too, because it was ridiculous to think a human being could be part fish. Such things did not exist but I was living proof of the contrary.

Thinking of my father made me recount the poem. So much was a mystery.

Where the land lay low,
the seeds best grow;
let die the life I hide from you.
Protect you as a father must,
into that world you'll not be thrust.

I tried to decipher its meaning. The first few lines were elusive. We never had a garden to speak of, a few flowerbeds at best. Most of the plants were perennials and my father rarely bothered with the upkeep. Gardening was more my grandmother's hobby. Before the *John F. Kennedy*'s demise, the middle line would have puzzled me as well. The life he hid from me was quite obviously the life of a mermaid—an existence I apparently needed protection from; as stated in the fourth line. The world of fish-people was evidently not where he wanted me.

⁂

On the flight home, the representative from CORE promised I could have my old job back. The following morning, I went to work. They assured me I would no longer have to clean the research vessels, though I told them that it was not an issue. They had a huge "Welcome Back" gathering in the cafeteria at lunch, which was embarrassing. Mrs. Keyes seemed relieved to see me and explained how she had car trouble the evening of the crew call. She was stuck on the mainland with no means of communication. I told her it was okay, because it was.

The happiest person to see me was Ethan Cottington, which was a little surprising. True, we had become friends in those days leading up to the *John F. Kennedy.* Even on board he was quite helpful, but unexpected were the bear hugs he greeted me with. It was very different from the hug I gave him on graduation day. I was the one standing with my arms to my sides. Dramatically, he recapped his worry and how he refused to leave the ship. Apparently, the Coast Guard made him, forcing him into the rescue basket and onto the helicopter. He relived, in great detail, the following day and how he so willingly joined the search and rescue teams. They patrolled the area where the *John F. Kennedy* went down for nearly a week. It felt good to have someone worry and I thanked him for caring so much.

It wasn't long before Joseph consumed my thoughts. If I had the notion I would be able to lead a normal life after the *John F. Kennedy*, I was sorely mistaken. The questions in my head began to nag. I wondered if Joseph had the answer. We didn't have a chance to talk much before he dove into the Gulf of Taranto, frenzied with Nasani's safety. Days passed and I wondered if I would see him again. I watched the evening news and after a while, new stories replaced the 'MERMAID GIRL' headlines. For this, I was grateful. However, it also meant that hope was running thin. The CORE employees were positive he would be found after they welcomed me home but they grew somber quickly as there was still no sign of their top researcher, Jay Mason. Often I passed by his office and grew sad.

One evening after work, I went to Keyes Market and wandered for almost an hour. Mr. Keyes finally approached with unease. "Can I help you find something, Seraphin?"

"No thank you. I'm not sure what I'm looking for." I kept my head down, an empty shopping basket hung over my forearm. I'm certain I looked miserable, because I was.

Instead of pushing with more questions he made small talk.

"Mrs. Keyes tells me that since your return you've been doing remarkably well. At first she was worried but she says you're tough."

It was amusing because I didn't feel tough. I felt lost. Shrugging my shoulders, I gave a half-smile in response.

"So, did you decide who you are bringing to the anniversary celebration?"

The event had slipped my mind. "Nothing has changed Mr. Keyes; I am not bringing a date."

"Oh, I see. There are no young men you'd like to bring?"

"No."

"What a shame." He turned and began straightening the candy display.

I turned with the intent on wandering a while longer.

"Before you leave, I've been saving some things for you." Stepping behind the cashier's desk he bent down and came up with a stack of at least 10 tabloids. "I have been keeping these for you. I know how much you enjoy reading this nonsense."

"Thank you so much. These often keep me smiling."

"You're in a few of them."

"Oh. In that case, please don't be offended but I'd rather not read about myself. Thank you so much for saving them but I'm worn out with all the media coverage."

"Sure dear. You don't have to explain." He took them from the counter and placed them below. You should know though, they're calling you a mermaid."

A fake laugh escaped. "I know. Isn't that ridiculous?"

"Sure."

Again, I turned away.

"You should also know that in one, a lady claims to have seen you and that boy who is missing. She claims that the two of you were near the cliff in Taranto, Italy. Can you believe it?"

"Barely," my stomach twisted. "Is that all she said?"

"No. That crazy woman says she saw him dive into the ocean after he clubbed you over the head with a baseball bat." Mr. Keyes gave a curious chuckle.

Someone saw us? I tried desperately to hide my thoughts. "That is—how could we have—well, that's just outrageous." I fidgeted, unsure of what to say next.

Mr. Keyes spoke so casually that I almost didn't catch it. "Right, why would Joseph hit you over the head with a baseball bat?"

All the air in the room seemed to enter my lungs as I gasped with shock. "MR. KEYES?"

"We have been here for you Seraphin. This neighborhood, these people, they're all for you."

"I don't understand what's happening. How do you know Joseph?" It was surreal.

"I don't know him, per say. I know of him. I saw you with the boy, running through the storm. He's Merrick's son, looks just like his mother, has her eyes. This photo doesn't do them justice." He laid one of the tabloids on the counter. Joseph's CORE employee photo was on the front page.

"You know Joseph's mother?" I questioned, still not believing.

"I've only met her once. Well, it wasn't that I met her but more like walked past her. Mrs. Keyes and I were on our honeymoon in Venice. We love the brackish water in Venice—the Venetian people are so welcoming too. Did you know that Venice is sinking? Saw it with my own eyes."

"Mr. Keyes—I, uh, didn't know…can you explain more about how you know the Merrick family? Are you—is Mrs. Keyes—different?"

"Oh yes. Sorry. We are—uh, water-dwellers, if you will."

Speechless, I watched as he casually straightened a few packs of gum that were slightly misaligned. *This was unbelievable. First Gianni and now Mr. Keyes—was everyone leading a double life?*

"If you don't mind explaining something, how'd you figure it out? The neighbors and I were all under the impression that you still didn't know. That's why your grandma sent you to live with the Cottington family. She didn't trust that we'd keep the secret."

My head grew light as I tried to process what Mr. Keyes was saying. I was overwhelmingly confused. NO, I didn't want to blackout, I wanted to know more. What did Mr. Keyes know about my life that I didn't? It was a surprise to hear that he knew Joseph's mother. I wondered if he knew mine too? "No. Stay here, stay here." I whispered, clutching onto Mr. Keyes' arm as I felt my conscious slipping.

"No Seraphin. Don't fight it." I heard him whisper.

I blacked out.

I saw the same scene play out, like always. The monster was sickening; my father was alarmed when he became aware of what I was doing. There was something unusual; someone was in the water, not far from me. I could hear a voice other than my father's speaking and laughing. The voice was evil. *I've found you.*

When I woke, I laid still for a moment trying to comprehend what my memories had revealed. My father wasn't scared of the ocean—he was frightened of what was *in* the ocean. Or should I say *whom*? I opened my eyes to see Mrs. Keyes reading a book and Mr. Keyes sitting at his desk working on invoices. They glanced up as worry filled their faces.

"What do you see when you black-out?" Mr. Keyes asked.

"I see the day he died." As I sat up, Mrs. Keyes moved onto the couch beside me. Her arms wrapped around my shoulders, comforting me. I welcomed it. Terror remained when I thought of the voice.

"Seraphin no one should have to endure this much emotional pain in their life, especially someone so young." She turned to Mr. Keyes. "Alexander, that's enough questioning. She's been through so much this summer. The poor girl just graduated high school and should be enjoying herself; instead she's battling a vision of her father's death. And besides that, she was lost at sea for over a month. Thank goodness Merrick's boy was there to help her get home."

Weakly, I spoke. "Joseph didn't help me get home. I don't think he was planning on letting me come home. He kept telling me how dangerous it was for me to leave."

That surprised Mr. Keyes and his brow furrowed but Mrs. Keyes shook her head at him. He looked at his invoices and continued to work.

"Mrs. Keyes, you work with Joseph. Did you know all along that his name wasn't Jay Mason?" I asked.

"I suspected he wasn't who he claimed to be. I assumed he was one of us, he knew too much about the ocean to be an ordinary human. It wasn't until Alexander pointed out how similar he looked to Lady Marietta that I thought him to be a Merrick. It's been years since they have appeared with Joseph, not since the death of his brother, Joshua. God rest his soul."

"God rest his soul." Mr. Keyes repeated without taking his focus off the stack of paperwork awaiting his attention.

"Joshua?"

"The poor boy," she shook her head and closed her eyes, "such a tragedy."

"Joseph had a brother? Will you tell me about him?"

They met each other's stare. Mr. Keyes gave a nod. She spoke gently.

"Nearly 8 years ago he died. Joseph was just a young boy at 14; Joshua, was 4 years his elder. We don't know the details but it was an accident. Some blame Joseph for his death. What a horrible burden to bear. No wonder he disappeared and has been hiding under an assumed name."

Joseph *was* hiding from his past. I wondered if he was responsible for his brother's death. I quickly erased that thought from my mind and spoke to his defense. "Surely Joseph wouldn't have killed his own brother. What reason would he have?"

"Jealousy, if Joshua lived he would have been the next Guardian. Rumor is he was born with the Rune of the Sea. Remember that photo of his neck, Alexander?"

"That was unfortunate. Those silly tabloids at it again, messing with people's lives. After that the poor boy couldn't escape the media attention." Mr. Keyes shook his head in disgust.

There was that word again, *rune*. I thought back to the tattoo on the nape of his neck. "Joseph has a mark on his neck too, is it the same one?"

"Oh yes, it's the same, though his *is* a tattoo, not *the* rune. It's a tribute to Joshua. The skeptics feel he secretly wanted to be a Guardian—they say he was covetous of his brother's fame. I don't believe a bit of that." Mrs. Keyes said with a tad of distaste.

I thought for a moment. "Why couldn't they both have been Guardians?"

They laughed. "We're sorry darling. It's just that we forget you don't know all the legends yet. There must be only a male and a female Guardian. And, besides, never has a second born son had the Rune."

"If that's the case and Joshua was the male Guardian, who is the female?" It was just a question though the response I received was shocking.

Mrs. Keyes came to her feet. "Well that's useless information now that there is no longer a male Guardian. You can't have one without the other."

Mr. Keyes shuffled his papers. "Nope, it doesn't really matter who she is. We should head home Tabitha, it's getting late."

"Seraphin, you've got to work in the morning. I need you rested—it's a big day we have to clean the *George Washington*. They're heading out this Monday for whale tagging week."

They led me out of their office, practically shoving. "Wait! I have more questions."

"Questions can be answered anytime but sleep, sleep is very important. You must get your rest now Seraphin." They sounded crazy and I wondered what had gotten into them.

I sat in my car for almost 30 minutes, digesting what the Keyes had told me about Joseph. Trying to process the things they told me about myself. Mr. Keyes said the neighborhood was there for me. I longed to know more and for once hated having to go home.

At 4am I was still awake. I couldn't take it any longer. There would be little sleep that night. After everything the Keyes had presented it was impossible for my brain to rest—it was spinning with confusion. There had never been a time that I longed to hear my father's voice as much as I did that very moment. I carried my broken self from my bedroom to his; climbing into his bed and surrounding my body with his pillows and blankets.

I felt my head grow light and I knew I was heading for another blackout. That time I fought it. With every ounce of mental ability, I pushed away the blackness. Instead of blacking out, I cried. It had been so long since my emotions were out of control. It was more like sobbing—inconsolable and uncontrollable sobbing; immersed for the fist time in sorrow. I hadn't allowed myself to cry immediately following his death. I had to protect Grandma so I tried to control my emotions and when I couldn't; my body controlled them for me. For 8 years, whenever I was upset, the world went black. Not that time though.

Thunder cracked outside the window—lightning lit up the sky. Rain poured down and the hale storm soon followed—the pings against the glass window were steady and hard. The wind howled through the creeks in the attic. The loss of my father, grandmother and, possibly Ms. Z came together in my mind like a typhoon—destroying memories and blending thoughts until all I could do was collapse—exhausted. In a strange way, I felt free. It was the first time I controlled my own thoughts. I didn't want to see my father's death again—and so I didn't.

The thunder sounded further away and the flashes of lightning dimmed. The rain slowed to a drizzle. I calmed myself.

TWELVE

The back door flew open with a bang.

I jumped out of my father's bed, throwing pillows and blankets onto the floor. I stood, frozen with fear.

"Seraphin, I know you're here." A voice whispered. "Are you alright? The storm."

It was Joseph. A wave of relief washed through me. I shouted his name and ran the rest of the way down the stairs and into the living room.

I'd be lying if I said I was upset with him for breaking into my house in the middle of the night. Every inch of my body tingled with excitement. I thanked God that the power was out due to the storm as he was unable to see the silly grin on my face. The moonlight from the window highlighted the drops of water on his skin. He was barefoot and shirtless, which didn't come as a surprise and he smelled like the ocean.

He let out a deep sigh when he saw me and as I stepped closer his expression softened. "Seraphin, I can't begin to tell you how sorry I am for leaving you."

My eyes shifted away from his. To be honest, I was still a little angry, however, there was no use being dramatic about the whole thing. He had come back and I was grateful to see him again. "Joseph, it's not worth dwelling over. I'm safe; you're safe—Nasani is she safe?"

Relief crossed his face. "Nasani is a strong woman; I should have trusted that she would take care of herself."

While it was nice to hear his concern, it bothered me when he said Nasani could take care of herself. *Did this mean that I couldn't?* "You would not believe the last few days, it's a media circus. They're calling me the mermaid girl. Oh and—" I was going to tell him about the Keyes when he stopped me.

"Seraphin, something is going on and you're part of it. Nasani took this from a merman she knocked out at the cavern. She's outside and can't get in—actually, she can't even see your house."

He held up a small metal key on a chain with the number 504 etched in it. I took the key and walked into the living room, by the front door my house key hung on a hook. The same 504 was etched in it. I knew both of the keys as well as the chain connected to the one Joseph found. My heart sank. I said nothing as he continued to explain.

"When I got back to the cavern, Nasani was hiding in the Cosa Identica, she was able to lure the man there and tricked him into diving head first into the mirage on the stone wall. It knocked him out cold. He showed up right after you and I left, I thought he was looking for me but—well, I'm not so sure I was the target this time. When I saw the key, I thought it was the one I used the day I brought you home. I was so worried something horrible had happened to you." He moved closer and wrapped his arms around me, any other time that gesture would have made me overjoyed but my body was numb and I could not feel his arms. He stepped back, holding my shoulders.

I was frozen. My face void of all color; I could barely speak. "Was the man bald with a tattoo across his face?"

"Yes. Do you know him?"

"This chain hung around the man's neck I saw drive Ms. Z's car from the high school parking lot. Why would my father's key be on a chain around a strange man's neck?"

"That was your father's key?" He was just as confused.

"Yes." I was without sensation as I sat on my couch.

When I was 5 years old I wanted a house key so my father and I went to the hardware store where he made me a copy of his key. I had a hard time remembering what number our house was on Briarwood Court and just like any parent; he used to quiz me on things like our phone number and address. He asked the man in the hardware store to etch 504 into the key for me. I was upset that our keys were no longer identical so he had his etched as well.

Joseph moved beside me, placing his hand over my hand and the two keys. "I don't know what's going on Seraphin but I think that perhaps you're more than just a misplaced mermaid. What do you know about your parents, other than their names?"

"I know my father's dead and my mother loved me so little that she left two days after giving birth." Letting out a huge sigh; it was difficult to talk about my parents.

"Seraphin, I'm so sorry and I know this has to be really tough but the more details you can give, the better. Both of your parents had to have been merpeople, otherwise, you wouldn't be so faultless when you transform. Your tail is ideal, your gills function perfectly and your senses are remarkable—all the signs of a full-blooded mermaid." He was so sure of himself.

I struggled to make sense of it all. "Do you think this merman was the man who killed my father? There was someone behind his death. I see it when I black-out."

"What do you mean you see it?" Suddenly, he was very interested.

I told Joseph everything from the moment my foot touched the water that dreadful day, explaining how I also blacked out earlier that night at Keyes Market and heard the evil voice of a stranger. He listened close; I could tell certain details excited him. When I talked about the sea creature that dragged my father to his death, his face turned.

"Leviathan," he whispered. "The sea creature is Leviathan. If he faced it, he didn't stand a chance—merman or not."

"You mean my crazy visions are true? There really is a sea monster?" Such a thing seemed outrageous, until I remembered that I was a mermaid.

The color of his eyes darkened. "Yes, I'm afraid so. It only comes out to do horrible deeds. If you want someone to die bad enough you can make a trade with Leviathan. It's not a trade most would make, his price is very high."

"You think someone paid to have my father killed? It had to be someone with a lot of money then, right?" As I said it, I knew that couldn't have been the case. What would a sea monster want with money? I shook my head.

Joseph laughed when he realized I knew how ridiculous my question had been. "Yes, it had to be someone with *loads* of money. Perhaps Leviathan wanted to buy a new yacht?" He teased then explained. "Let me put it this way, he is said to guard the gates of Hell."

"Oh. That's a hefty price." I swallowed hard realizing that someone wanted my father dead so badly that they traded their soul to Leviathan.

"I've never known anyone to do such a thing but there are instances throughout history—old tales my brother used to tell me when we were kids. Most of them were made up, I'm sure."

It was the first time he mentioned his brother. It took me by surprise. It angered me to think that someone wanted my father—Samuel Shedd—the nicest man I had ever known, dead. "Why would someone want him dead? And at such a high cost?"

He thought for a moment before he answered. "You ARE more than just a misplaced mermaid. Think about it. You're senses are far superior to most—you were put in hiding as a child—your father died protecting you. Seraphin, you're the *one* and your father knew it."

"What are you rambling on about? I was not put in hiding either. I've been here my entire life." I attempted to reason.

"In a house that Nasani can't see!" He was excited. "Seraphin! You are the female Guardian."

"No, I am not. I haven't a mark on my body. I know the story of your brother Joseph. What could be your motive for claiming such a thing?" I was frightened, recalling how Mrs. Keyes said there were some skeptics that believed he killed his brother out of jealousy. *What if I was the Guardian? Would he harm me too?*

In an instant the enthusiasm was replaced with fury as his fists clenched. "What could YOU possibly know about Joshua? AND what do you mean MOTIVE?"

Since I had known Joseph, never had his temper been like that. His eyes changed to a deep cerulean. They were the color of an angry sea. "I know he was the Guardian and that he died in an accident. I know that people blame you for his death."

"Do you think I could kill a person? Do you think I could kill my own brother?" He asked through his teeth.

The life he had was dedicated to saving others and I was no stranger to his miraculous gift of healing. Why did I doubt him? Disappointment filled me for falling victim to rumors. "No. I don't think you would kill anyone, especially your brother."

His eyes turned softer as he calmed.

Ashamed that I had offended him and embarrassed of my weakness, I couldn't meet his eyes.

"You're lucky Seraphin," he whispered. "Your father cared enough to shield you from this life, at least until you were old enough to understand it. He knew to keep you hidden from the rest of us. It's unfortunate that he lost his life in the process; he must have been a wonderful man—so much different than my own."

"Thank you for saying that." Those words I meant. After a long pause I finally met his eyes. They were lighter and his expression softer. I glanced at the key in my hand. "Are there people trying to find me? Do they know where I live?"

"I can only assume. If they know who you are then eventually they are going to come looking for you but you can't worry about that. You can't be frightened of this. We are finally together. At last, I've found you." As he said it, a smile crossed his face. "I've found you."

That couldn't be true; I had to be frightened and I was. "Who are they; who is trying to find me?"

"My parents," he confessed, bowing his head in shame.

That's not who I expected. "What could they possibly want with me?"

"Together we are more powerful than they are. They are the current rulers but now that we've found each other, we rule over them. At least we will, once we emerge." His face lit with excitement. "We are the Guardians of the Sea."

At last he found me? We're finally together? I thought as his words registered. "Your brother was the Guardian."

"That's what he wanted the world to think." He turned away, showing me the mark on the back of his neck. Raising my hand to his skin, I touched it. The lines began to glow a soft blue hue. "Is it glowing?"

"Yes." I pulled my hand away. "Why is it glowing?"

"It is the Rune of the Sea, I was born with it. It glows because we are together now. Your touch is the only thing that can make it glow like this." He only grinned. "I found you. Well—actually Aunt Doreh found you for me."

"But your brother…"

Interrupting me, he explained. "My brother was not the true Guardian. He died protecting me."

Instead of Joseph who was his father's intended target, Joshua was killed. When Joshua heard of the plans to have his younger brother murdered, he had a replica tattooed on the nape of his neck. Then, like a *true* guardian, he showed it to the world. Sacrificing himself to save Joseph, he declared himself the next Guardian. When their father, Lord Merrick, gave orders—the killer failed to eliminate the correct son.

"Why would your father do such a thing?" I was appalled.

"He couldn't stand the idea of his second born son being more powerful than he was. It was bad enough that people knew a Guardian had been born to the current rulers. It meant that they were somehow flawed. Guardians only live when they are needed, when the sea is no longer safe. It's their job to oversee the marine territories, if my father was doing his job correctly, we would have never been born."

"Oh." My heart sank. If it cost Joseph's brother his life, it was likely the reason my father's life ended as well. The possibility of someone taking my father's life on purpose opened fresh wounds deep in my soul. The thought of it hurt so badly I could barely catch my breath. Anger swelled inside me.

Then I heard a scream.

We ran outside. He was faster and I heard him say, "Not her. If she's gone I can't go on."

We passed through the ivy arch that separated my front walk from the back yard and all heads turned our way. My neighbors, Charlie Lamange and Fred Nulant, each had one of Nasani's arms, lifting her off the ground. Her long black hair flew in their faces and she struggled. She tried to kick her way free but they held her small frame with almost no effort.

Joseph stopped and sighed with a sense of relief. "My goodness Nasani, I thought you were in trouble."

"I AM IN TROUBLE! These creeps think I'm trespassing." She was shouting.

Mr. Lamange spoke. "Seraphin, do you know this girl?"

I nodded my head and they let her go. She dropped to the ground and remained there until Joseph reached his hand to help her up. Nasani straightened her hair and mumbled insults at her captors. Many of the other neighbors heard the scream and gathered to determine if there was anything worth watching.

Joseph reached into a small bag that hung on Nasani's back. He took out a black t-shirt. I stared as he pulled it over his muscular chest. Nasani looked at me curiously and I felt ashamed that I had been caught gawking.

The neighbors were gawking as well, but for another reason. The woman that had most recently moved into the blue house across the street whispered to Mr. Rigby who lived in the brick ranch next to her. "Is that Lord Merrick's youngest boy?"

The old man pushed his glasses up onto the ridge of his nose and took a shaky glance at Joseph. "It seems to be. He's got Lady Marietta's eyes."

Mr. Lamange spoke again. "We're sorry Seraphin, when we realized that she couldn't see the house, we thought she could be trouble." He turned to Joseph and held out his hand to shake it. "My boy, it's good to see you're well. Some of us were wondering where you'd turn up after we saw your face next to Seraphin's in the news. By now you probably know why we've been hiding her all these years. It's a shame your brother is no longer with us. She'll never be able to fulfill her destiny now." Then he seemed to regret what he said. "I mean no offense to your parents. They're doing a great job."

"Sir, if they were doing a great job we all know that new Guardians would not have been born." Mr. Lamange along with the rest of the neighbors seemed shocked that Joseph spoke out against his father and mother. Obviously they didn't know the horrible secret, how Lord Merrick had his own son killed.

Nasani suddenly burst into tears. Everyone watched Joseph comfort her, he was irritated, but not at her emotional outburst. I noticed his eyes were a shade darker with a bit of green mixed in. "I think that's enough talk of my family. What I'd like to know is how can this be possible?"

No one spoke. Nasani continued to cry. I wondered why she was crying but decided not to ask. Since I finished my very own crying fit just moments before, I knew first hand that anything could trigger such a display. Instead I made Joseph elaborate. It was ironic that *he* thought something was impossible. "How can what be possible?"

"This neighborhood—all of you—hiding in plain sight." He held one arm around Nasani and stretched the other, gesturing to the group. I still wasn't sure what he meant until Mr. Rigby stepped through the crowd.

He paused for a moment at Mr. Lamange. They shared a look of concern then he spoke. "Well, I suppose it's alright to explain a few things. The boy seems to have a general distaste for his parents." At this, the group of them shook their heads and whispered to each other—falling silent only when the old man spoke again.

"We are the Sons of Sailors." As he spoke everyone, simultaneously made a fist with their right hand and placed it over their own heart.

A woman standing in the back shouted, "daughters too."

There was a rumbling amongst the females wondering why they still had to be called by sons when clearly it was a mixed batch. One man reminded them that 'Children of Sailors' was vetoed at their last monthly meeting because the acronym SOS meant something and COS meant nothing. A boy that I recognized as the cashier from Keyes Market told the woman that it would be too costly to redesign all the hats and t-shirts they just had printed.

Nasani stopped crying and the three of us watched in utter confusion.

Mr. Rigby spoke again. "Knock it off. We're not giving a real good impression of ourselves."

"Sons of Sailors? I've never heard of you." Joseph doubted.

"That's a good thing. Makes it easier to sneak up and attack." The cashier shouted to Joseph. Everyone nodded his or her head in agreement.

"You all are harmless. There's not an evil one of you in this group." He said with confidence.

Joseph's assessment of the crowd was met with nods and an overall acceptance of their inability to do real harm to others. I thought back to Louie the manta and how I understood that he was harmless. When Joseph rushed out of the house after Nasani screamed, once he saw Mr. Lamange and Mr. Nulant, he knew she was not in danger. *Was this a gift we shared?*

The old man continued to explain. "We might not be tough and we sure are not evil, that's for certain but we protect each other. Our fathers—"

The woman from the back interrupted him. "And mothers."

"Yes, our fathers and mothers were seduced by your kind. They were made to believe they'd have a life with their loves but instead they were left behind—their children mutants and their hearts broken." A few people put their arms around the person next to them. Tears rolled down the lady in the blue house's cheeks. She was the newest addition to the neighborhood and I wondered what kind of life she lived before she found these people. "We're the lucky ones. We found each other and Seraphin is our inspiration. To think that a mutant's destiny was to be a Guardian gave us all hope that one day we would no longer have to hide. Of course, now she'll never fully be a Guardian without your brother."

Nasani began to wail again. I didn't realize how emotionally unstable she was. What on earth upset her now? If anyone should be crying, it should be me. I couldn't possibly live up to the expectations placed upon me by this wholehearted group of mutants. "Is that what I am? A mutant?"

"No Seraphin. You're amazing and powerful. There is nothing wrong with you. You can transform perfectly. BOTH of your parents are merpeople." Joseph was shouting but only because Nasani was crying so loud.

"Oh no, that's where you're wrong boy." Mr. Lamange spoke. "I knew both of her parents and she's definitely a mutant. Besides, she wouldn't be able to see her own house if she wasn't."

"She's NOT a goonch." Joseph shouted, angry.

The crowd fell silent. The old man explained that they didn't use that word. It was insulting.

Joseph laughed. "Are we to call a shark something gentler if it thinks its name too vicious? How about the poor crab that is assumed to always be a grump? Shall we call them all *glads* so we don't offend? You're a goonch. It's the name for your species. What else are we supposed to call you?"

No one answered him. They were clearly hurt by his rant.

I was mad at him for insulting them. They were wonderful—whatever they were. I did my best to redirect the conversation. "What would prohibit me from seeing my own house?" I looked at the house. My lovely butter-cream yellow house and I wanted to run for it and shut those people out; even Joseph—especially Nasani.

"Full breeds can't see it. A spell falls over it to protect you from their kind. A man named Orin conjured it so we could easily keep you hidden. After your father died we worried that they would find you." Mr. Nulat answered.

"Bindolestiv? You mean to tell me that Orin knew where she was all along? Is he here now?" Joseph was looking through the crowd—stretching his neck to see all their faces.

"Oh, you won't find him. He doesn't come here any longer." Mr. Rigby said.

"You know this man—this Orin?" I asked Joseph.

"He used to work for my father but left soon after Joshua's death. The things he was able to do—well, he's a genius. I don't doubt he hid your house. Every entrance that exists in the ocean is hidden by shroud. He's one of only a few who have this ability. I remember how angry my father was when Orin refused to work for him any longer." He had a strange look of satisfaction on his face. "I would venture to guess that he came looking for you, worried for your life. I mean, if they could take Joshua's life than what protection did you have? You're lucky Seraphin. Even Orin wanted to keep you safe."

"What entrances and why would they need to be hidden?" Thinking back to the waterfall in the cavern and how it mysteriously disappeared once I crossed through it.

Mr. Rigby answered instead of Joseph. "There are passages to underground cities. Communities that exist in the deepest depths of this Earth, under the oceans, lakes, and rivers—well, pretty much any body of water. Only a few of us have seen them. Merrick Law falls over the ocean communities—our kind is no longer welcome."

They turned to Joseph when he spoke. "Most of you wouldn't physically be able to live that deep anyhow. Your bodies don't transform the way ours do. Your abilities are weaker."

And like that, Joseph dismissed those good people once again.

The neighbors looked at one another, thwarted by his opinion of them.

He continued speaking of Orin. "Since he disappeared, not one has been able to conjure a shroud as secure as his. That's why there have been so many Lost City of Atlantis sightings. When humans stumble upon one of our underground communities they almost always assume they've found the lost city. It's really quite humorous." Everyone seemed to agree with Joseph on his point. For just an instant he lightened their spirits only to crush them once again. "Orin's shrouds are meant to keep goonches and humans out. They never fail either. He's the best."

The corners of their mouths dropped.

I cringed. Was he knowingly offending or did he really believe that they should be referred to by a name they didn't desire?

"So, the one on my house is just the opposite then. It's meant to keep full-blooded merpeople out. Right? This explains why Nasani can't see it." Both he and I turned to look at the house but soon after our eyes met each other's with the same curious gaze. "If his shrouds are as flawless as you declare them to be—"

"Then why can I see it?" He finished—startled by the realization.

They waited for Joseph to answer his own question while I watched them.

They were in their pajamas and bathrobes. A few had shoes on but most where barefoot. The neighbors that I grew up with were like me, half-person—half-fish. Not once had I seen those people at the beach or in the water. The shoreline that ran along our houses was always deserted. I thought of my father's constant warning to stay away from the ocean. I wondered if my mother seduced him into falling in love with her. I hated her for what she did to me, to my father. She had a child with him, a mutant child and then she left. It was her fault that I was this thing. I didn't care what Joseph said, I was a mutant—my father was NOT a merman.

Joseph broke my train of thought. "I don't know why I can see it. Maybe it's because…" Pausing, he reached up to his neck, rubbing it, whispering. "Maybe it's because I'm a Guardian."

"Did he just say he was a Guardian?" The cashier from Keyes Market snickered. "Who's he trying to fool? Joshua Merrick was the Guardian."

Nasani's cries became louder and she ran for the beach. Joseph stepped towards her but instead stayed to face the accusation. Anger filled his eyes and his jaw tightened.

"What do you know goonch? You're not part of my world." His voice was mean.

For the first time he used the word in a derogatory context. It was too much for me to tolerate. Appalled by the way he addressed them, anger swelled inside me. "Joseph, he's right. You said it yourself; Joshua had everyone thinking he was the Guardian. Why would you think less of them for believing?" I glanced at the crowd. They were listening intently. Some wondered if Joseph could indeed be their lost Guardian.

How dare he talk down to them? They were my father's friends. They wept at his memorial service; cooked casseroles for months so Grandma didn't have to lift a finger while she mourned her son. *Her son.* Yes, my father was her son. She was no mermaid, I was sure of it. I was a goonch, not a mermaid. That bothered me less than it bothered him. Joseph was mistaken in the way he addressed those people and he was mistaken about me as well.

I trust them. I know them. They shoveled the sidewalk in the dead of winter when Grandma was too sick and I too tired from staying up all night comforting her. I watched the woman who lived two doors down. She held her daughters hand. Her daughter was no more than 10 years old and stood in a nightgown with matted hair. I knew the girl's name was Celia. I smiled at her and she shyly returned my gesture. They trust me. They know me. I had to defend them. "You owe these people an apology for speaking to them that way."

Mr. Rigby turned to leave, muttering under his breath. "He's a Merrick; he shares his father's opinion of our kind." Shuffling away with his shoulders slightly slumped in defeat.

"No. Wait. He owes you an apology." I insisted. Looking at Joseph, aghast at the way he treated the harmless group.

"I owe them nothing." He said with his jaw still clenched.

I watched Celia catch her mother's expression. She shook her head and the girl let a tear fall. They placed their arms around each other before turning to leave. Slowly the group hung their heads in disappointment before backing away.

He gently placed his hand on me, trying to guide me away from the crowd and towards the beach where Nasani was still bawling her eyes out. "Let's get out of here."

I refused, carefully removing his hand from my arm. He grabbed it, holding tight—leaning into me when he spoke. "We should go. You don't need their protection any longer. We've found each other, it's our destiny."

"No. I don't treat people the way you have. These are good people, you said yourself they are harmless. What could you gain by hurting their spirit? What could you gain by leaving here with their opinions being so low of you?"

"Remember Seraphin, you're new here. You don't know how these people came to be. You don't know the lives they destroyed by simply being born. Their father's or mother's birthed them against all restrictions. They shouldn't exist. They're not like us." He sounded so sure of himself.

"Like us? These people didn't have a choice. Do you think they want to be treated this way? Look at them. Look at their tears." He wouldn't look. His eyes remained locked on my face. I found it difficult to look at him so instead I watched my neighbors, wrecked. "I didn't choose this life and I'm sure not proud of it. My father—he hid me. There had to be a reason. And, he trusted these people with my life. How can you expect me to just walk away from them—from everything—from my home?"

"FINE!" He threw his arms in the air. "Stay."

Walking down to the beach, he met Nasani. His arms wrapped around her as he led her into the oncoming waves.

The woman who lived in the blue house approached. She wiped a tear from her eye and spoke softly. "Thank you." She hugged me.

Then Mr. Lamange patted my shoulder like I had just made the winning touchdown for his football team. "Good job. Thanks kid."

Mrs. Nulant who was silent up until then had tears streaming down her cheeks. "I'm proud of the man I married. He may be different but that's what I love about him." Mr. Nulant grabbed her hand and pulled her into his arms. They walked home together, not allowing any space to enter between them.

I watched as my neighbors returned to their homes. Remembering something Mr. Lamange said. I yelled after him. "You said you knew my mother."

He stopped but didn't turn to face me. "Did I say that? What I meant to say was that I knew her through your father's words. He spoke of her often."

I ran to him, standing in his way. "No. You said you KNEW both of my parents."

"It's been a long night dear. You should get some rest." He stepped around me. "Goodnight Seraphin."

I stood alone in the middle of Briarwood Court and watched the sun rise.

THIRTEEN

At 7am, I arrived on the CORE campus having not slept the night before. Exhausted was an understatement. My first priority was caffeine. As I was pouring my coffee, I noticed Ethan with his head down on a table in the cafeteria. Seeing him sleeping, reminded me of the Spanish class we took together in high school, he slept the entire term. Before I left, I noted the time. His lab shift usually started at 7:15. Worried that he may have missed the beginning of his shift, I gently tried to wake him. As I shook his shoulder, the hand that rested over the back of his neck moved to reveal the Rune of the Sea. It wasn't Ethan. It was Joseph. Confused at how I could mistake one for the other, I turned to leave.

Before I could take a step, he raised his head, still groggy from his slumber. "Seraphin?"

A girl shouted from across the cafeteria. "JAY!" She came running to the table. The room erupted with excitement. "Jay's back."

People were shouting and running to him. Hugs and questions from everyone followed. He kept his eyes locked on mine. "Wait." He called after me but I backed away and let the crowd take over. I wasn't ready to face him. The entire room was buzzing as everyone was filled with relief to see that Jay Mason had survived the *John F. Kennedy*.

Joseph was swept away to the management offices shortly after he was discovered in the cafeteria. An announcement came over the entire campus that a 2:00 press conference would be held. Jay Mason had come back to CORE on his own abilities.

Everyone was speculating where he might have been. There was talk of pirates in Somalia holding him prisoner. One woman told how she heard through the receptionist in human resources that he was stranded on an island for weeks until a Japanese couple on Jet Skis stumbled across his starving, unconscious body. When I heard that, I laughed and wondered what story he really came up with to cover his tracks.

I walked to the press conference with Ethan. It was being held in the exterior courtyard on the main campus. Reporters were swarming; one recognized me as the other lost crew person from the *John F. Kennedy* and tried to get an exclusive interview. Ethan threatened the guy with bodily harm until he left me alone. He then took off his baseball cap and put it on my head, hoping it would be enough to hide my image. After that, I kept the brim low and my head down. Ethan wrapped his arm around me, leading through the pack, adding an additional layer of protection from the story hungry media.

We stayed to the right of the stage. Joseph sat casually in a folding chair next to the Managing Director of CORE. She was briefing him, but he looked uninterested. Instead he scanned the forming mass of curious minds. I was no exception. My curiosity was at its highest.

"He looks nervous, don't you think?" A voice came up behind us. Ethan and I both turned, his arm remained around me until he realized who was speaking. He dropped it and took a step away from me. Nasani stared at Joseph while Ethan couldn't take his eyes off of her.

"Perrine—uh, hey. How goes it?" He muttered out.

How goes it? Who talks like that? He was the nervous one, not Joseph. I wondered why he was acting so odd.

Nasani ignored Ethan, which bothered me.

"Actually, Perrine—I think he looks surprisingly calm and healthy for having been lost at sea for nearly 6 weeks." I was sarcastic in my answer and she cracked a smile. "I didn't know you were back to work too. Mrs. Keyes said you were on a leave of absence."

"I just returned today. I was a little—well, I just needed to take a break after the *John F. Kennedy*. Jay is a good friend of mine and I found it difficult to be here without him. Dr. Radski called me this morning when she heard he was back—thought I might want to see him."

"Yes—of course." Ethan fumbled in. "I'm so glad—I mean we're so glad you're back here at CORE. The lab just hasn't been the same without you."

She turned serious. "What do you mean the lab hasn't been the same? What's wrong with it?"

"No—nothing is wrong. The atmosphere in the lab is what I meant. The overall mood is a little low when you're not there." Fumbling even more with his words, his usual confidence was no where to be found.

She waited—started to respond and then dismissed him once more. Again, it upset me but what bothered me even more was the way Ethan was acting, like he had never seen a pretty girl. He glanced at her often while the Managing Director of CORE introduced Jay Mason.

"I'd like to allow Jay to recount the amazing journey where he was lost at sea and struggled to survive, knowing he had to get back to his family here at CORE." Everyone cheered except for Nasani whose eyes I caught in mid-roll.

As Joseph stepped to the microphone, he spoke soft and clear. His shoulders were back and his head was high. The expression on his face was enthusiastic and his eyes were electric blue. Above all else he was sincere; even though he was lying.

He recounted the whole ordeal—me falling over, and him stopping Ethan from diving in. At this, Ethan reminded me that he was willing to dive in. I assured him I knew that fact. Then he repeated it to Nasani who ignored him.

Joseph then told an amazing tale of how he was rescued by an orca. It was an impossible account to believe but his audience bought the entire thing. The orca allowed him to swim on her back; she took him to an old decrepit fishing boat whose nets had just been cast. She became entangled in the nets.

The crowd gasped. He had them on the edge of their seats as he said, "And there she was, trying to save my life while risking her own."

The fictional fisherman heard his cries for help and assumed she was trying to eat him. He explained how orcas are wrongly referred to as 'killer whales' even though they did not hunt humans. The men were frightened by the orca and could not understand Joseph's pleas because they spoke Burmese. Which happened to be one of only three languages Joseph claimed to not know; the other two being Gujarati and Yoruba.

The orca tangled her massive body further in their nets. Finally, they were able to drag her on board and to Joseph's horror; they were going to kill her. He recounted fighting with the men, punching the captain square in the nose and cutting the orca free. He was held captive on their vessel for weeks until he was able to prove his worth by helping the fisherman develop a safer more effective fishing pod that they could use instead of dangerous nets.

I laughed. Nasani laughed. Ethan was captivated with Joseph's lie.

Jay Mason, Top Researcher at Coastal Oceanic Research Expeditions then finished his tall tale by asking for donations to, 'The Orca Awareness Fund', that he had set up in honor of his imaginary hero.

I wondered if sea horses were an endangered species and if they were, would he have spun the story differently in order to raise money to protect them as well. All joking aside, he was charming and brilliant. The media hung on his every word and in no time there were people pulling out their wallets and writing checks made payable to The OAF.

How could this delightful man be the same person who called my neighbors by that horrible name? I watched him calmly raise his arm and wave to the crowd as photographers captured the moment on film. That photo would no doubt appear beside every news headline for at least a week.

Then a reporter shouted. "Are we going to hear from Seraphin Shedd?"

The crowd was silent and Joseph deferred the question to the Managing Director. She took the microphone, explaining that the interview was only with Jay Mason but assured the reporters that Ms. Shedd was doing remarkably well and had returned to work.

I took that as my cue to leave, sneaking past the back of the stage and onto the boardwalk. Keeping Ethan's hat pulled down over my face, the only thing I could see were my own feet.

Then I saw another pair of feet, felt arms wrap around me and lift me off the ground. Next thing I knew I had been tackled off the boardwalk and into the water.

Joseph's face was just inches from mine. He held me tight as we freely sank in the Gulf of Maine. We landed on a rocky shelf covered in algae that was slick to the touch. Neither one of us had transformed. Ethan's hat floated to the water's surface. My hair swirled around our faces. Fish swam by, curious. The sunlight flickered nearly 20 feet above. Below, the Gulf continued to drop to further depths; a dark ravine sprawled next to us.

So now what? I thought, wondering if he could hear me.

You can be quite stubborn at times Seraphin. Admit it. I heard his voice.

You can be quite cruel at times Joseph. Admit that. I argued back.

I was wrong and I apologize.

Apparently, he could hear my thoughts. *Tell that to my neighbors.*

I've searched so long for you Seraphin and I don't want to lose you because of some stupid word. His voice was full of sorrow.

It's not about the word Joseph. It's the way you treated them, like they are beneath us when their only wish is to be treated as equals. They are my friends. Joseph's opinion would not change that fact.

But they're not equals.

I couldn't believe what he was saying. *Says who? Your father? The man who tried to have you killed. The man who killed your brother? If anything, you should be against every belief he possesses.*

His face turned somber.

My face was unyielding. *You owe them an apology.*

I know. I promise I'll set things right. For now though, I need you with me. He held my hands and my gaze.

There are too many unanswered questions. I confessed my reluctance.

It was hard to believe that I, Seraphin Shedd, was sitting under that much water having a perfectly average conversation, feeling calm. All those years of panic and anxiety seemed so preventable. Had I known, perhaps I could have lived 18 years with less fear. Sure my father and grandmother, along with the entire neighborhood, spent their lives trying to look after me, but were their efforts as successful as they would have hoped? My father was so overbearing that he might have caused more pain than not.

He was listening to my thoughts. When I tried to listen to his, I heard nothing.

Can you teach me how this works? Why is it that I can only hear the things you want me to hear but you can hear all my thoughts?

I can block. He answered.

Can you teach me how to do the same? I asked.

I'm not sure I want to, I kind of like hearing you—unfiltered. Though, it's probably safer seeing how anyone in a 5-mile radius can hone in on your thoughts as well.

I agreed with him.

He went on to explain how the telepathic communication that merpeople use is different than that of other marine animals. We have the ability to hear the voice and feel the emotions of another while underwater, where other animals can only receive signals indicating an emotional state.

While Joseph was not able to identify all emotions on land, he was able to sense if a person or animal intended harm. Nature had embedded instincts in him; like a rabbit that could feel a fox stalking or a bear who knew hunters were near—Joseph was programmed to detect danger in any person or animal. I was not—it was disappointing.

We stayed beneath the surface for most of the afternoon. He helped me learn to focus and block my thoughts. I was grateful he could no longer hear my thoughts when he proceeded to remove his shirt; twisting it around his wrist. His body was incredible and I tried not to stare.

I want you to see. His hand lifted my chin and my eyes traveled back to his body. Then he showed me how he transformed. A layer of silver scales emerged from near his ankles and his feet grew into a caudal fin with blue highlights. The scales moved up his legs, sliding tight over the shorts he wore. Small gills emerged near his hips. He floated over the dark drop-off. I sat crossed legged on the edge; his eyes were level to mine. *It's your turn now.*

To my surprise he grabbed the bottom of my oversized green MOLE shirt—revealing my tank top underneath. I raised my arms and let him slip it over my head. The look he gave me was intense. Pulling me close, he carried me like a child. My legs bent over his arm as I gripped his neck. He carried me into the open water, far from the safety of the algae covered shelf.

You have to want it Seraphin. Do you want it? Or should I drop you and make you want it?

My arms tightened around his neck, fearful of his threat. I knew what he meant but I put more meaning behind his words. *Did I want it? This life?* At that moment, my answer was yes. The water was comforting as were Joseph's arms. However, what lay ahead of that moment was so uncertain. *Where was this life going to take me and could I live up to the expectations, whatever they may be?*

You have to feel it; crave it; deep within yourself. He urged.

The only thing I was certain of is that I wanted to share that moment with Joseph and be like he was—strong and confident. I held on to that thought. *I do want it.* I let him hear me.

Then do it. Make yourself into the magnificent mermaid you were born to be.

I turned to him and our eyes locked—those incredible eyes. Butterflies fluttered through me and my heart raced. I wanted it more than anything. Very slowly, I began to transform. We both watched, as my feet grew long and thin, transparent and sparkling into a lovely purplish-blue caudal fin. As the silvery scales emerged, Joseph continued to hold me near. It wasn't until my gills formed that he finally let go.

That was the happiest I had felt in a very long time. So sure of myself in the new form—I twirled with excitement and together we laughed.

HEADS UP—INCOMING. I heard Nasani. Her voice sounded panicked. There was a disturbance above. Joseph darted in front of me and pushed towards the surface. There was a large splash and he came face to face with Ethan. I watched as his scales retracted and once again his shorts and legs were visible. Ethan's thoughts were not readable but the expression on his face said more than words could possibly convey.

He saw me, and my tail. I tried to make my scales go back but it was too late.

Nasani came from underneath—*had she been in the water listening to us?* Together she and Joseph pulled a struggling Ethan under the rocky overhang. I followed but they were extremely fast. I could listen to their thoughts though.

What is this kid trying to do? Joseph asked Nasani.

He saw the hat she was wearing and her shirt floating on the surface along the boardwalk after spending the entire afternoon looking around campus for her. The first thing he thought was that she had drowned again. I guess the lug has a sweet spot for her or something because before I could warn you, he dove in. She sounded annoyed.

I asked you to make sure he left us alone.

Honestly, he's exhausting to follow. What was taking you two so long?

That's none of your business. He snapped. *Looks like we might have to do some damage control—do you think he saw Seraphin?*

I don't appreciate your tone. She snapped back. *I'll go get HER and you deal with him.*

I didn't like the way she referred to me but I disliked the way she spoke of Ethan even more. Obviously, he was concerned with my safety and who could blame him? One moment I was standing next to him and the next I had disappeared leaving nothing but a floating hat and shirt.

Instantly, I felt responsible.

Nasani appeared and waved for me to swim to her. She led me under the boardwalk until we came to a dead end. A large wall made of stone, stretched out in front of us.

Go on. She signaled. *It's a walkway. Trust me.*

I didn't want to trust her. Instead I used my senses and listened for Joseph's voice. I could hear him talking just a few feet past the wall made of stone. Ethan's voice rang through as well.

First I put my hand to the stone, feeling nothing but open space. My arm met no resistance. Then I could see the difference between the stone on either side and the mirage concealing the walkway. It was a shroud.

Orin Bindolestiv *was* a genius. *What do I do?* I asked Nasani.

Just swim through, you'll see what happens next. She was bossy.

There was no choice but to trust. She swam past first; entering the shrouded area with ease. I followed, eyes closed; worried. When my body made contact with the paper-thin mirage that hid the underground cavern, a jolt of static electricity passed through me. My scales instantly retracted and my gills closed. It was so unexpected that I fell onto the rocky floor; landing hard on my side and gasping for air.

"NASANI—what the—? It was her first time transforming through a shroud!" Joseph's voice echoed through the cavern.

It was difficult to catch my breath—Joseph helped; he placed his hands on my shoulder blades. A rush of air filled my lungs.

"Thank you." I whispered.

He helped me to my feet. Together we walked to Ethan who was sitting on the ground, sopping wet and shouting. Nasani did not speak and followed close behind.

"What did you do to her? What is going on?" He saw me. "PHIN? What was on you? Were you wearing at tail or something?"

"Great. He did see her." Nasani muttered.

"Perrine?" Ethan's eyes were as wide as silver dollars.

"Well, no use keeping up the charade. Kid, my name is Nasani. I'm a mermaid." She held her hand out and gestured first to me and then to Joseph. "She's a mermaid and he's a goonch."

She was mad at Joseph and I wondered if it had anything to do with yours truly.

Joseph gave Nasani a disapproving look and stepped forward, reaching out his hand to help Ethan. "Not that there is anything wrong with being a goonch—but I'm a merman." He glanced to me. I was amused at his sudden care for the word.

"I don't know what a goonch is." Ethan was even more confused.

"Hey Ethan—uh, thanks for being worried about me. I'm sorry I didn't tell you when I was leaving the press conference. I ran into Joseph—it's just that there are some unbelievable things—" *How could I even begin to explain the turn my summer had taken?*

"Who is Joseph?" He looked around the cavern and held his arms out, baffled.

"Oh, that's me. Jay is an alias." Joseph gave a pathetic half wave.

"Again, I ask—what the hell is going on here?" Ethan started shouting.

The three of us seemed to be waiting for the other two to explain things. After a few minutes Joseph stepped to the task. "Alright, FINE. But the only reason I'm including him is because my Aunt Doreh said he could probably help me with my family. Not that I need any help, especially from a kid who can barely swim."

"I'm a great swimmer." Responding to least important part of Joseph's statement, Ethan's ego was obviously bruised.

"Sure. You're great. C'mon, let's get inside."

We followed Joseph through a long hallway. As we walked side-by-side, Ethan shot quizzical glances my way. I tried to ignore him.

The hallway opened into a cavern—not unlike the one under the Ionian Sea. It looked a bit more lived in. Maps littered the walls and were spread out onto a table but what caught my attention was a large bulletin board with hundreds of photos of young women and a list of crossed out names.

"Welcome to my world." Joseph held his arms in a half-hearted gesture.

"Who are these women?" I was standing at the wall of photos.

"They're evidence." He was close behind and put his hand on my shoulder. I could feel his warm breath on my neck. "Proof that for years I have been searching for you Seraphin."

Ethan abruptly appeared beside us while Nasani joined us opposite him. "Great, now that you've found her, please enlighten me. Is this some kind of joke?"

Nasani chimed in. "No joke kid."

"Stop calling me kid. I'm like only two years younger than you. Seriously!" Ethan snapped.

Maybe he wasn't as smitten with her as I had originally thought.

She crossed her arms, turned her face away from his and gracefully strutted across the room to pout in the corner.

Joseph took Ethan to the large table. "My Aunt Doreh, you know her as Ms. Zebedee, said your father was a marine scientist, is that true?"

"Yeah. Why?"

"Did he talk to you about his work?"

"Nah."

"But you want to be a marine scientist, right?"

"Yeah."

"And that has nothing to do with your father?"

Ethan grew uncomfortable, the relationship with his father was even more nonexistent than the one he had with his mother. If he wanted to be a marine scientist, it probably had very little to do with Gomer Cottington.

"Is leaving various marine science magazines lying around the house considered molding the mind of your son? I guess they were his, right? So sure, let's go with the idea that he inspired my career choice." Ethan said, anger present in his voice.

"I gather you have a general distaste for your father. I knew I liked you for some reason." Joseph patted Ethan on the shoulder like an older brother would.

They smiled at each other—I noticed how similar the two were.

Nasani chimed in. "Such a touching moment—you've both got Daddy trouble."

"What is your problem lady? You're a jerk to me in the lab, you totally ignore any compliment I fling your way and now you can't even resist throwing your two cents into a conversation that has nothing to do with you." Ethan raised his voice.

She left the room.

Joseph gave me a pitiful look. "Will you go talk to her? She really likes you."

Shrugging my shoulders and pointing to myself, I turned to be certain he was talking to me. Unfortunately, I was still the only other person in the room. *He wants me to console her?*

"Of course," my answer lacked eagerness.

When I approached the end of the walkway I found her sitting against the wall. "What?" She asked.

"If you want to be left alone, just say so and I'll leave." I said. "BUT, if you want to talk I'm a pretty good listener."

"I'm sorry." She said in defeat. A tear rolled down her cheek. "I don't mean to be difficult, especially with Ethan. He puts me in a state, for some reason. It's been since the moment I met him."

"I don't understand what you have against Ethan; he's a really nice guy."

"I know, that's the problem—he's too nice." Her shoulders slumped.

"Can you elaborate? I'm having a hard time understanding why being nice deserves so little respect." I jumped to Ethan's defense.

She wouldn't look at me. "Seraphin, how do you feel about Ethan? Are you two—you know?"

"Ethan's my friend."

"And that's all?"

"YES! Why is everyone so interested in my feelings for Ethan?" Joseph ran me through similar questions on the *John F. Kennedy*.

"I don't know." She was on the verge of tears.

I felt bad for raising my voice.

Then she sighed and sorrow took over her expression. "I miss him; my Joshua." Collapsing with grief, tears streamed down her cheeks.

I understood then why Joseph and Nasani were so close. A strange mix of sadness and joy churned inside. Shame surfaced for feeling jealous. He loved her, there was no denying, but he didn't love her like his brother had. I thought back to her crying outside of my house and the way he comforted her each time the neighbors mentioned Joshua's name. "I'm sorry Nasani. I didn't know."

"He was—he was my all. They took him from me—from us. Joseph has you now. I see the way he looks at you and honest, it makes me happy. The search for you has been his way of coping all these years. He deserves this—to be the Guardian; he's the most honorable man I've ever known—well, aside from Joshua. Where do you think he got it from though?

"They were quite the pair. They protected each other until the end." As she wiped tears from her face she turned her head from side to side, trying to shake away her sadness. "I've got to pull myself together. It's been too many years but the wound feels fresh."

If anyone knew how she felt it was me. The pain of my father's death will never fade. "Nasani, no amount of time can heal the heartache associated with losing someone so dear. We just have to take it one day at a time and let their memories bring us comfort when no one else can. Do you have a memory of Joshua that makes you smile?"

"Yes." Her face lit up as she explained the last time she saw Joshua. It was a clear night and the stars were visible on the Australian shore where they held one another. Her father and Lord Merrick were attending an environmental conference in Sydney. Their families decided to make a vacation out of it. She knew it was past curfew and her father was going to be furious but for some reason she could not pull herself away from Joshua that night. It was as if she knew it was their last hour together. A giggle escaped as she recounted a small sand crab that had attached itself to Joshua's toe. "He squealed like a child; jumping around on the sand until I managed to pry the little critter off. The bravest man I knew was reduced to a frightened boy all because of a tiny pinch. But, he didn't need to be valiant and exciting for my sake; I loved every moment of monotony or imperfection he let slip through."

I wiped a lone tear from my eye before it could drop. "Thank you for sharing that with me."

"Seraphin, I want you to know that I won't get in the way of your life with Joseph. I won't allow myself to be the third wheel. He belongs to you and I know this." She spoke as if it was an absolute that Joseph and I would share our lives with one another. It seemed a little extreme as she went on to assure me. "Joseph has and will always be yours."

Uncomfortable with the drastic turn our conversation took and how unconditional she approached the relationship between Joseph and I, my head grew light. "Nasani, please let's talk about something else.

Joseph and I are not like that. I'm not even sure we're friends. To think of him as mine, to make him sound like a possession is ridiculous."

"He *is* yours though. The two of you are destined to be together as—"

I didn't allow her to finish. "As Guardians, I know."

"NO. I mean, *yes*. But not just that, you and Joseph are to be together. You and he will be the ultimate team of two…as long as you both shall live."

"Married! You think we're going to be married?" I was in hysterics. "I assure you that will not happen."

She defended Joseph. "But why? Even if the Legend didn't dictate it, *which it does*, Joseph is wonderful. A girl couldn't ask for a more trustworthy, devoted and loving person to share their life with. And, you can't tell me he's not handsome enough. Have you seen the effect he has on women? Knees buckle when his blue eyes meet their stares."

"It's not that, I know how wonderful he is. It's just—what did you say about the Legend dictating our future?" *If so, where could I find a copy of the Legend so I could uncover my so called future?*

"Maybe I've got it wrong. I've never actually read it, as a matter of fact; no one knows where it is. History has misplaced it. What I know has been handed down through generations by way of bedtime stories and merfolk tales." She tried to ease my panic but failed to do so. Instead she changed the subject. "Speaking of tales, I wonder how Ethan is processing all the new information Joseph is presenting him with."

"Maybe we should go find out." I suggested.

She stood and fussed with her long black braid which had purple ribbons threaded through it, as always, she looked ravishing. Her hand extended and I took it, she helped me to my feet. "Thanks for this."

I hugged her and we walked back to Joseph and Ethan with our arms still wrapped around one another.

"Oh good. You're back." Joseph mumbled with little enthusiasm. They were bent over the table looking at the maps. "Ethan's in."

"Phin, how cool is this? I am SO glad I didn't go to Michigan with my parents. My summer is going to kick butt. I can't believe you're fish people—and Ms. Z too."

"I guess it's somewhat cool." A little dumbfounded that Ethan accepted the existence of merpeople better than I had—he was almost excited. "ETHAN? Nothing about this seems impossible to you?"

"No. Should it?"

"We are half-fish people. Your awareness of truth has been altered and you're okay with it—just like that? Everything you knew to be true is now false." A part of me wanted Ethan to doubt as heavily as I had.

He stopped looking at the map and picked up a globe—spinning it around. "Phin, history is filled with false realities. If we stopped at what we know to be true—we'll never discover that it's actually false. The earth would still be flat."

Ethan spun the globe again.

The sphere quivered a bit before detaching from the brass brackets holding it to the base. We watched it smash into the ground; the earth cracked apart like an egg. The northern hemisphere lay at my feet while the southern hemisphere continued to spin. I watched Australia pass five times before it came to a wobbly halt.

"Sorry Joey." He muttered. "I'll fix the earth."

Joseph held a wide smile. "What a relief—and here I thought we were going to have to save the planet all by ourselves." He winked at me and though I would have thought it impossible, his smile grew even wider and he let out a laugh. *Was this the man I would marry? Did he already know this?*

The four of us gathered around the table.

Ethan held both hemispheres, shifting them first so that the top half of Africa lined up with the bottom half of South America. He realized his mistake and continued to rotate the pieces—aligning the continents properly. From where I sat, only blue was visible. The great span of the Atlantic Ocean—a mystery to that day; what wonders it held. He then rolled it along the equator, the arctic twisted before me. The earth was an ocean and the continents islands—how could we be expected to protect such a vast area?

"So, what now?" I reached, taking the two halves from Ethan. "Where do we begin Joseph? Are you ready to share your secrets with us?"

"What secrets?" Nasani perked up. "Joseph?"

"I'm not sure what you mean Seraphin." He gave an innocent glance in Nasani's direction. Her expression didn't change.

"*I mean*, are you finally going to tell us where my favorite teacher is?" I was trying my best to be tough. "Don't you think priority number #1 is finding her? Do you have a plan?"

Pushing his chair back and standing, he didn't answer but instead pulled a milk crate out from under the table. It was filled with black tubes. We watched him take several from the crate before he found the one he was looking for. He placed the crate beneath the table and sat back down.

"I've searched for this scroll for years." He began.

"And you just found it? Under your table?" Ethan joked.

"No." Obviously annoyed, Joseph continued. "It was given to me—the day I met Seraphin I also met an old—I suppose you could call him an acquaintance. He is the reason I was late helping my aunt. Anyway, he handed this to me and then left—without saying a word. I was in shock but managed to chase him for miles before he disappeared—just vanished."

"What is it?" I asked.

"It's *the* Legend. I don't know where he found it or why he surrendered it to me—it was unexpected." He was genuinely perplexed as he stood staring at the official rules of our lives. I wondered which block of text held our wedding vows.

"Who gave it to you Joseph?" Nasani was very interested. "I can't believe you had this and didn't tell me."

"Trite," Joseph answered. Irritation was in his voice. "I've been a little busy Nasani—sorry, it slipped my mind."

"Nicholas Trite? Is that the crewman missing from the vessel that went down earlier this summer? I think I remember the name from the news report." Ethan sat forward. "Did his disappearance have anything to do with—I mean—did he just swim away, like you and Phin?"

"ETHAN!? I didn't just swim away. I was really drowning." I defended myself.

They ignored me.

"Of course he swam away, he's a merman, but I don't know why he wanted to disappear. His actions are out of the ordinary." He spoke only to Ethan.

Since no one was listening to me, I slouched back into the chair and crossed my arms. I felt a little out of place—Ethan seemed to fit in better than I did.

"Can I see it?" Nasani sat forward.

Joseph carefully removed a worn piece of parchment from the black tube. Gently he laid it on the table for us to see. The edges were torn and stained dark brown. The text was unreadable—instead of letters, neatly lined rows of delicate brush strokes flowed across the page. In the center, an illustration featured a long necklace and a thick-banded bracelet—exactly like the ones from the mosaic that Ms. Z showed me.

"The carcanet and cuff," I whispered.

Nasani spoke, eager. "You know the relics, Seraphin! Do you have them?"

"I have seen them—"

Joseph interrupted. "Where are they?" His manner spirited.

"I don't know."

"But you just said you saw them." Nasani questioned.

"No I didn't. He interrupted me. I was trying to say that I've seen them—and so has every student that attended our high school." I pointed to Ethan, asking him. "Do you remember the mosaic?"

"A housefly?"

"Ethan? What?" I was confused.

"Mosaic is housefly in Spanish, right?"

Laughing, I corrected him. "Not quite. Perhaps you should have stayed awake in class more often. Mosca—that's the word you're thinking of."

"Yeah—isn't that what you said?" His smile was sly.

Nasani laughed.

After a few jokes at Ethan's expense I explained the mosaic featuring the Guardians at the bottom of the high school pool. Nasani and Joseph were surprised to find that such a piece of art existed and even more shocked that it was in a public place that held no significant relation to merpeople—other than the fact that Ms. Z taught at the school.

They were disappointed to find that I had no knowledge regarding the whereabouts of the relics.

"But you're supposed to have them. Joseph has the Rune of the Sea and you have the heirlooms. That's what this piece of paper says." Nasani lifted the corner of the brittle parchment. A piece broke off between her fingers. "OH—no—I didn't mean to—"

"Nasani, be careful!" Joseph raised his voice—taking the piece from her. "This thing is older than time."

"I can't imagine the condition that jewelry is in. I mean the fact that this thing has a drawing of the necklace and bracelet—that's got to make them older than it. I bet they're all worn out now, like in the Indiana Jones movie where he finds the Holy Grail and it's just a beat up old metal cup—nothing fancy about the thing. You probably don't even know you have them Seraphin—or what if your Grandma sold them at the garage sale she had a few years ago? My mom bought a bunch of her old jewelry—maybe she has them? If she does, good luck getting them back. She wouldn't care if they could save the world—the name Mara may as well mean greed; it already means bitter, which is dead right if you ask me." Ethan finished babbling—we looked at him with blank stares. "What? It's plausible."

"As fun as that might sound, I don't think the relics belonging to Guardians of the Sea could have been purchased at a garage sale." Joseph patted Ethan on the back. "Though, you might have a point when it comes to the condition they're in. Old *is* an understatement—these things are ancient. At one time they had to have been in your possession Seraphin. It's the only way your father—your neighbors would have known you were the Guardian. From what I recall, the last line of the Legend says that they will take their true form once we seek their power." Joseph began rolling the parchment, placing it back into the black tube. "Without a translator, this thing is useless. There is only one man who knows exactly what this says, and I have no idea how to find him."

Our conversation had gotten a little too off track for my comfort—I only had one concern. It was the same one I had all along. Legends and relics meant very little to me—family and friends meant everything. "How about your aunt, do you know how to find her?"

Ethan raised his eyebrows, listening intently. Nasani waited for an answer as well.

"We have to find the relics before we can face—before we can find my aunt. Seraphin and I need their power, we will fail without them." He placed the tube in the crate under the table then paced across the room—his fingers ran through his hair then locked behind his head;

elbows bent on either side, he turned and faced a blank wall. "We need the carcanet and cuff."

"Sorry but I don't have them." Irritation slipped into my voice.

"Yeah, I get it." Joseph sounded equally as irritated.

Ethan continued his questions, ignoring the increasing tension between Joseph and me. "Try and think Phin, I mean an old lady's life hangs in balance here."

"Ms. Z would not appreciate you calling her an old lady." Turning my attention away from Joseph's tense stare, I found solace in Ethan's relaxed expression.

His unwavering dedication to the brand-new mission was amusing and without even trying, he lightened the mood of the room. "She gave me a B+ last year instead of the A I deserved. She's lucky that's all I'm calling her. So, what *do* you know?" He pressed further.

"I'm not sure. I mean, bits and pieces of things come to me—mostly when I black-out."

"And you've never seen a vision of where the relics could be?" Joseph interjected.

"No. I only see that day—the day my father died. I've had—" I was just about to recount the dream, the one where he and I were in a tunnel but decided it wasn't important. "I mean, I've never had a vision that involved the relics."

They sighed.

I grew curious. "Joseph, have you ever had visions like mine?"

His expression softened and he looked to Nasani who gave him an approving glance. "I do—but they're not important, just silly things—more lighthearted than the ones you have and they're not about the past, they're a glimpse of the future. At least, I think—*hope* they are." He would reveal no more. "We should go back to your house and begin our search there. It's a start."

"But I can't see her house. I won't be able to go in." Nasani complained.

"I'll stay outside with you—if that's alright, I mean. If you're alone and you want someone to keep you company than I'll be the one—but if not just—" Ethan awkwardly tried to lend assistance.

I expected her to dismiss his offer but instead she responded quite pleasantly, stopping him before he could make an even larger fool of himself.

"I'd like that." She smiled at him and his face turned redder than a radish. Without hesitation she began down the walkway. Ethan stood, slightly dumbfounded.

Joseph threw his arm into Ethan's side, shoving him after Nasani. "Go on Romeo."

We followed Nasani as Joseph filled us in on his plan. He would bring Ethan back to the boardwalk so I could drive him to my house. My confidence remained low so it was a relief to hear I would not be responsible for bringing Ethan to the surface. While we drove, he and Nasani were going to swim along the coast. They would meet us at the house.

At the edge of the walkway I stopped, unsure of my ability to transform.

Nasani dove into the water and Ethan was about to but Joseph noticed my hesitation. "Ethan, wait." He approached, concerned. "You'll be great, just do what you did before."

"You mean stare longingly into your eyes until I want it bad enough?"

"If that's what works. However, eventually you'll have to do it without assistance from my good looks." He teased.

"Phin, show me your stuff. Let's see this fish tail." Ethan seemed to put my mind at ease. "She doesn't have it in her Jay—I mean Joey. I think you've found the wrong girl."

"Oh, I *am* the Guardian—Ethan Cottington."

"Then prove it." He challenged, standing at the edge of the opening, where Orin created his shroud. It was magnificent; Nasani's tail floated in a wall of water, just beyond the opening. The paper-thin magic was strong enough to prevent the Gulf of Maine from rushing into the underground cavern.

I grew stubborn—determined to prove my worth. "If I were you, I'd take a deep breath."

He drew in air and clenched his mouth, plugging his nose for added effect.

"Here we go." I skipped to him and together we dove through the opening—straight into the water. I pulled my legs together and with one strong kick I transformed.

Ethan's eyes grew wide.

Joseph entered the water and I could hear him laughing. *Showoff.* He teased. *Since you're obviously an old pro at this—take him up to the surface. I'll be watching if you need me.*

I held Ethan close, aware that he had a limited supply of oxygen. Unlike the rest of us, he could very easily drown. It wasn't until Ethan became distracted by Nasani's tail, that things went wrong. Reaching out, he touched her, making contact with where her upper thigh was hiding under the smooth scales. Instinctually, she slapped with her tail, knocking him from my grip. He tumbled head over heels, freely sinking and unconscious.

Oh no! No. I didn't mean to hit him that hard. She cried.

I watched in horror as the air from his lungs escaped. I dove to him but she was faster, grabbing and pulling him to the surface.

Huh? Change of plans; let's let them deal with each other. No point in waiting around for him to regain consciousness. Joseph reached his hand to me and I grabbed it. *It's a lovely night for a swim, don't you agree?*

I took his hand

FOURTEEN

It was almost like dancing, the way we swam together. Looping around each other with our bodies intertwined, we were playful. He took the opportunity to show me some moves; teaching me to accelerate to unimaginable speeds. Joseph was quite charming and I found myself wondering if I could indeed spend the rest of my life beside him.

We reached the shore behind my house too quickly, I wanted more time alone in the water with him but he recalled his task of retrieving the relics so playtime was over. We surfaced and swam the rest of the way side by side, walking the same way along the beach. For a long time we were silent until we reached a tiny fish that had been left behind when the tide pulled out. It was dead.

"Should we have been here to save it?" I asked.

"No Seraphin. We can't possibly save every little fish that misjudges the tide." Dropping his voice lower—more serious, he admitted. "I waited for you that night."

"What night?"

"The night we argued down here. I wanted to apologize for mocking you—I was confused."

"Confused? I believe you were more along the lines of arrogant."

He laughed. "I am royalty—arrogance is in my blood. I can't stop it from showing sometimes."

"How are you royalty? Please enlighten me your highness." I curtsied and he bowed back. When he bent I tousled his hair with my hand. "I can't seem to find a crown in that mess of hair."

He tried to grab me but I was faster than him on land. I ran along the beach as he chased, reveling in the attention. The tide came in quick—before I knew it, the water was above my knees. Joseph was able to catch up and when he did, he tackled me into a large wave. As the wave cleared I tried to stand up but he pulled me back down onto him.

"Things will be better now that you're here." A serious look came over his face. "I'm no longer confused."

I slowed my laughter. "I wish I could say the same."

"Anything I can help clear up?" He offered.

"Can you fill me in on—well; let's see—just about everything?" I shyly looked away and pulled myself off of him. "It's just that you know so much, you already know your mission and what to expect. You know who your parents are and who you should trust—I feel so in the dark."

He took my hand and we helped each other up. "I'll tell you everything. Where would you like me to begin?"

"I don't know," and I didn't. There were so many questions floating around in my mind.

"Great. Then how about we start with the most important factor in this equation; me." He nudged jokingly. "It's also what I know best."

"That's as good a place as any to start. Sure. Tell me first how Joseph Merrick is royalty."

As we walked up the hill to my house he explained that the sea has different rulers than the countries on land. He compared it to having a ruler over all the countries, saying that they didn't divide the ocean. To them, it's one large underwater country. The Merrick family reigns over the salt bodies of water *only*—however, this excludes anything that's land locked. Most sea-merpeople are not permitted in The Great Salt Lake in Utah or The Caspian Sea which is bordered to the northeast by Russia and to the south by Iran; as well as various other land locked bodies of water. Sea-merpeople are not only unwelcome when it comes to fresh water, they are also putting their lives at risk for they cannot take fresh water into their gills. They must hold their breath like a human and can very easily drown. He went on to explain that most mutants, like my neighbors, don't have that problem. Their gills can tolerate fresh water. The largest population of mutants or fresh water nymphs reside in the 5 Great Lakes—land locked by the United States and Canada. Which is why he was shocked to find a group of them in my neighborhood.

It was refreshing to hear him use the word mutant, though it still seemed degrading. "So your father is like a President or a King—and you're a Prince?"

"I suppose, though, we don't like to give them those titles. I'm just their son, Joshua was their prince.

"President's and Kings rule the land. We respect the Laws of Land and follow these when we surface. At times, their laws stretch out to sea and this is where they become murky. My parents, Lord Merrick and Lady Marietta Merrick, write the Laws of the Sea. When the Presidents and Kings fail to protect the waters from pollution, this is when the Lord and Lady are supposed to step in. First and foremost it is their responsibility to prohibit these types of things. They have failed and continue to do so by letting humans have access to waters that in the past have been forbidden. For example, my parents have the ability to hide the wonders of the sea from harm; instead, they have turned money hungry and dine with those who seek to strip the ocean from all its treasure."

"How can they hide part of the sea? Would they use a shroud?"

"More powerful—they could hide an endangered whale traveling at great speeds or conceal miles upon miles of underwater crude oil deposits from careless oil companies. Instead, they make deals with poachers and drillers—profiting from the destruction of our home." He was angry.

"I get why you're here. You're powerful and knowledgeable and have all the resources of CORE at your fingertips. But—what I don't understand is how I have anything to do with this. I mean, couldn't the Universe have picked a better candidate? How am I supposed to do this? What is expected of me?"

"We don't have to go around saving every fish that gets caught in a net Seraphin." He tried to convince me. "At least, I don't think we do. I mean, that'd be pretty exhausting."

We both let out a stressful laugh.

Then he continued. "To be honest, I'm not sure what to do either. I knew I was supposed to find you but—well, I guess I thought—"

"I'm not what you expected." My thoughts slipped out, interrupting.

"No. That's not it at all."

"It's alright—"

He stopped, placing his hand on my shoulder. "Don't say that. I didn't know what to expect. You're exceptional in every way. You're strong and intelligent. Whatever our purpose is, I feel confident that you'll be phenomenal."

The look on his face was difficult to read and his eyes swirled with both light and dark blues. He continued. "I thought that you would already know about the Legend—that maybe you were out there looking for me too. It just makes things a little more complicated."

"At least we're disappointed in the same thing." I said. "I wish I knew more about this life too."

We reached the top of the hill and I could see my neighbor's homes, their house lights on—hiding in plain sight—trying to lead normal lives. While I fished for the spare key that was hidden beneath a cedar shingle. Joseph lectured me about how I needed to take my personal safety a little more serious. Then he went on to say that a girl my age shouldn't be living alone. I suggested that he no longer comment on the way that I live when, for all I knew, he lived in a cave.

"I don't live in a cave." He seemed appalled.

"Oh, I'm sorry. Would you prefer to call it a cavern?"

"Seraphin, I have a house—a real place of residence—with a street address and everything." He revealed.

"And how was I supposed to know that?" It was difficult to picture Joseph living in an everyway ordinary house. "And where is this house?"

"It's in a neighborhood."

"You're being vague."

He only laughed.

We entered the house, both of us barefoot and wet. Joseph stayed on the small piece of carpeting that lay by the front door. "I don't want to drip all over the floors. It's one of the downsides to traveling by water. No shirt, no shoes and sopping wet."

I glanced at the puddle of water pooling at my own feet. "Will I ever get used to this?"

He shrugged. "The pros outweigh the cons."

"I hope you're right. I'll grab some towels."

Upstairs, I took two large beach towels from the linen closet but before I returned to the main floor, I noticed that the door to my father's room was open. It was strange since I thought it was closed when I left for work that morning. Slowly, I peeked into the vacant space. Perhaps I was mistaken? I pulled it shut, making sure the latch caught.

As Joseph and I dried ourselves, I heard what I thought to be the roar of my Gran Torino. Before I could peek out the window, there was a knock. We gave each other a puzzling glance. He stepped to the door. It was Ethan; his mouth gave him away before Joseph could look through the peep hole. "HEY—you guys in there?"

I pushed past Joseph and opened the door. They managed to bring my car home, but how? The keys were in my CORE locker and the spare set resided on a hook by the back door. "Ethan, what did you do to my car to get it here?"

"Wasn't me. It was Nasani, she hotwired your car. Pretty awesome, right?" When he turned I saw the red outline of Nasani's caudal fin on his cheek. Obviously, the fact that she slapped him unconscious didn't bother him.

Joseph interjected. "I'm the one who taught her that."

I shook my head at him. "That's not something to be proud of." But it was too late; Ethan gave him a fist bump, solidifying the brag.

Nasani was shouting from the neighbor's yard. "This isn't funny guys. Where are you? Can someone come and get me?"

Apparently, her knight in shining armor was too distracted with the hot-wiring tutorial Joseph was talking him through. I tried to remind him of his earlier commitment to stay with her, but he could not be bothered. After failing to interrupt the two men, I rushed outside to help Nasani. She was standing with her back to my house and her hand flat across her forehead.

"I'm on my way," I assured her.

"I hear you but I can't see you." She turned. "Oh, there you are."

"If I take your hand and lead you to my house, will you be able to go inside?"

"I think so. If we take people, like we did Ethan, into the caverns they're able to see beyond the shrouded area."

"Let's try it." Taking Nasani's hand I led her onto my porch, she had her eyes closed and her other arm extended, feeling—balancing herself. I told her when there were steps but she still stumbled—laughing.

Joseph and Ethan watched momentarily but quickly lost interest in our giggling. As I helped Nasani through the front door, I watched down the main hallway of the house and into the kitchen where the two were helping themselves to the plate of chocolate-chip cookies.

Mrs. Nulant brought them by early that morning in an effort to thank me, once again, for defending the neighborhood against Joseph's harsh words. It was almost mocking her that he was the very person enjoying the cookies. I wondered if the neighbors saw us together and what they thought of it. He promised to apologize and I hoped he would do so soon.

Nasani opened her eyes once we crossed the threshold. "Hey, this is a nice house Seraphin."

"Thanks." It *was* a nice house—my mind wandered again to what Joseph's house might be like, "Nasani, where do you live?"

"I live on the CORE campus, of course. I'm in the older apartments though; I put in a request for the new housing where Ethan is staying. Those apartments are so much nicer," she mindlessly fidgeted with my grandmother's knitting kit then went on to feel the fabric of the curtains like she was inspecting her surroundings.

"Is that where Joseph lives too?" In a way, I was conducting my own inspection.

"No." She didn't elaborate, even though I waited for her to say more.

"Then where does he live?"

Suddenly, she took interest in the bookshelf. "He has a house."

"I know. He told me that much. Where is the house?" I peeked around the corner to be sure he was still engaged in conversation with Ethan. I didn't want him to overhear my questioning.

"I don't know. I've never been there," she answered.

"But you're his closest friend."

"Yes. I think so."

"And you've never been to his house?"

"Never."

"Why?"

"He's never invited me," she was matter-of-fact.

Joseph stood with his arms crossed, smiling. "Doing a little investigative work Seraphin? We're not here to find my house, we're here to find the relics, remember?"

"Right," I was embarrassed that he caught me digging.

Ethan came into the room. "What's going on?"

Joseph answered him. "We're just waiting for Seraphin to give us any details she might have that will lead us to the carcanet and cuff."

The three of them stared at me.

I paused. Feeling pressure to produce some clues—but my mind was blank. "I'm sorry but I don't even know where to start looking. I've cleaned this house from top to bottom. I would have come across them if they were here."

"You're right. I don't think your father would have endangered your life by hiding them in the house." Joseph paced the living room.

Nasani was still browsing through the bookshelf. "*Den lille havfrue!*" She slid a small worn book from the shelf—holding it with care she brought it close to her chest; closing her eyes and sighing.

"What?" Ethan questioned.

She opened the book, showing him the pages. "The Little Mermaid by Hans Christian Andersen—I haven't seen this in years. My mother used to read this to me." Saddness filled her eyes.

Ethan glanced at the book. "It's not written in English."

"I know. The story was Dutch—I have never seen an original print before. This is a treasure," she opened the book, "look."

Inside the front cover, written in ink were the words;

"If you looked down to the bottom of my soul, you would understand fully the source of my longing and—pity me. Even the open, transparent lake has its unknown depths, which no divers know."

"This is an excerpt from the writing—the words of Hans Christian Andersen." Nasani said with excitement.

"What do they mean? Is it a clue?" Ethan asked.

"All words are clues." She answered—still full of intrigue as she held the book.

Joseph stepped forward. "But do you think it's a clue to where the relics are hidden? Are they at the bottom of a lake?" He sounded desperate.

"The words give clue to how Andersen's own life was full of heartache and misunderstanding. For example, the Little Mermaid longs for—"

Joseph cut her off. "Nasani, this is interesting and all but if it doesn't have to do with the relics, I don't care."

I broke in. "I care. I always wondered about that book. For the longest time I thought it was my grandmothers but she didn't know where it came from. I forgot all about it. I love that it's The Little Mermaid—even if it's not a clue to the relics, it might be a clue to my hidden life. The hand that wrote that was not my fathers, it is too delicate—maybe it was my mother's."

But Nasani's enthusiasm had already been extinguished. She placed the book on the fireplace mantle without saying another word then folded her arms across her chest; turning her back to Joseph. His one track mind was disheartening and I found that even though I noticed a discrepancy in my surroundings, I did not make it known.

I discreetly moved near Nasani. Ethan and Joseph continued perusing the bookshelf. The photo that belonged in my father's bedroom had been placed on the mantle—not by me. It was the second indication that someone had been in my house while I was away. Holding the snapshot, I examined it. I was 7-years-old. I sat on my father's lap as we rode the Northeast Harbor ferry to Great Cranberry Island. In the background a house on the shore of the island was visible.

Nasani had left my side and wandered the house. I heard her in the kitchen; then in the dining room and finally I heard the hardwood floor creak as she climbed the stairs. Joseph stood upright and ran his fingers through his hair, exhaling.

Battling with both my conscious for hiding information and fear of an unknown intruder, I reluctantly came clean. "This right here—it doesn't belong. It usually sits upstairs on my father's shelf. I didn't move it."

"Creepy!" Ethan exclaimed.

"That is a problem. Are you certain you didn't move it?" Joseph asked.

"There is no doubt in my mind. Also, when I went upstairs to get towels earlier, my father's bedroom door was open. Usually, I keep it closed."

Nasani screamed from upstairs and a then we heard a big thump. She continued to scream as the three of us raced up the stairs. Joseph and Ethan pushed in front, nearly knocking me down. I watched as they elbowed each other in narrow stairwell. Ethan won out and got to Nasani first. She was standing in my father's bedroom, screaming with her hands over her face. On the floor at her feet, a man with wild gray hair and crooked glasses was unconscious. Lying next to him was my father's hard cover copy of *Mysteries of the Great Submarine Grounds, volume II.*

"That's two for two, Nasani." Ethan teased. "Although, I think this poor guy got it worse than I did—the knot on his forehead is already taking over his face."

"Who is he?" I asked.

The four of us stood over him.

"I don't know." Nasani and Ethan answered at the same time.

"I do." Joseph said; his voice uneasy. "Let me introduce you to Orin Bindolestiv, the originator of the shroud."

"Oh." I said, tilting my head in pity. I could almost make out the word *'Great'* in the red blotch across his forehead.

"Is that supposed to mean something?" Ethan said irritated. "He broke into Phin's house. The guy deserved what was coming to him. Great work Nasani."

"Thanks," She said reluctantly, "I think I should try to fix him up now though."

"Good idea," Joseph agreed, "he may have come here to tell Seraphin something important. He's not a threat which is why I didn't pick up on him when we first got here. Nasani, can you bring him to a conscious state so we can find out why he's come?"

The three of us waited for her answer but she just stared at the old man.

"Nasani?" Joseph moved next to her, his voice was low. "What is bothering you?"

She whispered back, barely audible. "Something about this feels off, you know? I can't quite put my finger on it."

Ethan and I stepped closer to eavesdrop.

"You have no reason to doubt your abilities—Seraphin is standing here because of you. Ethan too." He assured her.

"I do not doubt my abilities Joseph." Her voice was much louder. "Just go. I'll figure it out."

"You want me to leave?" He was obviously taken aback.

She didn't look at Joseph when she gave her answer. "I want you to leave."

"But what if you need me?"

"I won't," she snapped.

"Ethan, Seraphin let's go. Apparently, she doesn't need us." Joseph snapped back.

Ethan paused. "I—well, I don't like the idea of leaving Nasani alone with this guy. What if he wakes up in a bad mood?"

"I can take care of myself." Nasani eyes met Ethan's.

Without hesitation he moved close to her and repeated himself. "I don't like the idea of leaving you alone with a guy who just broke into a house. It's not that I doubt your ability to take care of yourself. Obviously, you've managed to knock him out with no help and I'm certain you could do it again. But what kind of man would I be if I knowingly left a young lady alone with the complete stranger she just finished attacking?"

At first she seemed at a loss for words as they stood just inches away from one another. When she finally did respond, her voice was softer. "That would be nice if you stayed." Joseph's head whipped around in disbelief. I put my hand on his shoulder and began to move towards the door. His feet were firmly planted on the ground and my efforts went unnoticed.

Finally, Joseph muttered something under his breath and turned to leave.

I began to follow until I remembered the poem on my father wrote. I stepped over Orin—excusing myself to the unconscious man. To my horror, the paper was not where I left it. Frantically, I searched the floor. It was nowhere to be found.

"What are you looking for?" Joseph asked, realizing I was no longer behind him.

"The poem," I started to panic.

Nasani and Ethan ignored me, both of them working to arrange Orin into a more comfortable position. Ethan grabbed pillows off of my father's bed, placing them between the floor and the man's head.

Joseph stepped over Orin, willing to help. "What does it look like?"

"It's a small folded piece of paper."

"What's on it?"

"A poem that my father wrote—I think to me."

"Is this it?" Ethan was kneeling over Orin, holding my father's poem in his hand. "This guy apparently likes poetry too."

I practically dove over Joseph to get it—snapping it out of Ethan's hand.

"Sheesh!" Ethan exclaimed.

"If you don't mind, I need some quiet so I can concentrate." Nasani kneeled at Orin's head behind the pillows.

"That means leave." Ethan translated.

Joseph and I shared a look and then casually stepped back over the unconscious man and into the hallway, closing the bedroom door behind us.

"They are shaping up to be quite the team."   I laughed.

"Does that bother you?" He suspiciously asked.

"No. Does it bother you?" Nasani made clear her feelings towards Joseph, however, I wondered if he felt more for her.

He shrugged.

I pressed further. "I think Ethan has a thing for her. He's a good guy. Nasani is lucky to have his attention. Don't you think?"

Again, he shrugged—obviously bothered.

"You are jealous," stating my observations. I knew it was a bold move.

He laughed. "That's ridiculous."

"Sure." Going past him, I gave a sarcastic smile. "Ridiculous."

"It's not jealousy. It's—just that—forget it, you won't understand," frustrated he sat on the first step with his elbows on his knees.

"Really? Why don't you try me?" I turned, already half-way down the stairs.

Speaking to his knees; he began explaining his feelings. "Nasani is my friend—my best friend. We've been together since we were just kids—she's always been a part of my life." He swallowed hard and lifted his head to meet my eyes. They were sad.

I remained quiet—terrified of what he might reveal.

"I love Nasani—"

I cut him off. "You know what; I don't need to hear this. There is no need to explain."

He put his head back down; his hands went into his thick messy hair. "I want you to know."

I swallowed hard. If Joseph was in love with her—I already knew that she did not share the feeling.

He went on to explain. "We love each other as families do. I protect her and she protects me."

Relief filled me. I didn't want Joseph to be in love with Nasani. Though, I wasn't sure I wanted him to be in love with me either. "I know that much Joseph. It's obvious that you care deeply for each other."

"I don't know if Nasani told you about Joshua," saying with a sigh.

"She told me that he was her love."

"They were more than in love Seraphin. She tried to end her own life when he died. After his death she slipped into a deep depression—she mourned Joshua and the life they were supposed to share."

Suddenly, Romeo and Juliet seemed more emotionally unstable than romantic. I said nothing and he continued.

"Right now, her life is one of seclusion and heartache. When I fled and she came, she left everyone behind—the only person she stays in contact with is her father. So many times I had wished for her to go back but she's stubborn and will not. Anger keeps her up at night for what they did to my brother. Her way of punishing them is to stay away and no longer bless them with her gift of healing. You were the first person she healed since—" He paused, taking a deep breath. "Since the day she could not save Joshua."

Learning that she tried to save Joshua but failed broke my heart. I wondered if Joseph had tried as well.

He answered my silent question. "When Joshua was dying, I didn't know how to heal. It wasn't until after that I asked Nasani to teach me. Usually it's passed only through blood relatives; but I was able to learn." Tears filled his eyes, he looked away.

"Why does it bother you that Ethan is in there?"

He gave a sad laugh, and then let out a deep sigh. "It's hard to see her sweet on someone other than Joshua—Ethan might be his replacement. He might be the person she spends the rest of her life with."

"Wow. Maybe I'm wrong but Ethan probably isn't ready to propose." I let out a giggle—an attempt at lightening the mood. It didn't work. "I mean, he's still in high school. That kind of thinking is sure to scare a guy off."

"Not all men are scared off by commitment." Again, our eyes met.

Butterflies would have flown from my stomach and out of my mouth had it been open. I swallowed, just too be certain they stayed down. *Did he mean that he was ready for a commitment? Did he know that I knew about the Legend?* I needed to be clear with him. "I suppose that can go both ways."

"What do you mean?" He seemed confused.

"The stereotype is that while all women want a solid commitment from their man, men tend to avoid one like the plague. I just mean that it's possible for a woman to be equally as terrified when it comes to promising the rest of her life to a man." I thought that was clear enough. *Hopefully he's caught on.*

"That never occurred to me." He was genuine with his response.

Fresh air sounded good. Before I realized it, I had begun down the stairs.

"And you Seraphin…" He spoke confidently, getting to his feet and following me. "What are your thoughts on marriage?"

"It's not something I think about. It never has been." Besides, I had no father to walk me down the aisle. The thought of it made me not only uncomfortable but sad as well.

He questioned me, "Never?"

I reassured him as I reached the bottom of the stairs that I never purposefully thought about marriage and headed for the front door—I needed fresh air. My fingers fumbled with the lock. As the door opened his hand came from behind—pushing it closed. I held on to the knob, keeping my back to him. Escape was the only thing I could think of.

"Think about it now then."

"Think about what?" I played dumb.

"About committing yourself to someone—could it ever happen?" He was so close I could feel the heat from his body.

My heart pounded—I was confused. It wasn't something I wanted to think about. For goodness sakes, I was just an 18-year-old girl.

What did he want from me, a declaration of my unwavering love? "I need some air." It came out as a whisper.

"You need some air or some space?" His hand slipped across the front of my body; slowly removing my fingers from the knob—with one fluid movement he turned me. We were face to face, my back against the door. With his other hand, he held it closed—I was trapped between his arms.

"I don't know," still whispering.

A mischievous smile cracked from the corner of his lips. His arm slid down the door and he moved in closer. I froze—terrified but surprisingly a little excited.

Joseph lowered his lips to my ear. I drew a deep breath and closed my eyes; taking in his scent. The knob clicked and felt the door open against my back, pushing me closer to him.

"Then, by all means, don't let me trap you." Stepping aside, he opened the door.

A breeze blew in.

I blushed and turned into the cool night air—alone. The door shut behind me.

The neighborhood was silent and only one porch light burned. Mr. Rigby who lived across the street sat in his recliner facing the television, his living room blinds remained open even though his eyes were probably closed. He was a lonely man. An elderly woman lived with him years ago—it might have been his mother. When she passed away my father and I went to the funeral. It was my first one and I didn't quite understand the idea of death. To be honest, I didn't grasp it until my father was dead.

It was difficult to watch the old man. He had no one to close the blinds or to turn the unwatched television off. There was a very good chance that he wouldn't move from that spot until morning—his loneliness would remain on exhibit for anyone to observe throughout the night. How does a person end up a window display selling loneliness? Could the old man's life one day be my own? It was certainly possible that I'd end up alone. Especially with the way I had been thinking. I wondered if Mr. Rigby had ever been given an opportunity in love.

In the house, Joseph was leaning against the living room wall; arms folded across his chest—staring at the displaced photo on the mantle. I watched from the corner of the window—he didn't see me. Occasionally he would shift his weight or put his hands in his pockets—a few times he reached up and ran his fingers through his hair. It wasn't until he took his eyes off of the photo and bowed his head that I saw the tiny glisten of a tear on his cheek.

He was upset, it bothered me. Maybe I should have been more receptive to his questions instead of running like a scared fool.

It was difficult to see him as vulnerable—I quietly stepped through the door, unsure of what to do or say. For several minutes I stood a few feet away—watching every breath he drew. Why was I confused? Perhaps I was still an immature little girl—uncomfortable with the thought of growing up?

Though, it didn't feel that way.

Deep down I knew the reason I was reluctant to feel more. The words of Gianni—the claim that Joseph was no friend still haunted my thoughts. He sure felt like a friend, but so did Gianni.

"I know you're back there." He spoke softly.

Of course he knew—he knew everything. I didn't know how to respond.

He kept his head low. Suddenly, I wanted to throw my arms around him and tell him I was sorry—but for what, I still wasn't sure. Instead I focused on Nasani's voice; it seeped down the stairway. "How do you think it's going up there?"

"From the sound of it, she's struggling. The tones are very powerful but I can hear some despair in her notes. She breaks occasionally—that's unlike her. She shouldn't be struggling; it's a quick fix. He just had a bump on his head; I doubt there was even a concussion. I bet Ethan is a distraction. She shouldn't have let him stay."

"Is that why you're upset?"

"I'm not upset," his tone was less than friendly.

Frustrated, I walked down the hallway and into the kitchen to get a drink of water. Joseph came through the dining room and into the kitchen door opposite to where I was standing. He opened the refrigerator and pulled out a can of Coke—cracking it open. I watched as he took a drink.

He realized I was staring. "Do you mind if I have a Coke?" It was not meant to be polite.

"What's mine is yours." I said with thick sarcasm.

Tipping the can back he muttered as he walked out of the room. "If only that was the case."

I followed, unwilling to let it go. "What is that supposed to mean?"

"What?" Casually he plopped down onto the couch.

"If you have something to say to me, I'm listening," ready for him to air his grievances.

He thought for a moment, placed the can of Coke onto the side table and stood up. "Alright, I think you don't want this. I think you're being selfish and I can't for the life of me figure out why."

"Unbelievable! Who is selfish?—NO wait! More like self-centered! Is that what's wrong? You're feeling rejected? Not used to coming in second? Nasani has Ethan and I'm not interested so now you're going to mope." Assuming he was appalled because I didn't throw myself at him, I was angry.

He took a step back. "Wow."

We stared at one another. A strong wind blew in from the open window and the drapes fluttered into the space between us. It was out of place. My hair swirled and the front of Joseph's shirt rippled in the breeze.

"You think I mean ME. Well, at least I know how you feel. I won't waste my time on those thoughts any longer." There was no hiding his anger.

I began to speak but he stopped me.

"That's enough. You've made your point, now let me make mine. By 'this' I mean 'the life of a Guardian'. I don't think you understand what an honor you have been given. It's a gift. Only you Seraphin and only me; that's it—we are the only two who have been chosen. By God; by the Universe; by whatever higher power you believe in—He; She; It picked us. It's a shame to see such a gift go to waste on someone who doesn't appreciate it."

"I...I don't—just because I..." Fumbling for the right words, my anger grew. *How dare he suggest that I wasn't worthy?* "What did you think would happen, Joseph? Was I supposed to jump for joy when I found out my entire life was a lie?"

"Your life hasn't been a lie Seraphin. It's called PROTECTION. The truth was kept from you in order to keep you alive—realize that!" Joseph was heated and I watched as his eyes changed to a deep, dark blue that swirled.

Wind whipped through the room. Neither of us paid it any attention. Both were too focused on the other.

"PROTECTED? You must think my life has been full of cupcakes and rainbows compared to your hard existence." Ethan and Nasani probably could hear me, I was loud.

"I'm not trying to compare our lives. I'm simply saying that *you* don't realize how many people care for you. Or maybe you're not willing to know." They could probably hear him as well.

"Or maybe I'm CONFUSED. I don't know what I want right now. You've had years to contemplate; to doubt—not to mention all the knowledge of this life at your fingertips. I've had days. I still don't know who to trust—what being a Guardian REALLY means—or why I, of all people, have been chosen." As I hollered, the drapes from the window violently thrashed. Unknowingly, I pushed them aside, keeping my focus on Joseph.

"You're upset." Suddenly, he was calm.

"YES!"

Joseph's expression puzzled me. He crossed the room. "Seraphin, you're just a silly girl. You'll never be a Guardian. How can you protect the sea when you can't even keep your emotions under control?"

I gasped at his words. They tore through me. "Joseph, what are you saying?" Yes, we were arguing but those words crossed a line with me. I wanted to be the one who decided if I was worthy, not him.

"I'm saying that I was better off before I found you." He turned; his eyes were a light shade of blue but his brow furrowed and his expression was stern. The contrast was confusing and so were his words. "It's a huge mistake having you as the other Guardian."

"You don't mean that." I sputtered and turned away.

He was silent for a few moments. I expected an apology; an admission that he was exhausted like I was; that we should stop arguing and get some rest. Instead, he hit me where he knew it would hurt. "You're nothing—no better than your neighbors. You're a worthless GOONCH!"

My jaw clenched, my eyes narrowed. A loud crack of thunder shook Joseph from his defensive stance. "GET OUT. Get out of my house." I spoke through my teeth.

"I'm RIGHT! Don't you get it?" He moved to the window—the drapes swirled around him. "Look at what you did."

"I've done nothing, Joseph. How can you be so cruel?"

He started laughing and put his hands in front of his body—like he was trying to calm an angry bear. His eyes were the cool blue that fascinated me, so I focused on them—still confused. "Seraphin, I'm trying to show you something. Look. Listen."

Rain pelted. Lightning flashed. Joseph waited.

I realized what was happening. "You think I'm doing this?"

"No—I *know* you're doing this." With his hands remaining out in front of him, he approached. "You're emotions are tied to the storm—to the weather. No wonder you blackout the minute things get tough. It's Mother Nature's way of protecting herself."

Surprisingly, I didn't care if I had the ability to make my house fly through the air. I only cared about one thing; Joseph's opinion. "Do you really think I'm worthless?"

"Would I be standing here if I did?" He was laughing.

My shoulders relaxed, but only a little. Outside the storm paralleled my emotions. My breathing remained quick and sharp. My emotions were tied to the weather—to the storm, like the girl in the story Joseph mentioned. Then, my thoughts quickly turned to the massive storm that overtook the *John F. Kennedy*. I gasped. "Joseph—do you think? I had a nightmare and was upset—is it a possibility?" My mind raced. Could I have been responsible for such a tragedy?

He understood what I was suggesting. "Seraphin, you can't blame yourself. Since the beginning of time earth has had storms. Horrible terrifying bouts of weather—"

Stopping his explanation, I knew he was just trying to make me feel better. I could see the curiosity in his eyes. "But you and Nasani said that the storm was an attack. What if it was an unintentional inside job? What if I was the reason that the boat sank?"

His words were gentle but quizzical. "I suppose it's possible that whatever emotions you experience during sleep could affect the weather. When you blackout you're completely unconscious, so your emotions are trapped inside your head—your body completely shuts down when things get difficult. So, why the change? Why all the sudden are you conscious during your emotional breakdowns?"

I knew the answer. "Because I fought it—the night you came here during the storm; I didn't allow myself to blackout. For so many years I was numb and I wanted to feel again. What have I done?"

"The day I found you jogging though, I thought we were being followed—it felt like an attack. My senses told me I was being threatened," still confused.

"You were being threatened—by me. I was angry with you but I fought it that day too. I didn't want to blackout again." I admitted. Explanations were what I needed. "What does this mean Joseph? Am I a freak? Do you know of anyone else? You said there was a girl who had eyes like mine. Who was she?"

"You mean to say that you don't already consider yourself a freak?" He laughed. "Or do you mean that now you're a freak amongst freaks?"

"Joseph, I'm serious!"

"She was a story Seraphin. That's all. It was an old tale to stop kids from throwing temper tantrums in public." His voice changed to a high pitched mocking. "You'll drown in your tears if you don't dry those eyes…"

I collapsed into my father's chair. "I could have killed all those people—Ethan was on the boat. What if the Coast Guard didn't get there in time? What if—"

"What if accidents happen and you try not to blame yourself. There was no way of knowing what you were capable of." He was trying to protect my feelings.

Deep down, I knew that it was my fault. What if my destiny was not to guard but rather destroy? Was I Joseph's opposite? Joseph was a healer and I could only devastate. No good could come of having such abilities. The world was at the mercy of my emotions.

Very naturally he walked over to the chair. He reached down to brush the hair out of my face but stopped before doing so. Instead, he awkwardly put his hand into his pocket and wandered to the couch. "You shouldn't feel bad. I told you before; storms are good for the environment—"

"But bad for the people," finishing before he could try and lift my spirits.

Shaking his head, he settled onto the couch and tried to change the subject. "Let's not jump to conclusions before we can do a little research. This is new to me too Seraphin—but maybe it's not new to Orin. Let's hope that Nasani wakes him up soon so we can ask him some questions, he's the smartest man I know.

"We've had a long couple of days. You're tired, it's getting late and I don't know about you but I'm starving. Do you mind if I raid your kitchen? I can cook. How about I make some pasta?" Joseph was doing his duty and guarding me from myself. I was thankful for it.

"That sounds really great." I closed my eyes, hoping to drift off to sleep.

Joseph wandered into the kitchen. Metal pans clanked. "Where is the colander?"

Before I could answer, Ethan came running down the stairs, shouting. "He's awake! Nasani wants you two upstairs, *NOW*."

FIFTEEN

*J*oseph came from the kitchen while I jumped out of the chair; the three of us ran up the stairs, wasting no time. I had so many questions for Orin. *Did he know about my ability to control the weather? Why was he here? Did he know my father well? How did he get in my house?*

Orin was in my father's bed and immediately my heart sank. He was in no shape to answer my questions. Nasani held his hand, the lump on his head remained. His skin looked ashen; he was soaking from sweat and breathing heavy. She spoke softly to him. "They're here Mr. Bindolestiv. The Guardians are here to see you."

We were the *Guardians*, Joseph and I. The realization hit me and instantly I felt uneasy. Standing in a pair of shorts and a tank-top, I didn't feel like the next ruler of the sea but more like a frumpy 18-year-old girl; which is precisely what I was. Joseph, on the other hand, stood tall and strong and although he was wearing just a pair of shorts and a basic t-shirt, he looked like he deserved respect and honor.

Slowly Orin lifted his free hand and gestured for us to join him. He tried to take a deep breath to speak but instead he gagged and winced in pain.

"My goodness Nasani, what did you do to him?" Joseph whispered.

Orin shook his head.

"This wasn't my fault. He is sick. Joseph, there's poison in his body. It's just like Joshua. I can't help him." Nasani began sobbing.

A tear dropped from Joseph's eye.

I wanted to hold and reassure him. Instead I gently ran my open hand across the back of his shoulder, hoping he would know how I ached for his loss. He pulled away from my touch. Shame filled me for having accused him of being self centered earlier. Unsure of what to do next, I crossed the room to the side of my father's bed where the strange man was dying. "I'm Seraphin Shedd, daughter of Samuel Shedd. This is my home."

Orin winced in pain then choked out, "aa—pIG—chur."

"The picture?" I questioned.

He nodded his head in agreement.

"Do you mean the picture of my father and me? Did you move it? Did you put it on the mantle?" I grew excited.

He nodded again then sputtered "RAHnn—beh"

I didn't understand what he was saying, looking at Joseph and Nasani for help, I shrugged my shoulders. They shrugged theirs in return.

He shifted his weight and tried speaking again. We all listened—hanging on his every syllable. "CRRann—"

Ethan shouted. "CRANBERRY!"

"Great Cranberry Island?" I asked. "My father and I were on the ferry to Great Cranberry Island when that picture was taken."

Orin nodded his head.

My mind swirled. Finally the words of the poem came to mean something. "Where the land lay low, the seeds best grow."

Nasani held a puzzled expression.

Orin smiled and sighed.

"I don't know why I didn't think of this before." I turned to Joseph who was wiping another tear from just below his eye. "Joseph, I know where the relics are."

"You do?" Relief crossed his face.

Ethan chimed in. "Awesome Phin. Now we can go save Ms. Z."

There was a choking sound. We turned our attention to Orin. Frantically shaking his head, he tried to speak but then only made a low grumble. Tears filled his eyes. Nasani rushed to his side, placed her hands on the feeble man and began to hum a low tone. It was too late though. She couldn't do anything to save him.

His eyes closed.

Joseph began to shake him. "NO!—Nasani bring him back."

"I can't Joseph. I can't." She sobbed. "I'm useless and so are you. We can't save him."

Joseph's eyes turned dark blue. His expression was hard. "Leave me."

Nasani and Ethan looked to me. "You heard him. Let's go." I said.

We silently shuffled out of the room, closing Joseph in with Orin. It wasn't until we got to the main floor that the most beautiful tones began to ring through the house.

"That dude can sing." Ethan threw himself onto the couch and cuddled up to a pillow. "You think he can bring this guy back from the dead?"

"Orin had very little life left in him, if any at all. I'm not sure Joseph will be able to do anymore than I could. If he had the cuff his abilities would be heightened. He'll try though. Joseph doesn't let lives slip through his fingers and he doesn't like to lose. Who ever poisoned that man was sending a very clear message by using the venom of a blue-ringed octopus. It's the same poison that was used on Joshua; I am useless against it." Nasani blotted her eyes with a tissue and, with ease, slid next to Ethan on the couch. He moved to give her more room but still kept his body close. He offered her the pillow but she waved it away.

"Nasani," Ethan asked "Joshua was pretty special to you, wasn't he?"

She slowly nodded her head. If she allowed herself to speak a flood of tears would have been set free.

"I know it's not much but I'm really sorry. I've never experienced the loss of someone close but I imagine that the pain is unbearable." He looked in my direction—his eyes filled with understanding and sympathy.

Nasani smiled and shifted her weight closer to Ethan who had casually stretched out his arm and placed it around her shoulders. He closed his eyes and yawned, within minutes his breathing deepened; he had fallen asleep.

I was tired, but found it difficult to relax. Nasani held a look of exhaustion but I got the feeling she didn't want to give in to sleep.

"Can I ask you a question?" I broke the long, silence.

She nodded.

"How is it that you have healing abilities?"

She shifted away from Ethan, as to not disturb him, leaning forward to answer. "My family has a long history of healing abilities, so it comes naturally. However, I don't think just anyone can learn. I'm not too sure why it worked with Joseph. He's always had the urge to save people, animals or anything really. I suppose it comes from something within. He heals differently than I do, I saw this when he worked on you. It's much more passionate—like he feels the pain of those he's healing. It's almost as if he absorbs it. I don't experience any of the pain and suffering that the wounded or sick are feeling."

"Do you think he'll be able to save Orin?" I knew I wouldn't like her answer the second I asked my question.

"What I'm more concerned with is that he might harm himself in the process. He won't give up Seraphin. Just like he didn't give up with you—healing you took so much. What's worse is that he knows Orin and respects him. His emotions are already woven—did you see how intense Joseph's eyes were?"

"I did." Immediately I wanted to rush to the bedroom and pull him away from Orin's dying body. His voice rang through the house, more powerful than Nasani's. "Surely he would stop before he put himself in danger."

Nasani shrugged her shoulders. She leaned into Ethan's arm, closing her eyes.

I listened to Joseph's voice for hours. It was well into the morning when I tip-toed up the stairs. For another 30 minutes, I waited in the hallway outside the bedroom. Finally, my worry for Joseph had taken hold. Quietly, I opened the door and slipped in—my fears were confirmed. Joseph was hunched over Orin, singing his sounds of healing tones, but his skin had turned pale. Sweat poured from his body and his legs were shaking. Death had already captured Orin. There was no rise and fall of his chest and the sweat that had been on his skin earlier was dry, but Joseph wouldn't see.

I moved across the room, he didn't break his focus from the old man. Taking a deep breath, I slowly wrapped my arms around Joseph from behind, laying my hands over his. At my touch, his voice turned from a soothing tone to a low moan. I felt the pain he was in—both emotionally and physically. My heart ached as his did. When I closed my eyes, I began to see why the man meant so much to Joseph. Like a movie clip, I saw young Orin in a library reading. He wore the same glasses but his hair was full with bushy brown curls. Another man joined him, placing his hand on Orin's shoulder. A boy no more than 5 years of age, with bright blue eyes and curly blonde hair ran into the room and pounced onto Orin's lap, throwing his small arms around the man's neck.

The scene changed. Orin was older with white streaks in his hair. He looked nervous as he paced outside a tall building. There were 3 beautiful women standing in the background, watching him like hawks watch prey. It was cold and snow fell from the sky. A woman wearing a black scarf around her head held the hand of a boy—too young to be a man but too old to be a child. His eyes stayed down as they approached. The woman kissed the top of the boy's head then left. Orin placed his hand on the boy's shoulder and the two sulked away as the hawk-like women watched. I caught a final glimpse of the boy's face and his deep-sad blue eyes.

Then I gasped at the next scene that filled my head. Orin stood on the beach with a man and a woman. The woman held an infant child. Her face was filled with sadness. The man turned and I saw his face. Orin held a silver box in the palm of his hand.

My mind returned to the bedroom where Orin lay dying. "We have to save him." I whispered.

A blue glow filled the room. The Rune of the Sea on Joseph's neck illuminated and was spreading light over the surface of his skin. It was so vibrant that I turned my head to the side—catching a glimpse of my own reflection in the mirror. I was glowing. The light traveled down my arms—it soon followed Joseph's arms as well. When it reached our hands on Orin's chest, a burst of blue energy filled the room. The pressure was too much; it threw us against the wall.

A deep breath drew from Orin's lips.

Joseph and I remained on the floor; in shock. "Joseph, did you see?"

"Yes." He sounded unsure. "Did he show us those things?"

"I think. Was the boy you?"

"Yes. That was my father with Orin in his library and the woman with the scarf is my mother—I remember that day very clearly but it wasn't my memory that we just saw. The three women standing; watching, could you see them? Who were they? We were alone that day—my mother, myself and Orin."

"I don't know but they didn't look friendly. They were watching the three of you with intent." Chills moved through me as I recalled their sharp faces. Their features were nearly birdlike and they wore thick coats of feathers.

"The woman on the beach, with the child—she looked like you Seraphin; was that your mother?"

Even though I had never seen my mother, he was right. Her hair; her face; we were so much a like. A low moan came from Orin as we helped each other to our feet. We went to the bedside and the old man spoke.

"What is the child's name?" He said weakly but remained unresponsive when we tried to wake him. He was talking in his sleep.

Joseph was shocked. "I think we saved his life Seraphin."

"You mean—you saved his life."

"No. I wasn't strong enough. I was losing him—his life was slipping away. When you came in I had nearly given up. Then I felt you—your energy. We did this together." The look he gave me was full of admiration.

Orin began to shout. "NO—woman—stay back." His breathing increased and I took a step back. Joseph stepped forward and placed his hands on the man's chest. His blue eyes grew wide and his face was full of fear.

"Joseph, what is it?" I was alarmed.

Not answering, he began to shake his head from side-to-side. Orin screamed in terror and his torso shot forward, throwing Joseph's hands into the air. They stared at one another. Joseph continued to shake his head. Orin panted like a dog as sweat soaked through his clothing. Neither spoke for what seemed like an eternity. Orin returned to laying, closing his eyes he remained unconscious.

Finally, I broke the silence. "What just happened?"

"I was there." He spoke to no one then turned his attention to me. Disturbance filled his face and he looked frightened. "Seraphin, something happened to your mother. Orin knows."

"My mother?"

"The memory is so foggy. I was just a child. She was holding you, but there was a flash of light and I heard a man yell." He was frustrated as he searched for the memory. "The next thing I remember is Vanita Caro's voice, Nasani's mother; healing me."

"What did he do to her JOSEPH?" I was shouting, suddenly protective of a mother I never knew. *Could Orin be the reason why she wasn't a part of my life?*

"Orin didn't do anything," he defended, "It wasn't his fault. It wasn't anyone's fault. I wasn't supposed to be there, my parents didn't know. Seraphin, do you know what this means?"

"It means this guy needs to wake up!" Shaking Orin, I repeated myself. "WAKE UP!"

Joseph took my arm, stopping me. "It means your parent's knew you were a Guardian and that they brought us together as children. I remember your little toes dangling down from your mother's arms. You were the baby that Orin brought me to see."

Tears filled my eyes. "So what happened to her Joseph? Did she leave me?"

"I'm so sorry," he moved closer, standing beside me. "I'd give so much to know the answer to that question. All I remember is what I've already told you. Orin showed me my own memory, he reminded me of the day. When he wakes up we'll know more, he'll tell us everything."

Orin was breathing but remained unresponsive. "I think we should let him rest," Joseph suggested.

We left the room together; both exhausted. Neither of us had slept the night before. The days were beginning to blend together.

"You should rest too. I'll stay here and keep watch in case Orin wakes up again." He slid down the wall and onto the hard wood floor.

"You're not going to sleep on a wooden floor Joseph. Don't be silly." I reached out my hand for him to take.

"Honestly Seraphin, I'm fine. I'm not sure I'll be able to sleep much as it is." He ignored my hand.

I looked at my feet and then around the hallway. A painting hung on the wall between my bedroom and my father's. It was a blue canvas with the negative silhouette of a mitten. Little plus signs were scattered around the edges of the mitten. I took interest in it. My mind spun with thoughts of my mother. I craved more information but knew it was impossible until Orin woke. While I was lost in my thoughts, Joseph moved to be near me. I felt him standing close.

"You need to rest Seraphin," urging, his breath was warm on my neck.

Of course, he was right but I couldn't bring myself to leave. Or maybe I couldn't bring myself to leave him. I wasn't sure. "I don't want to be alone."

A long silence stretched between us. I continued looking at the painting and he remained just inches away. The wooden floorboards creaked as he shifted his weight from one side to the other.

He drew a deep breath and exhaled. "You should go downstairs with Nasani and Ethan."

"Do you want me to go downstairs?" I was surprised at my own words.

It occurred to me that he was holding back. It was my doing. I had made a mistake when I rejected him so blatantly earlier.

"I want you to get some rest and if that means going downstairs, then yes." He stepped away when I turned. His head was down and I watched as he slid his hands into the pockets of his shorts. "It's been a long couple of days Seraphin."

"You're right." It was hard to leave him at the top of the stairs but I did. He watched as I walked down—on the last step, I turned. "Do me a favor and sleep in my room. It will be more comfortable and you'll still be able to hear Orin if he wakes."

"Thanks."

"Goodnight Joseph."

"See you in a few hours Seraphin."

I made my way into the living room where the faint light of a candle burned. Ethan and Nasani slept—and from the looks of it, uncomfortably. Ethan was at one end of the couch with his mouth wide open and his limbs sprawled freely. Nasani was covered in a knit blanket and had her head resting on Ethan's leg. Her body curled into a ball.

I blew out the candle and locked the doors but left the window beside the chair open. The cool breeze was refreshing and within no time I fell into a deep sleep.

It seemed like only a few minutes before the sun was shining through the window. I was awake but the rest of the house remained asleep. Glancing at Ethan and Nasani, I had to laugh. At some point they had completely changed positions. Ethan was on the floor, curled in a ball and gripping a throw pillow. Nasani had the entire couch and knew it by the way she was sleeping. As I stepped over him, Ethan let out a few choking snores.

After I made a pot of coffee, I walked down to the beach. The water was calm and I found it hard to resist. I waded in, waist deep then fell back into the calm ocean. For several moments, there was nothing but the sound of my hair gently swaying in the rippling water. A few small fish were swimming nearby and a school of minnows was feasting on seaweed about 100 yards away. I focused, pushing further—like sonar, bouncing signals. More fish; a large colony of lobster—I had to be sensing almost a mile off shore. It was exciting to have such capabilities. I pushed even more. A worm wiggled on a fishing hook cast out from a small aluminum boat and just a few feet below that, Joseph was in a heated discussion with Ms. Z.

Was I sensing this correctly?

My first thoughts were naive. I was so relieved to see Ms. Z alive that it took time for reality to soak in. Ms. Z and Joseph were face to face, both fully transformed. She wore a floral swim top that accentuated her chubbiness—he was shirtless.

Was it an illusion like the one that Orin showed? I let myself sink into the water fully. No—I was not mistaken. I felt Joseph; his presence.

They didn't sense me and I kept my thoughts blocked so they wouldn't hear either. My heart was racing. I could tell that Joseph was upset but I couldn't hear his words.

Though, it didn't matter what they were saying. Joseph had been lying—Ms. Z had been lying. Was Nasani lying too? What a fool I had been to think Ms. Z needed rescuing—to think that Joseph and Nasani were my friends.

Their conversation ended and Ms. Z disappeared.

Joseph began to swim to the house—then I let him hear me. *You liar! You're not welcome in my home—in my life. Stay away from me.*

It shocked him. The last thing I heard before I ran to the shore was his pleading. *Seraphin, it's not what you think. Please let me explain. Seraphin, please!*

As fast as my legs could go, I ran up the hill and to the house. I knew it would take Joseph only minutes to swim the distance back to shore. Quietly, I woke Ethan. He was confused. I grabbed his hand and my car keys. Soaking wet and shivering, I convinced him to get in my car. We pulled out of the driveway as Joseph crossed through the ivy covered trellis. I drove away from my home on Briarwood Court while he stood in the middle of the street with a look of defeat.

SIXTEEN

"What is going on Phin?" Ethan rubbed his eyes—still groggy.

"They're lying to us."

"Who?"

"They are—the people in my house, the fish people."

"You're one of them."

"No. I'm not. I'm not a liar." I was shouting and speeding.

"Alright. Calm down. I don't think Joey can catch us on his bare feet. You can slow down to at least 10 over the speed limit." Ethan was logical, which is exactly what I needed.

I let my foot ease off the gas pedal. My heart was racing and my mind was going even faster. Every moment that Joseph and I spent together was a lie—but no, that wasn't the worst part. The only woman I trusted—my dear, sweet teacher had lied to me as well, and for so many years. What a fool I had been; an absolute fool.

Raindrops began to pelt the windshield and a violent wind whipped through so hard that I found it difficult to steer the car straight. I realized what was happening. "I need to calm down."

"That's more like it. How about you pull over and let me drive?" He suggested.

We stopped in the parking lot of Keyes Market. Mr. and Mrs. Keyes pulled in behind us. When I got out of the car, Mr. Keyes shouted over the thunder. "Seraphin, the store doesn't open for another hour. If you need something, I'll get it for you."

Seeing Mrs. Keyes reminded me that I had less than an hour to get to work. I ran to the car and she rolled her window down. "What dear?"

"Mrs. Keyes, I'm so sorry to do this to you today but I can't come to work. There is something very important that I have to do. It's about the Guardian thing," hoping she would understand.

"Don't worry. Do what you must—just make sure you get out of this rain before you catch a cold. You're soaking…." She rolled up the window before she finished her own sentence.

I climbed into the passenger side of my car. Ethan started to pull out of the parking lot but stopped. "Where am I supposed to go?"

"Drive to Northeast Harbor. We're going to spend the day on Great Cranberry Island."

"You just told Mrs. Keyes that you needed the day off," he was dumbfounded.

"Ethan. I know where my father hid the relics."

During the car ride, I explained to Ethan how I saw Joseph and Ms. Z secretly meeting.

"So what were they saying?" He asked the obvious question that couldn't be answered.

"I wasn't able to hear anything," sheepishly admitting.

"If you couldn't hear what they were saying then how do you know that they've been lying to us? I get that you're upset but stop and think for a minute, Phin. Maybe they are letting Ms. Z see Joseph? Did he tell you where they are keeping her?"

"No."

"He didn't tell me either. She could be close-by for all we know." Again, his thinking was very logical but I didn't want to think that way.

Bottom line: Joseph lied.

We drove along the coast. The water was rough and dark; unwelcoming. Only minutes before it was calm and peaceful. I hated it; the ocean was my enemy again—I felt betrayed and wanted to be far from it. For a long time, we didn't speak.

Ethan broke the silence. "I'll consider that perhaps Joseph is hiding a few bits and pieces of the truth from us. But, can you accept that he's not as horrible as you're making him out to be?"

Could I accept? I had been acknowledging things that were scientifically impossible. The existence of merpeople was something that I suddenly had to admit. Could I consider that Joseph wasn't a horrible person? I didn't want to.

"Phin, you're being stubborn." Ethan stopped the car in the middle of the road. Cars behind us squealed and swerved as horns blared with anger. We were stopped along Route 3, a two-lane road that ran along the coast from Bar Harbor all the way to Northeast Harbor. The car sat on the bridge where Long Pond met Bracy Cove.

"You're not thinking logically." Ethan spoke with a sense of calm. "You need to think about this. Really think. Don't let your emotions get in the way."

Cars drove around us; a driver shot foul looks in our direction.

I could not admit that what I saw was a mistake.

"SeraPHIN!" That was the first time Ethan used my full name. It was startling and I gave him my attention. "You can't do this. You don't know all the details. We need Joseph and Nasani."

"We need them for what? Obviously, our initial objective has changed. Ms. Z no longer needs to be rescued." My arms were folded over my chest like a stubborn child.

"How can you be so sure? What if she still needs help? Ms. Z has always been there for you. Even if you don't trust Joseph, the least you can do is trust in her."

Darn it. He was right. Ms. Z remained a loyal friend—unless I considered the fact that she knew I was a mermaid and never said a word about it. Though, she was probably doing me a favor; I wouldn't have believed anyhow. Perhaps I was being misled—but not by Ms. Z, I decided. She would never do such a thing.

Joseph was strange when we met. He stalked me for days after—showing up randomly. During one of the first arguments we had, he admitted to being jealous of the time Ms. Z devoted to me. When asked, he would not disclose any details relating to her disappearance—could the kidnapper be Joseph? And I still couldn't shake Gianni's words. *Joseph was no friend.* "Ethan, you're right."

"I'm glad you're seeing things a little clearer. Let's go back to your house so we can pick up—"

Before Ethan could finish I climbed out of the car.

"—Phin! WHAT ARE YOU DOING?"

I perched myself along the railing of Route 3. Below, a twisted whirlpool churned. A few weeks prior, I would have blacked-out at such a sight.

Ethan opened the driver side door and was standing in the flow of traffic. Horns and profanities blared. A man driving by hollered, "Lady, you're crazy."

The word crazy didn't touch the way I felt. My life was ignominious. I had turned into a fantasy—any 5-year-old girl would give everything to be me. . But however outlandish it was, being a mermaid was my reality. I had to face it. I was through being manipulated. Yes, Joseph helped me to discover who I was—but my life did not belong to him. As a matter of fact, he needed me more than I needed him. The relics had been given to me; I am my father and now my mother's secret. I recalled Joseph's words the night before. My parents knew I was a Guardian. In a way, that fact solidified everything. I was no longer just a scared girl. "Here's something even crazier; I am Guardian of the Sea, chosen to protect. It's time I started living my ludicrous life."

Falling into a backward dive, I spread my arms wide. As I cut through the surface of the water a hysterical laugh rang through my head. It was my own. Transforming easily; I powered toward Great Cranberry Island. Sounds, scents and sonar came from all directions. I ignored them all—nothing could take my focus off of the island. The message my father left was clear thanks to Orin. I knew the place he referenced. We spent hours collecting the low bush cranberries year after year. The seeds grew best in his favorite place to pick—that is where I would find the relics. I was certain.

It took minutes before the island was in sight. The bottoms of research vessels lined the boardwalk that ran along the CORE property. I avoided that area—my destination was on the other side of the island. Only a few homes remained but most of the shoreline opposite CORE was vacant, waiting to be developed. When I reached the rocky beach, I was careful that no wandering eyes watched when I emerged from the surf.

"Alright Dad—it's just you and me now." I muttered while trekking though the overgrowth covering a once maintained path leading to an abandoned house. The house from the photo—I was close to our cranberry gathering site.

The rocks and twigs covering the ground created a rough surface and a sharp edge sliced the bottom of my foot. The lack of shoes was another downside to traveling by sea—so much of the lifestyle was inconvenient. Blood seeped from the wound. I had nothing to bandage it with. I continued on—a bit crazed. Limping, I made my way to the site my father referred to. Low-bush cranberry plants littered a large clearing—though none were ripe, they held lush green leaves and the beginnings of berry-buds. I nearly melted at the sight. Memories came flooding back and any anger I held turned to sorrow.

An enormous flat boulder—20 feet in diameter sat just above the earth. I made my way to it. Years had no effect there. A picnic lunch atop the rock; a game of tag in the neighboring field; and a roll down the hill that seemed so much bigger years ago—I closed my eyes and there we were. I envisioned my father and I living our lives, our once ordinary lives. "Why here? Why did you have to bring me back to this place?" I whispered to my father. Pains of loss stabbed.

A low breeze blew. Gentle arms wrapped around my waist. Joseph was holding me. I didn't have to open my eyes to know he was there.

We were connected—my body knew his—there was no other way to explain the feeling of his touch.

"You lied." I said—my eyes remained closed.

He didn't speak. Instead he placed his head against the nape of my neck. I felt the wet of his hair.

"I don't need you." My mood was a bit combative and the stubborn side was not ready to forgive. A truer statement would have been *I don't want to need you.*

Still, he remained silent though he held me tighter.

"Have you nothing to say for yourself?" I turned to face him but instead gasped at the sight of his battered face. Blood dripped from his eyebrow and mouth—his eyes were nearly swollen shut. I took his hands into mine; his knuckles were raw and bloodied, claw marks ran down his arms. "Joseph? Who did this to you?"

He only shook his head.

I shouted. "ANSWER ME."

His head jerked up.

Before I knew what was happening he was pulling me through the field telling me to run. I tried to pull my arm from his grip but it was no use—he would not let go or slow down. Crazed, he looked toward the shoreline—a loud screech came from the clearing. Joseph ran faster; nearly dragging me as I stumbled over the rough brush with my injured foot.

We were only a few feet from the shore when a whirlwind surrounded us. Joseph continued pulling towards the water. Sand and pebbles pelted at my skin. The force of the wind was direct—like a weapon. He stumbled and I tripped over him; we both lay flat on the rocky sand—the water washed over my right arm. Joseph still gripped my left. His body lay twisted and bruised.

Another loud screech filled the air.

Joseph tried to stand but his knees buckled. He let go of my arm. "Go." He mumbled.

I knew we were in danger. The screeching was not human—nothing friendly could have made such a horrid sound.

Our eyes connected, for the first time panic filled his. I lifted mine to see three, winged creatures. They flew side-by-side and when the center creature lifted her wings, the outside creatures dropped theirs. Beautiful was an understatement. Their bodies were covered with a coat of creamy white feathers—like three clouds moving swiftly through the sky.

The screeching turned to a soft melody that was calming. I relaxed at the sound. Time slowed and even though the wind remained violent—it didn't matter, nothing mattered. Joseph was crawling on his elbows—dragging his lower body though the sand. He was shouting—I smiled. He was handsome—I wondered if he liked the flying ladies. Drunk with pleasure, I asked him, "Do you like them? I do. They're so pretty."

He continued to shout but I couldn't make out what he was saying.

Like a dream, Ethan appeared.

I wondered if Ethan liked the flying ladies. He ran past me, into the water. It didn't matter if he liked them. Everything was going to be wonderful—I could just feel it.

The sand moved underneath my body—the cool rush of water and Ethan's arms around me. He was pulling me into the water—but I didn't want to go. I wanted to stay and listen to the bird ladies sing. They were singing for me. Ethan was too strong. I struggled to get away but failed.

The instant my head dipped below the surface of the water, reality reared. Joseph was lying on the beach—blood pouring from his wounds. Ethan held his breath and would soon need air. I had been tricked by their melody—they put me in a peace coma. The world was falling apart and they made me forget all my worries. *What magic was this?*

Their sharp talons fit the claw marks on Joseph's arm.

I tried to get a closer look at the creatures; lifting my head above the water. Ethan pulled me down—pointing to his ears and shaking his head. I resurfaced again, making sure to keep my hands over my ears. Ethan broke the surface, took a deep breath and went back under.

I watched the middle creature tuck her wings and fly dangerously close to Joseph on the beach. He took a handful of sand—throwing it in her face. She pulled back in anger but then reached out blindly with her claw; slashing his back. His body arched in pain.

My heart screamed. *No.*

The other two creatures tucked their wings. They were preparing to attack—I had to stop them before they killed him.

I concentrated on the anger; on the ache. The sky turned dark—churning with thick black clouds. Hurricane force winds moved in from the ocean, as the waves built a wall behind me. "Hang on Ethan. Things are about to get rough." And I meant it. The power of the storm was revitalizing. My guard fell. All the years of blacking out—protecting myself from the terrifying emotions—meant nothing. The only thing that mattered was the man who needed my help—the man who had helped me so many times—I owed Joseph.

The creatures found it difficult to maintain their flight—they landed on the beach, just a few feet away from their target. Black clouds billowed and hail began to fall—pelting the attackers. Nothing distracted them from Joseph. *Who was I fooling?* I was no match. I was making things uncomfortable but I wasn't yet a threat.

They surrounded Joseph—he didn't cower. Though his eyes showed fear his actions were brave.

I ran—Ethan ran. We were side-by-side. He was shouting. "PHIN! The waves!" He stopped.

I stopped. We were 20 feet from where we started but the ocean was still only inches behind. The waves swirled and crashed at my ankles. The water seemed to be attached—but I didn't have time to figure it out. Joseph needed us.

Focusing on his eyes, I dove through the white feathers. He reached out his arms, grabbing me and falling—the wave swallowed us all. White feathers blurred—angry screeching bubbled from their mouths. The three creatures tried to escape the surf but Ethan pulled at their wings, legs or whatever else he could grab hold of.

I sheltered Joseph's injured body with mine. Claws met my skin only once but the pain was excruciating. It wasn't hard to imagine what Joseph had gone through before he met me on the island. I cringed when I thought about the pain he must have been in.

The water moved us out to sea.

The creatures had enough and as Ethan grew weary he released them one at a time. They shot out of the water like cannons. He surfaced.

Joseph and I floated in each other's arms. His eyes were closed. I traced his swollen face—his lips parted under my fingertips. He mouthed, 'thank you'.

I wanted to lean in closer—but his lies kept me back. My heart sought to forgive but my head reminded of his betrayal.

We kicked to the surface, both silent until we broke through. Ethan was only a few feet away. He was waving his fist in the air, taunting the creatures to come back and fight. They were far off in the distance—fleeing to safety.

"Ethan, don't invite them back. Let's be satisfied knowing we scared them away for now." I urged.

Joseph clung to me. He could barely hold his head up. His eyes opened and closed sporadically and when he finally spoke it was to ask for Nasani. There was nothing more I could do for him. My powers stopped there. We needed her.

Ethan helped me to bring Joseph to the house I passed earlier. We knocked and no one answered; Ethan kicked in the door. It was clear the house had been vacant for a long time.

Joseph collapsed onto the floor.

Ethan gave me a weary look—worried for his friend. "I'll get Nasani. You stay with him. Try to stop the bleeding." He left.

I stared at the broken man sitting before me. "Joseph."

He lifted his head. Sadness filled his eyes.

"Don't die, please," I knew it was an empty request that neither of us could promise true.

A crack of a smile slipped through his swollen mouth and his eyes lightened just a little.

I looked around the house, gathering a few items that had been left behind; a large beach towel and a blanket. I tried the faucet but no water flowed. Returning to Joseph, I spread the blanket on the pine floor. It was a poor attempt at adding a little comfort to his aching body.

He lay on his side—exposing his raw, bloodied back. It was all I could do not to wince at the sight. Three distinct and deep claw marks ran the length of his body. I tore the towel into smaller pieces of cloth to bandage his injuries.

"Does it look as bad as it feels?" He asked weakly.

Blinking back my tears and swallowing hard I tried to hide my fear. "Nothing Nasani can't fix." I assured him though we both doubted my optimism.

The day passed; Joseph slept and I worried. Outside a light drizzle consistently fell—I wondered if it was a result of my sadness. Occasionally he would moan with pain. I'd rush to his side though there was nothing I could do to ease it.

He watched as I paced the room. Joseph wasn't the only one hurting though he was by far the most critical patient. The cut on my foot burned and so did the scratch from the creature's claws that ran down my arm.

"Seraphin, you're hurt."

Disputing his claim, I tried not to limp but it was difficult. The last thing I wanted was for him to be concerned with me.

It was not the time to ask about Ms. Z, though it consumed my thoughts. He was in no shape to speak at length about anything—rest is what he needed. I'd question him after Nasani worked her magic.

Night fell and there was still no sign of Ethan and Nasani. The side of the island that we were on was remote and no streetlights lit the way. I worried that they would not be able to find us in the dark. The rain drizzled as I continued to agonize.

Finally I sat near Joseph on the blanket. He had fallen back to sleep and his breathing was labored. Beads of sweat formed on his brow. The loss of blood was great—I feared for his life. Taking his head, I lifted it carefully onto my thigh. Running my fingers through this hair I wondered why the creatures would attack Joseph with such fury. They were the women in Orin's vision—that much was certain. I prayed that they would stay away until Nasani arrived.

I shifted my weight, bending at the knee and pulling my foot closer. He turned his head, my fingers continued to mindlessly twist his wavy hair. I didn't notice when he reached his hand to my foot and could barely hear the low humming. After everything he had been through, he was doing for me the one thing I couldn't do in return. The wound on my foot slowly began to close—the stinging stopped. I felt a force push from the bottom of my foot, up my leg, through my torso until it found the wounds on my arm.

I pleaded with him. "Stop—don't waste your energy." My words meant nothing; he continued to hum his healing tones. I wanted to do the same for him.

The wounds on my arm closed—I could feel the power that Joseph used. I willed it to my hand. Placing my fingers to his battered face, the healing energy moved through my body and into his. I was a conductor. With my help, he was healing. The cuts closed, the swelling went down and the bruising of his face began to fade but those were only his minor injuries. I wanted to help heal his back, where blood continued to seep. My hands moved to the nape of his neck, the Rune of the Sea was glowing.

Joseph caught on to what was happening. The tones grew deeper and more intense. He summoned with meaning—sitting up and baring his back to me. As he bent forward his hands reached, grabbing my legs and folding them around so my feet rested across his lap. The energy continued to move from his hands to my feet, through my body; finally escaping out of my hands, like a complete circle.

I wanted to heal him—to feel his energy. Placing my right hand between his shoulder blades and my left hand just above his tailbone, I focused on drawing out his pain. His back arched, his head threw back; resting on my shoulder. Our cheeks touched and my face vibrated from the deep moans that came from his throat. I was supporting his weight and we were perfectly balanced.

My eyes closed. The clear colorless waves moved around our bodies—though they were not the same ones I saw when he healed me on the shoreline, or in the cavern under the Gulf of Taranto. They were more intense—intimate curves intertwined between the silhouettes of our bodies. Dark lines were being pulled from his wounds—disappearing into the tangled web of healing energy. When there were no more dark lines to pull, Joseph slowed his humming to a whisper and then to a stop. We remained still for several minutes, just breathing each other in. As I began moving away, his body twisted and his arms reached—pulling me around onto his lap.

I melted in his arms as he stroked my back with his finger tips.

We had healed one another with no help from a doctor, no assistance from Nasani. Our wounds were no longer gashes but smooth.

"Thank you Seraph…" His whispering voice trailed off; beginning again softly just seconds later. "That was ama…z…"

I only nodded my head, exhausted. I fell asleep in his arms.

SEVENTEEN

As the sun burst through the dusty windows of the old abandoned house, I woke. At first, it was startling to be in an unfamiliar place. After a few seconds my mind adjusted—recalling where I was and why. The blanket was wrapped tightly around my body and I was quite comfortable considering the fact that a pine floor was beneath. Joseph was no longer beside me but across the empty room, propped against the front door.

His bloodshot eyes revealed an all night watch though his face held a look of enthusiasm. "Good morning Seraphin. Did you sleep well?"

"I did."

"The Sirens stayed away last night." Standing up, he gave one final glance out the front window and then joined me on the floor.

I spread a bit of the blanket for him to sit on. "The Sirens?"

"The evil bird ladies that you thought were *so* pretty. Remember them?" Joking, he batted his eye lashes.

"Explain. Go slow and start from the beginning."

"It was a sunny May morning when Lady Marietta Merrick gave birth to a child that was destined to be the most powerful man in the sea—me," he was trying to be funny.

"Fast forward," while I appreciated his humor, I wanted specifics.

Joseph was in good spirits. His skin held no sign of his earlier abrasions—he was shirtless in only his shorts and even though he stayed up all night, he looked fantastic. I wished I could say the same for myself.

He went on to clarify how The Sirens are essentially part bird-part woman. They transform as we do and their song is impossible to resist. It captures the listener inside of a peaceful trance. The very trap I had fallen into at the beach—it was immobilizing. To feel that carefree—nothing to fret; no worries to burden, could have been deadly.

"Thank God Ethan showed up when he did or we both would have been toast." Joseph reasoned.

It didn't take long for my brain to connect the recurring dream I had to The Sirens. The screeching and my fear for Joseph's safety; though in the dream, we were in a tunnel. I didn't want to tell him about the dream—*not right then, at least.*

"Why didn't their song have an effect on you or Ethan?"

"It did have an effect on me, the first time they attacked. The second time I wised up and was humming to myself. It would have had an effect on Ethan as well if he stayed out of the water any longer. Luckily he heard my voice over the bitter screeching. You know, they don't actually sound beautiful? They sound like the horrid screech you first heard. It's just that a person's mind can't comprehend something so terrible—it searches for good and in the meantime blinds all the other senses. It really had an effect on you. I've never seen you so lovey-dovey." He mocked.

I ignored his teasing. "Why did they attack you?"

He was shrugging his shoulders, "I don't know."

"Could it have been your father's doing?" I couldn't make sense of the random attack.

"I don't think so," he explained. "Mr. Lamange said they would never work for my father and that they usually only attack when their land is being threatened. He said they've been at peace with the merpeople for many years. Usually they only lure sailors to their death—if they get too close to their island, that is. All of your neighbors were shocked to see The Sirens in such an unrestricted location. They don't usually attack unless they're provoked."

"My neighbors? Mr. Lamange? When did you talk to them?"

"After you jumped to conclusions and ran away—"

"Excuse me?" I interrupted.

"We'll get to that." He paused for a moment, holding his finger up as if to say 'just a minute'. "Anyway, before I could go back into your house to tell Nasani what had happened, The Sirens swooped down. Their screeching turned into the most beautiful melodies. I was mesmerized and, all the while, they were kicking my butt in front of your house. If it wasn't for Mr. Lamange coming to the rescue, I don't know what would have happened. He scared them away, I thought they were gone but they followed me here—and you know the rest."

"And, you have no hint of why they attacked?"

"No idea, it's not like they gave me a chance to ask either. I've never seen those things before—well, except in Orin's vision."

"Could your father be threatening their land? If they attacked you, perhaps they don't know you're at odds with him. My neighbors didn't know when they first met you. Maybe it's worth a public announcement—it could save you to declare yourself his estranged son."

"Perhaps—Aunt Doreh was always trying to get me to do that very thing," suddenly realizing we had come full circle and regretting the mention of his aunt. He knew he had some explaining to do.

"Speaking of your aunt, would you like to explain what I saw?" taking advantage of his slip-up.

Joseph took a deep breath then put his hands in his hair and lowered his head. At first he spoke low and into his elbows. "There's a lot you don't understand."

"Try me." I was stern.

"It's just that—", but before he could begin explaining, the door burst open and in flew Ethan pulling Nasani by her arm.

"Save him!" Ethan shouted.

Nasani looked bored. "Save him? From Seraphin?"

"What's going on? Joseph, you're supposed to be dying." Ethan declared, obviously confused.

"Sorry Ethan. I apologize. I'm sure with those bird ladies on the loose I'll have plenty of other near death experiences you can help me out of, but for now, Seraphin was able to step in and save my life." He patted me on the back; happy to not have to answer my questions about Ms. Z—for the moment, at least.

"What took you so long to get here?" I asked.

Ethan and Nasani glanced sideways at each other—a silent plea of not having to be the one to explain. Nasani pushed Ethan forward. He hung his head low and began mumbling. "Well….uh ya see…"

"WHAT?" I was growing angry. "Just come out with it!"

"I wrecked the Gran Torino on Route 3." Ethan sheepishly admitted.

I repeated in disbelief, "Wrecked the Gran Torino."

"I know. It's my fault and I'll get it fixed. I promise. It's just that I was so freaked out when I left here that—well I was shaking and worried. YOU SAW THOSE THINGS SERAPHIN! YOU SAW JOSEPH—he was going to die if I didn't hurry." His voice was pleading.

How could I be mad when I might have reacted the same way?

"And you could have died driving so recklessly." Nasani placed her hand on Ethan's shoulder.

The three of them looked my way—waiting for a reaction. "Don't worry about it. I'm glad you're safe—that we're all safe for the moment."

Ethan's shoulders relaxed and he hugged me. I returned the hug, assuring him that I was not upset but rather relieved that he was unharmed.

"Did you find the relics Seraphin?" Nasani asked with enthusiasm.

There had been no time and besides that, even though I knew the rough location; I didn't know where to begin digging. How was I going to locate a buried treasure with only a guess? "No. I could use some help."

"Where do we begin?" Ethan exclaimed.

I explained to them the field to which my father referred to in his poem. Joseph agreed that the area I spoke of was large and would be difficult to search. Ethan wandered the perimeter of the house; finding an axe and a busted shovel that had only half a handle. They would have to do. The four of us walked to the field. One area was lower, so we began our search there. Ethan and Nasani trailed behind—whispering to one another; I heard Ethan say Ms. Z and tried to listen closer but Joseph interrupted my eavesdropping.

"Seraphin, I don't know how the relics will change us. I know they're said to be powerful and that with them our senses and our gifts will be heightened. Once you put the carcanet on, there will be no going back. The life you know now can't exist. You'll have to join me—" He stopped, drawing in a deep breath before continuing. "I'll have to give up my life too. No more CORE; no more college. My job—our job will be protecting the sea and all its inhabitants."

My life had already changed and I wasn't exactly comfortable with it. To have it altered even more seemed crushing. Though from the sound of Joseph's voice, he wasn't as comfortable with his life being turned upside down as I had originally thought. "You love working for CORE and you're about to start the Master's program at the University. That seems like a lot of wasted time and effort, don't you think?"

"This is more important." Suddenly, he sounded sure.

I wasn't going to lie to myself or Joseph. "Well, I don't like it and if it means giving up my life, I'm not ready. And how do you know we can't continue to live our lives? Is there a rule somewhere that says we can't?"

"Well, no. But look at all that's happened. Our lives are far from average and having additional power means we'll draw extra attention. We can't keep hiding like we are. At some point we'll have to announce that the Guardians are alive—and since everyone thinks all hope died with Joshua—we're going to be in the spotlight for a while. And not only that, there will be people visiting us, asking for favors, asking to be healed. My father's not even a Guardian and people were dropping in at all hours." Just when his confidence began to waver, he adjusted his tone. It seemed as though he was trying to convince himself of something he wasn't sure of. "This is important to the world and I'm ready."

"Maybe we should wait?"

"No." He stepped in front of me and began kicking the cranberry plants aside, searching for a sign of the relics.

Ethan and Nasani caught up. "We have a question. Does Ms. Z still need our help, or not?"

Funny, I was wondering the same thing. The three of us waited for Joseph to answer.

"It's—well—things with my aunt are a little complicated at the moment," stumbling over his words.

"Joey, if you've got something to tell us than there's no time better than the present." Ethan walked over and put his hand on Joseph's shoulder. "Listen man, I like you but I'm not going to follow you off a cliff made out of lies. I'll only defend you and stand by your side if you're truthful. If I wanted to be sheltered from reality, I'd move back home."

"You all deserve the truth—it's just that I'm afraid of what you'll think once you hear it. You've got to believe, I didn't know what her intentions were. I didn't even know Seraphin's emotions were tied to the weather. I figured it out the night before last and when I did—my aunt's plan became clear." Joseph was rambling and making very little sense. "I told her that I didn't want any part of it—but she wants me to convince Seraphin that it's what the world needs. She's always had this crazy premise that the world is infected but I never thought she'd take it so far. I still don't think she will actually go through with it—she doesn't have the means, without your powers."

Ethan and I were confused but Nasani caught on quickly. "Joseph, you can't mean—is she insane? All those innocent people," she knew Ms. Z's plan and it made her distraught.

"So is Ms. Z missing or not?" Ethan was growing impatient.

"Not in the sense that I lead you all to believe. She's disappeared on her own—she ran away, hoping to bring Seraphin and me closer together by doing so. Her plan worked and honestly, I didn't know at first. I didn't know until after the *John F. Kennedy* went down. After Seraphin was rescued by that jerk Enzio, Aunt Doreh came to see me. She was worried he—forget it, it's absurd," unwilling to finish his final thought.

Joseph knew Gianni was the one who rescued me. Ms. Z ran away in hopes that Joseph and I would bond over finding her. The information hit me like a ton of bricks but surprisingly, I responded to the least important thing he stated. "Gianni is not a jerk."

"Gianni?" His head tilted. "The two of you are on a first name basis? And how do you know he's not a jerk? Of course he'd be a perfect gentleman to you, you're a pretty girl. Maybe Aunt Doreh was right."

Ethan and Nasani looked at one another. Ethan shrugged his shoulders. Nasani spoke low. "Gianni Enzio is kind of a jerk." She said to Ethan only.

"Right about what?" My voice grew louder.

"She was worried about that slime-ball sweeping you off your feet." For the first time his eyes were green with no trace of blue.

"THE NERVE YOU HAVE!" I was shouting. A strong wind blew. "I'M JUST A SILLY GIRL IN YOUR EYES!"

Only Joseph stepped forward, the other two took four steps back each. "I suppose that's true if you're silly enough to fall for Gianni Enzio. Was it the uniform or the accent that roped you in?"

"It was his honesty, a trait that you have yet to show." Recalling Gianni's warning, I continued to argue. "Secrets don't make friends, JOSEPH!"

"So, you *do* have a thing for Enzio?" He was heated.

"If I did, it would be none of your concern." I spoke through my teeth knowing I had to calm down. The wind grew violent.

"Sorry to interrupt this but does anyone actually need our help? If not, I'm going to work. Dr. Radski is going to boot me out of the research program if I miss another day." Ethan was matter-of-fact.

"You see Joseph, life goes on. This isn't the most important thing in the world. We have everyday lives that need tending to." I turned to leave, following Ethan. "I'm done here. You can have the carcanet if you find it. It's all yours. Feel free to give it to whomever you deem worthy, your highness. I have an ordinary life to lead."

Joseph seemed surprised at my defiance. "But you can't just leave. We need to find—"

Nasani stopped him. "Joseph, let her go for now. It's alright. We need to talk, is it true? What Doreh is planning?"

I continued walking even though I regretted not sticking around to hear what Nasani had to say. Reasoning with myself and too flooded with pride, I decided it didn't matter.

Ethan remained a few steps in the lead as we trekked across the island and onto the CORE campus. We were nearly an hour late for our shifts but no one seemed to mind. Mrs. Keyes was welcoming. She even allowed extra time for me to shower and change. Later that afternoon when I saw Ethan in the cafeteria, he said Dr. Radski was too busy getting the gear set for whale tagging week to care about him being tardy.

I didn't see Joseph or Nasani the rest of that day. Since my car was out of commission, Mrs. Keyes offered to drive me home—I graciously accepted. She reminded me that the Keyes Market Anniversary Gala was the following weekend. Then she pressed me about bringing a date. I jokingly wondered to myself if Gianni had plans that evening.

Dread filled me when I arrived home, for two reasons. First, the Gran Torino was in the driveway; Ethan wasn't exaggerating when he said he wrecked it. A bill was taped to the front door from the towing company. All I could do was heave a sigh. Second, I had no idea who was in my house—my best guess was that Orin remained in my father's bed and that Nasani was tending to him. As far as Joseph goes, I couldn't begin to speculate his whereabouts.

When I opened the door, nothing was as I had predicted. The scent of a fresh dinner and the sound of a baseball game on the television startled me. Mr. and Mrs. Nulant were asked by Nasani to tend to Orin in her absence. Mrs. Nulant had taken it upon herself to make spinach lasagna for dinner and Mr. Nulant sat in my father's chair watching the New York Yankee's play ball. It was all so commonplace—so welcoming.

Mrs. Nulant raced to the door. "Seraphin dear—how are you? We've been so worried. Joseph said you were upset when you left. Then the Cottington boy came by in a huff to get the odd girl. He was going on about someone needing her help, then this morning your car shows up—*well*, what were we all to think?"

"I told you not to worry dear. She's the Guardian—perfectly able to take care of herself." Mr. Nulant didn't turn from the game.

I might have been able to take care of myself, however, at that moment; I wanted to be taken care of. I thanked her for being concerned and found it funny that she called Nasani odd. "The girl has a name—it's Nasani."

"Yes. Of course dear, we'll try and remember it. Now, go get cleaned up for dinner before it gets cold. I've got chocolate chip cookies ready to put in the oven as well." Mrs. Nulant dismissed me and went back to the kitchen repeating Nasani's name over and over again in an attempt to remember it.

How ordinary, I thought.

The Nulants sat with me during dinner and then helped clean up. It wasn't until after I finished three warm chocolate chip cookies that I realized not once did Mrs. Nulant actually check on Orin. "How is Mr. Bindolestiv? Has he made any progress in his recovery today?"

Mr. Nulant answered, "Seemed fine to me."

"Yes, he said he was feeling well and was disappointed that he wasn't able to thank you and Joseph in person for saving his life. I believe he left a note for you upstairs." Mrs. Nulant finished.

"WAIT! "Where did he go?"

"He didn't say." They both answered in a very unemotional manner.

I raced up the stairs as any hope of gathering information on my mother dissipated. My father's room had been neatly put back together; the pillows were arranged precisely. A small note was folded on the bedspread.

Joseph and Seraphin,

I fear that by coming here I have invited unwanted attention. I cannot thank you enough for saving my life. Your powers are extraordinary.

Perpetually in your debt,

Orin Bindolestiv

I thanked Mr. and Mrs. Nulant for their neighborly care before they left. The house was quiet and for this I should have been grateful; but for some reason, I was not. When night fell, I took a walk. The moon was lost behind a few clouds. *Were those clouds from me? I wondered how my gift worked—or was it a curse?*

When I finally returned to my empty house I found the copy of *Den lille havfrue,* that Nasani had been so excited about. Opening the page to the inscription, I ran my fingers over the elegant pen strokes that I hoped were my mother's. Before going to bed I placed the book, my father's poem, and the misplaced photo, inside a keepsake box along with the note Orin left behind. I longed to crawl into the box and hide as well.

EIGHTEEN

Mrs. Keyes first asked if I was willing to work the *George Washington* during Whale Tagging Week—after I turned her down, she scheduled me for the expedition anyway. She was listed to go but wanted to stay behind; Keyes' Market Anniversary Gala was the following weekend and she felt it important to help her husband prepare for the event.

I was reluctant to go. While my fear of water was no longer an issue, it worried me that neither Joseph nor Nasani had been on campus for several days. Going on a research mission with the lingering question of their whereabouts was disconcerting.

Ethan and I met for breakfast in the CORE cafeteria before crew call the morning we were scheduled to leave.

"What's weird about this whole thing is that we're the only ones who seem to care that Jay Mason and Perrine Canard haven't been to work all week." He finished his 6th link of breakfast sausage before I had time to take a bite of my oatmeal. "Dr. Radski is too wrapped up making sure we have the proper supplies that she's neglecting the fact that we don't have the proper people going. Nas—I mean, Perrine is the best lab tech at CORE—"

"That's the only reason you want her there? The fact that she's a great lab tech—I mean, it couldn't have anything to do with the fact you've got a massive crush on her?" I teased.

"That's ridiculous Phin. Of course I don't have a—seriously? No. We need her help in the lab. That's it." He rolled a pancake around the last sausage link; eating it in less than three bites.

"What's with the appetite? Is it because you missed dinner last night?" I asked.

"How do you know I missed dinner?" He was shocked.

"I stayed late, waiting for Mrs. Keyes so she could drive me home again. I was expecting you to show up here eventually, but I was wrong. What are you up to? I've never known you to skip a meal."

Before he leaned in close, he wiped the corners of his mouth with a napkin. "I went for a jog around the island—ended up in the field. I think I found something but I didn't want to tell you until I had time to verify. It was dark and I didn't have a flashlight."

"The relics?"

"No, but there is a flat stone that seems out of place—it reminds me of the Petoskey stone I picked up in Michigan when my parents were looking at houses last year. Look here." On the table he placed a smooth rock covered with a pattern of six sided segments. "This is the one I brought home after our visit. It's actually a fossil, not just a stone. They can only be found in Michigan—around the Great Lakes. So, it makes little sense that I would find one on an island along the Gulf of Maine. I was planning on checking it out this morning after breakfast."

I picked up the stone, studying the peculiar surface. "I'm going with you."

"Fine—but I'm leaving now. We only have an hour before we have to be on deck." Without a moment of hesitation he pushed his chair back—stopping only at the trash bin to deposit his tray.

Before leaving the campus on foot we went to the maintenance supply room and borrowed a shovel. We walked then jogged across the island to the field where the low-bush cranberries grew. Ethan led me to an even lower section that I hadn't noticed before. "I think it's around here."

We were on our hands and knees searching a 10-foot area when I felt a flat break in the earth. "Ethan, I think I found it."

He hurried over, we pulled the plants covering the area out by their roots—sure enough, a 4-inch long stone barely broke the surface of the soil—it was decorated with the same-segmented pattern as the one Ethan had.

Our fingers pushed and grabbed the soil around it—I lifted it, Ethan began digging with the shovel—he was nearly 4 feet down when he stopped. "How far down should I go?"

"Ethan—maybe this isn't the spot. Perhaps it's just a coincidence that stone is here. We could be wrong about this," reasoning that my father didn't seem the type to bury something more than 4 feet underground.

Leaning against the shovel, he sighed. "You might be right Phin—besides, we're running out of time, crew call is in 10 minutes."

We did our best to backfill the hole and returned to campus in time to grab our bags and board the *George Washington*. The Captain from the *John F. Kennedy* was manning the vessel and, I might have been imagining things but I'm certain he sighed when he saw I was on the boat.

The crew was much larger than the one before. Dr. Radski had assembled a team of professional divers and marine veterinarians aside from the regular CORE researchers and lab techs. With only 5 minutes left before leaving port, two men and a woman boarded the vessel. Ethan ran to the maintenance cabins to give me the news that Jay Mason and Perrine Canard were among the late arrivals. He didn't know the other man but said Dr. Radski seemed flustered that he was on board.

"Do you think its Mr. Anonymous, the founder of CORE? Was he young? Did Joseph and Nasani actually accompany him on board?" My curiosity was high.

Ethan didn't know any details about the mystery man. He had to get back to the lab—Dr. Radski was on a rampage and he didn't want to draw any extra attention.

While it put my mind at ease knowing he was safe—I wasn't exactly in a hurry to see Joseph. The thought made me nervous—when it came to him, the only thing I knew for sure was that I was unsure of everything.

Throughout my cleaning rounds, I didn't see Joseph, Nasani, or the mystery man and during lunch in the cafeteria, they were all absent. Ms. Radski hurried her researchers and techs through their meals so it was impossible to catch Ethan before he was rushed back to work. I cleared the tables, realigned the chairs and went back to patrolling the main deck for bird-droppings. As the day wore on, my curiosity grew.

Where were they staying? Why hadn't Joseph sought me out? Why wasn't Nasani working in the lab?

Before dinner I was called to the lab to help clean a frozen block of krill that someone dropped—it shattered into mushy melted pieces. It was my only chance to see Ethan.

While Dr. Radski had her back turned he filled me in on what he heard. "The guy is someone important—I'm just not sure who he is. Earlier he came through the lab but only stayed a few minutes. He speaks with a thick accent but I don't know where he's from; definitely not Maine. Nasani walked beside him the whole time and didn't say a word. Can you believe she didn't even acknowledge me? I mean, I thought we had something but I guess I was wrong."

"You do like her." I whispered while I cleaned.

"Well yeah. Isn't it obvious?" Ethan hurried to assist a researcher while I picked up the last bit of krill

☙

The cafeteria was empty during dinner. Dr. Radski ordered the food to be brought into the lab so the researchers could finish assembling and activating the tagging devices that were to be used if a whale happened to swim up to the *George Washington*. Instead of eating alone in the cafeteria, I opted for eating alone in my cabin; with a baked potato in one hand and a coke in another I made my way through the tiny hallway. Before I could see him, I knew he was there waiting. I sensed him. *What would I say? Was he upset with me—was I upset with him?*

His eyes caught mine as I rounded the corner and my heart skipped. Wearing a light gray shirt and a black thin tie, he stood with one hand in the pocket of his straight charcoal trousers and in the other he held a neatly folded sport coat. The corner of his mouth raised into a curious smile as he glanced at my pathetic dinner. "Eating alone?"

"Do you have a better idea?" I tilted my head; allowing a smile to crack through to the corners of my lips.

"As a matter of fact, I do." He looked me up and down. "Not that you don't look fantastic but is there a chance you have anything other than a green MOLE shirt to wear?"

I glanced down at my dirty work shirt where a few small pieces of krill remained. "I must have forgotten about the Whale Tagging Ball—silly me."

"I'll take that as a no."

"Oh wait, I know." The sarcasm was apparent in my voice. I closed my eyes. "Bippity-boppity-boo!"

His arm linked around my bent elbow. "Come with me, I have something better than a fairy godmother—I have a Nasani."

While leading me through sections of the *George Washington* that I didn't know existed; he remained silent. I asked him where he had been; where we were going; why he was avoiding my questions, but he said nothing. After riding in an elevator I had never seen before, we arrived at room #2. My cabin was #348. Across the hall was a door marked #1. Joseph knocked and Nasani answered the door to room #2. Instantly she smiled and squealed—hugging me and pulling me into the room, leaving Joseph to the hallway. She wore a long fitted gray satin skirt with a slight flair at the bottom—reminding me of her mermaid form. Her top was a simple purple sleeveless v-cut blouse and her hair was braided and twisted on top of her head in an elaborate up-do.

"I have the perfect dress for you!" She exclaimed. "But first you need to shower because you smell like a dirty fish tank."

"It's that bad?" I asked, curling my nose.

She only nodded her head.

Cabin #2 was a large space with a couch and two leather oversized chairs. A glass wall faced the black ocean. A small balcony hovered over the water. The Japanese inspired paper shade separated the main living space from the sleeping area and a bathroom larger than room #348 ran adjacent to a not so small kitchenette. Taking my baked potato and coke, she pushed a fresh-thick towel into my arms and shoved me into the bathroom. I showered with hot water and used lavender scented soap to wash. It must have been her favorite aroma.

I wrapped myself in a towel and called for Nasani. Not once did I complain as she plucked and primped me to perfection. Several times I asked her where we were going—but she didn't answer other than to say, "We can't very well leave the boat without ruining your hair?"

When she finished I was wearing a light gray wrap dress with a plunging neckline but a conservative fold around the collar. The sleeves cut off just before the elbows and my knees hid under the slight flare of the skirt. She tied a sapphire blue sash around my waist—made me slip on a pair of matching slides—tucked one side of my long wavy hair behind my ear and shoved me into the hallway where Joseph leaned against the wall patiently.

I turned quickly back to the door—wanting to ask more questions but she was gone and the door was shut.

"Are you ready?" Joseph asked softly.

When I turned, his hand awaited mine. I placed my hand in his and he led me to door #1. With a quick glance I noticed he had put the sport jacket on. His hair was still the usual mess and I found it charming, "Ready for what?"

"Dinner, I hope you don't mind but I already ordered." He reached for the door handle, twisting it. Placing his hand on the small of my back he gently pushed me forward. "Oh and by the way, you look absolutely amazing Seraphin."

The door opened into a waiting area with a shiny white tile floor. The room had a potted evergreen in each of its four corners; they were more like sculptures than trees with their branches twisted and trimmed. A long rectangular platform with a thick white cushion was suspended from the vaulted ceiling. Ivy twisted through the chains holding the unusual swing in place.

Joseph led me to the swing—gesturing for me to sit. "I'll let him know we are here." Before I could speak he passed through a sliding electronic door that closed tightly behind. The space was in great contrast to the rest of the *George Washington* décor and for a moment I forgot that we were on a boat in the middle of the Atlantic Ocean.

It took Joseph just a few minutes to return. "Alright, let's go in." He stood waiting by the door.

I didn't move.

"Oh," he walked over and held out his hand, "I'm sorry, not much of a gentleman, huh?"

I only turned my head away from his gaze.

Frustrated he took a step back and dropped his hand, "WHAT!?"

"Who is in that room? Why are we dressed up? What did you order me for dinner? I want all of those questions answered before I move from this fancy swing couch." I was stubborn.

"The man who's bank account your paycheck comes out of; because he's fancy, like his couch; fettuccini alfredo with a side of steamed asparagus. Is there anything else you'd like to know? I really don't think we should keep him waiting. He's a busy man." His hand reached for mine again but I ignored it.

When the electronic door opened I sauntered through in front of Joseph. I was going to meet the man on my own terms. The suite was extravagant and again I had to remind myself that we were on a boat. Two crystal chandeliers lit a dining area with a long table set for only two though eight chairs surrounded it. Instead of going to the table—as Joseph did, I wandered around the living area. Renaissance paintings of women decorated the walls; a sculpture of a mermaid was the centerpiece of the room. I blushed slightly when I realized that under the marble swirls of hair she was topless. *Thank goodness she had long hair.*

An incomplete painting of a woman caught my attention—part of her hand and pieces of the background remained colorless sketches while the rest of her body was fully rendered with deep hues. It was difficult to take my eyes off of her.

"Great choice, that one is my favorite as well—so, is an unfinished masterpiece still a masterpiece? Does it deserve to be next to those finished works of art or should it be unframed; forever trapped in incompleteness?" A deep voice with a thick accent traveled across the room—it was smooth and slow, every syllable accounted for. "What is your opinion?"

Without turning, I spoke. "The simple fact that the painting is incomplete, in my opinion, makes it a surprising success compared to the others—we are given a rare glimpse at the painter's process; train of thought and raw abilities."

The man moved closer to the painting, disregarding my personal space. For a stranger he stood too close but I didn't move. "Interesting observations for such a young, uneducated girl—so you're saying that it's perfectly acceptable to not finish something that has been started?"

Uneducated? "My words did not suggest anything of the sort."

"Do you know who I am?" He stood closer than a foot from me and he was nearly two feet taller. I finally looked at the middle-aged man. His black hair was longer but neatly pushed out of his face, the color of his skin was darker than tan with a yellowish tint and his eyes were shadowy and accusing.

"I do not."

"Do I know you?" He asked.

"While I am certain I've never met you, I cannot be sure if you know who I am or not. I work at this company and since, I think, you are the founder of CORE. My best guess is that you have come across my employee paperwork before. But does that constitute knowing someone? I barely think so." My voice was unwavering and I was proud.

"So you do know who I am?" He asked.

"My answer is the same, I do not."

Joseph entered the room and I caught his face from the corner of my eye. He shook his head from side to side—I did my best to ignore him.

"You know that I am the founder of CORE," trying to catch me in a lie, he responded.

"That was a lucky guess based on the fact that no other person would be staying in such an elaborate suite. For example, I am the lowest ranking employee on this boat—so my cabin is the size of a small walk-in closet. Just to clarify, I am not complaining—simply comparing." I stated my observations.

The man smirked. "Ms. Shedd, as it turns out I do know you and I knew your father as well. The man made poor choices and for that you are much like this painting; incomplete. Had you been born my daughter—a masterpiece you would surely be. Instead, we were cursed with families that are inferior to our own worth."

Joseph turned his attention to the electronic door.

I couldn't take my awareness off of the unpleasant man. *How did he know my father?*

"Father," A voice came from the half open door. "I am sorry to interrupt, but your helicopter is waiting."

Nasani stood with her shoulders back, her head high and a face that was vacant of emotion.

"Thank you darling," the man was polite to his daughter.

He turned to me, lifting my chin to meet his eyes. "If only God had gifted me with the female Guardian—she would have been perfection.

Ms. Shedd, make wise choices and try not to let your raw abilities go to waste."

Walking to Nasani he bent and kissed her on the top of the head. Before the electronic door closed he added one last thing. "Ms. Shedd, you may stay in my suite for the remainder of this research mission. Please, consider this your home at sea."

The three of us were silent for several moments, afraid to move in case he came back through the door. It wasn't until after the chopping of the helicopter blades passed that Nasani left the room. A tear rolled down her cheek as she left. Looking back, I wish I had said more, but I didn't and Joseph didn't. We let her leave without knowing the truth about what was troubling her.

A woman was standing on the other side of the door when Nasani passed through. She wore a white jacket and pushed a silver tray on wheels. "Room service," she announced to Joseph.

"Thank you, over there please." He pointed to the dining room table.

Wheeling the tray to the table, she placed two covered plates at each setting, asked if we wanted iced tea or Coke; what kind of salad dressing we preferred; lit the candles then left. Joseph led me to the table, pulling out the chair.

It felt like a date and I was suddenly very aware that we were alone in a beautiful penthouse suite, impeccably dressed. "Why isn't Nasani joining us for dinner? We should invite Ethan up, he'd love this place."

"Nasani ate with her father earlier." He took the seat directly across the table from where I sat. "If you'd like to invite Ethan, that's your decision—though I'm not certain Dr. Radski will let him leave the lab for more than 5 minutes at a time."

"Good point. She has been working the crew extremely hard. He probably wouldn't be able to sneak out." I took the silver lid off of the smaller plate first. It was a spinach salad sprinkled with walnuts and cranberries. My favorite—I noticed that Joseph had a house salad. "Did you order this salad for me?"

"Is it alright? I kind of guessed. We haven't had many meals together—well other than cafeteria food—if you don't like it you can have my salad."

Feeling bad for having said anything and fearful that he took my question the wrong way, I assured him. "This is perfect. If I had to, I wouldn't have known what to order for you."

His shoulders relaxed a bit and he took a sip of his iced tea. "I'll tell you what I like." Lifting the cover off of the larger plate and holding it on a slight angle so I could see the entire dish. "Eggplant parmesan is my favorite—or roasted portabella mushrooms or a black-bean burger on an onion roll. Actually, I'll eat just about anything—anything but an animal, that is."

"Good to know." I laughed. "I'm a little pickier, which is why I'm so impressed."

"It's much better than that baked potato." He laughed as well.

Dinner with Joseph was peaceful. We avoided any conversation that might be unpleasant—mainly anything having to do with being Guardians; recovering lost relics; flying bird ladies; Orin Bindolestiv; Ms. Z; mutant fish people; my father or his. Though, I did have questions, I held back until after we were done eating—I was certain he had his as well. We were nothing more than two friends sharing a meal. I would have thought it impossible for us to have a conversation about regular, everyday things but we did and I enjoyed myself.

Joseph talked about vacations he'd been on with his family. A trip to the Swiss Alps; an African safari; but his favorite, he said was when his mother brought him to Maine. He was only 10 the year they spent a weekend in a seaside bed and breakfast— the trip was a memory he cherished.

Marietta Merrick was from my hometown of Bar Harbor; her parents were buried in the same cemetery as my grandmother. Suddenly, Joseph seemed real—a person, with a family.

"It was just my mom and I. That weekend was the only time I had her all to myself." When he spoke of his mother his eyes changed to a soft blue. "She used to be great. I hope one day she will be again. Then you can meet her. Truth be told, not a day goes by that I don't miss her."

My life wasn't quite as exciting to talk about. I had never been on a vacation and the first time I left the shores of Maine; Joseph had been with me on the *John F. Kennedy*. I found myself, instead talking about my neighbors—sharing the memories I collected watching their lives from my front porch.

"…then there was this one time when Mr. Rigby was trying to trim the tree in his front yard. He didn't have a ladder high enough so he tied an arrow to a portable, hand chain saw and tried to shoot it up into the tree with a bow. It ended up going through his second story window screen—pinning his cat by the tail to his bedroom door. My father spent the rest of the day trimming Mr. Rigby's tree for him while he went to the emergency vet with the cat."

"Your father was great. Don't bother with Dr. Caro's opinion of him. He kept you in hiding in order to protect you, and that's admirable." Joseph stood and walked around the table, taking my hand—he led me to the living area. "I may just decide to keep you in hiding—only a fool would want to share you with the world."

An uncomfortable smile crossed my face and I quickly changed the subject. "Nasani's father—does he know what a powerful daughter he has?"

"He couldn't possibly know and if he does, he's an idiot to not appreciate her." We should have been telling Nasani those things but instead we were too wrapped up in each other. That was our mistake.

Joseph and I forgot about everything that evening. For the first time we simply enjoyed the other's company. Our conversation carried on into the early morning hours. It was easy to lay my head on his chest and I began to drift to sleep when he asked, "Do you think I should finish school?"

I was surprised and my answer was honest. "I think you should do what makes you feel fulfilled and happy."

Then he asked if still planned on not attending college. Again, my answer was honest. "I'm not opposed to college. As a matter of fact, it seems like a very average thing to do and at the moment, I find that I'm drawn to the ordinary things in life."

He let his opinion be known with only one word. "Good."

I fell asleep in his arms wondering if he was beginning to see things as differently as I was.

NINETEEN

When I woke, he remained asleep. I watched him; his tie pulled far away from his neck; the top two buttons of his shirt undone; his hair a mess. He took deep breaths, perfectly at ease. My head found his chest once more and I closed my eyes and listened to his heart beat. It was perfectly tranquil those moments with Joseph—he shifted slightly until his hand found mine. What more was there in the world? No worries; burdens or lies—only Joseph. He had managed to capture my attention, and not with his amazing powers and superhero like abilities. I was drawn in by the way he listened to my pointless sharing; the softness of his eyes when he spoke of his mother, and the fact that he ordered me a delicious dinner.

Did I fall into his trap? It didn't matter. Nothing mattered for a few perfect minutes.

With his eyes closed, he whispered. "What time does your shift start?"

A sense of comfort ran through me as I felt his voice vibrate through his chest. "Not until noon." I answered.

"Good." He didn't move and took several deep breaths before speaking again. "Let's go for a swim this morning. We're close to where the R.M.S Titanic met her demise. I'll take you down there. We'll be back before anyone notices. Besides, I could use a little freedom before Dr. Radski handcuffs herself to me for the rest of the week. I'm pretty sure she scheduled the briefing for 11:00 this morning so I have a few hours."

"Sounds like it could be interesting—and creepy."

"Don't worry; I'll protect you from all the ghosts." His arms tightened around me.

We remained on the couch, lying beside each other for another 15 minutes; neither of us wanting to be the first to move away from the other.

It wasn't until we heard the electronic door opened and a woman shouted, "Housekeeping", that we finally pulled away from each other's arms. Joseph kissed my forehead and whispered, "Thank you for allowing me to act like a human again, even if it was just for a few hours."

I wanted to ask what he meant but he disappeared into the bathroom—shouting through the door. "Seraphin, you should go down and get your bags. I'll meet you on the balcony so we can work on your dive." From the sound of his voice I could tell he was holding back laughter.

"I'll have you know, I've been practicing." I shouted back before passing the housekeeper and exiting through the electric door.

I could barely hear him call behind me, "Can't wait to see it!"

The woman wore headphones and whistled—pulling a cleaning cart behind her. I wondered where she came from. She looked familiar. *Wasn't it my job to clean the research vessel? She wasn't even wearing a MOLE shirt.* I dismissed my suspicions, deciding that Dr. Caro probably had his own staff that I knew nothing about.

On the way to my cabin, I passed Ethan; he was hauling equipment to the main deck. He looked exhausted. "Have you seen Nasani and what's with the dress? Did you go out dancing last night while I was stuck in the lab with that evil witch of a woman?"

"Dr. Radski got you down this morning?"

"That's an understatement. So, did you see her? Who is the guy?"

"I did see Nasani—though not for very long."

"Did she ask about me?"

I laughed. "No."

He looked disappointed. "Who's the mystery man?"

"You won't believe me but I'll tell you anyway. He's her father—and he's the founder of CORE. His name is Dr. Caro."

"You're right, I don't believe you. Why would she work under an assumed name at her own father's company? That doesn't make any sense."

"Sure it does, it makes perfect sense. She probably doesn't want anyone to know that he's her father—afraid she might be treated differently or something. Plus, we're not even supposed to know his name, so don't go spreading it around. I don't want to get Joseph and Nasani in trouble."

"Have I told anyone that you're half fish yet?"

"Ethan!"

"Well, have I?"

"No."

"Then I think your secret is safe with me."

Dr. Radski's voice came over the intercom. "ETHAN COTTINGTON REPORT ON DECK"

He cringed. "It's a good thing you're part fish because you are going to have to dive in and save her after she gets thrown overboard."

"Hang in there." I patted him on the shoulder.

"I'll try." He sighed. "Oh, tell Joseph that Jay Mason and Perrine Canard need to be at the briefing. It's been moved to 10:00. Everyone must attend. Well, except for me because apparently, all I'm good for is hauling equipment up the stairs."

"You should be flattered that she recognizes your brut strength," trying to focus on the positive.

"I'll *show* her brut strength. You had better get your fins ready, Phin. I mean it, she'll go overboard if she doesn't back off." With that, he lifted a large mechanical device that looked like a miniature space ship and continued up the stairs to the main deck.

I hurried to my cabin. Joseph had to attend the briefing an hour earlier, that left little time for our swim. Thank goodness I remembered to pack a swimsuit. I put it on—throwing a tank top and shorts on top. Overloaded with my poorly repacked bags, I threw Nasani's dress across my shoulder so I could return it. Before shutting the door I noticed the Petoskey stone that Ethan and I found in the field on Great Cranberry. It was on the cot, so I grabbed it. Even though it proved to be a worthless find, I felt the need to keep it.

To my disappointment Dr. Radski's voice came over the intercom again. "THERE HAS BEEN A CHANGE IN OUR SCHEDULE. ALL MUST REPORT TO THE BREIFING ON THE SECOND FLOOR IMMEDIATELY."

My shoulders hunched. Our swim would have to wait. Jay Mason had to get back to work.

I passed several groups of people I didn't know on my way back to room #1. I didn't see Nasani or Joseph—surely they would have heard the announcement. I thought about knocking on Nasani's door and returning her dress but instead I walked into room #1.

"Joseph, did you hear Dr. Radski? You have to be at the briefing, she moved the time. It's starting right now." He didn't answer. *Maybe he already went down, though I would have passed him on the way.*

It felt wrong. The cleaning cart sat in the middle of the living area—I could hear the faint whisper of music. I moved over to the cart slowly—a pair of headphones played. Turning, taking in the suite my heart began to race; an overturned chair at the table; the open cabinets, drawers, and doors. *What happened?*

"JOSEPH?" I panicked. "Where are you?"

I ran to the balcony, Ethan was visible on the deck below. A generator was close by, prohibiting him from hearing. In my hand was the Petoskey stone—I threw it, aiming for beside him but instead it hit him on the back of the shoulder. He shot around, angry. I continued to yell his name. Finally, he looked at the stone—realizing it had come from me. Looking up, he saw me, and turned the generator off.

"Have you seen Jay Mason? Do you know if he made it to the briefing?" I tried to hide the panic in my voice.

"He didn't. Dr. Radski was looking for him just a few minutes ago. She's super mad—she might explode if he doesn't get in there soon." Then he paused, cracking a smile. "Actually, if you see him, tell him to take his time." Ethan pocketed the stone and continued working, turning the loud generator on—but not before scolding me and rubbing his shoulder. "Next time you should aim for me so you'll be sure to miss."

Then, I turned around.

Ms. Z stood with her arms spread wide. "Seraphin! Thank goodness you're alright." She hugged me and patted the back of my head. A tear dropped from her eye. The cleaning lady was beside her. The woman had long white hair and I realized where I had seen her before. She was the woman from the diner who had been dressed in leather from head to toe.

"Ms. Z? Where is Joseph?" My arms remained at my sides; frozen.

"The briefing, didn't you hear the announcement?" She was at ease when she spoke. "He's gone back to work."

I wanted to believe it, but I knew it wasn't true. If he had gone to the briefing, I would have passed him in the hallway. The open balcony door nagged at me. There looked to be a struggle. I was confused and pulled away from her embrace. "Ms. Z, where have you been?"

She broke down, sobbing. I had never seen her so vulnerable and it caught me off guard. "It was horrible. Scientists treating me like an alien; poking and prodding. They experimented on me." She lifted her sleeve to reveal her arms; I was shocked to see that they were covered with bruises.

"But Joseph—I mean, he was with you. I saw the two of you together. Does he know?" Immediately, I was angry with Joseph for hiding the fact that Ms. Z was indeed in trouble. He had assured me many times that she was not in danger, had he lied to me?

Interrupting and wiping her tear-streaked face, "Joseph can't know. He can't afford to worry about me when times are so…" she stopped talking and shook her head. "Things are bad Seraphin. The humans know about us and they want to kill us all. Thank heavens Joseph found you—I suspected you were a mermaid from the moment we first met but I would have never imagined you were the other Guardian. The world is so lucky to have found you."

"You didn't know? But Joseph and I thought you introduced us because..." I couldn't finish my thought. Emotions ran wild. *Who do I trust?*

As if she could read my thoughts, her hands gripped my shoulders and her expression softened. "I've always treated you like family—you know that, right? You know that you've always been so special to me?"

"Of course Ms. Z, you have been a terrific teacher." Silent, I scolded myself for being such a silly love-struck girl the night before. I should have spent the evening pressing Joseph for the truth—*or his version of the truth.*

"And friend?" She asked, sympathetically.

"Yes. You've been a great friend as well." I assured her; meaning what I said.

My mind raced and before I could second guess anything she was saying, she had worked herself into a panic. She explained where she had been for so many weeks. And at first, it made perfect sense.

"I need your help. They are planning to take over our underwater sanctuaries. The humans know how to penetrate the shrouds—THEY WANT TO FORCE US OUT! FLOOD OUR HOMES!" Anger filled her voice. "They kept me in a lab for months. I didn't mean to give so much away but they tortured me. Secrets were revealed—innocent lives will be destroyed. We'll be herded into nets, captured like helpless fish."

"Ms. Z, it can't be true. Why would they treat us so horribly?" Adrenaline was rising; my heart raced as I began walking towards the electronic door. "We need to get Joseph and Nasani. They will help us figure out what to do. Dr. Caro too; he has resources that can be of assistance."

The woman with the white hair laughed but said nothing.

Ms. Z turned to her, "Vanita will go find your friends dear."

Vanita? Could it be the same Vanita who healed Joseph so many years ago? Nasani's mother?

Ms. Z's attention was on me again. "We don't have time to wait for them. You have to use your powers—you have to stop them before they destroy us all." Horrific screams came from outside. I hurried to the balcony in time to see nearly fifty heads emerge from the black surface of the ocean. Women and children held their heads in pain—they were shouting and incoherent.

"They've begun Seraphin! They are using sonic blasts to penetrate our hiding places. Look at what they are doing to those innocent merpeople. YOU HAVE TO HELP THEM!" She was screaming into my face and shaking me.

Trying to make sense of everything, I was numb. "How can I help them?"

"Use your anger." She urged.

I caught the face of a child in the water, no more than 10 years old. She cried with pain—drops of blood dripped from her ears. Injured merpeople surfaced faster than I could think.

Anger overtook me; thunder exploded; wind ripped.

"Yes…yes…YES! Only a tempest can destroy their plan. You're powerful enough; feel their pain and suffering, feed off of it." She leaned in close, whispering. "Lose control Seraphin. Show them how mighty you can be."

I did lose control. Power surged through my body. I created, for the first time, a storm of my own making. The *George Washington* and the hundreds of merpeople that continued to surface remained under protection, in eye of the storm. Wind twisted like a funnel cloud and I closed my eyes.

"Focus on the land—the wind will take the storm." She was directing me, helping me to focus my power but the rational part of me wouldn't let go.

"WHAT LAND?" We were in the middle of nowhere. "Where are the scientists?"

"They are everywhere Seraphin. This Earth belongs to the ocean. Flood the islands that foolish humans call their continents—cleanse the world of the human race. Bring about a massive flood to punish them; to show them they do not belong here." Her voice was disturbing.

This is wrong. I'm going to kill people. What is the matter with me? I dropped to the balcony, curling my arms around my knees—covering my ears. Only God should have such power.

"What are you doing? Why are you stopping?—help me rebuild the world."

I whispered, "by first destroying it?"

Ms. Z hollered in frustration. Her words were cruel. The truth hurt. "You stupid girl, what has this world given you but heartache. I've been the only one there for you and you turn your back on me?" She moved past me on the balcony and I watched; not knowing exactly what she was capable of. "KILL HIM!"

Two men pulled Ethan into my line of sight. He struggled.

Ms. Z's voice was suddenly softer, "Will this make you angry enough dear?"

I jumped to my feet and charged the woman. She was no longer my beloved teacher. In a matter of seconds she had turned into an enemy—threatening Ethan's life. A mass came from the shadows before I could grab her. My feet dangling as the man with the tattoo across his face lifted me in the air. I kicked at him—trying to free myself. "You can't do this. Let him go!"

"That boy is inferior to us Seraphin. They all are. Why should they freely walk this planet while we hide in caves?"

Did she really believe that? Ethan was her student.

I watched as the two men pulled Ethan across the deck to the stern of the boat. They stood directly over the propellers. Pleading with the merpeople in the water, I shouted, "Please save him."

No one could hear. They were still holding their heads in pain, oblivious to the situation playing out. The men lifted Ethan—I screamed, hiding my face in the burly arms that held me prisoner.

Ms. Z commanded. "JOSEPH, STOP!"

When I opened my eyes, Joseph shot out of the water like a cannon. Transforming back to two legs, mid-air; he landed on one of the men, knocking him down. A crow bar was near the area where Ethan had been working earlier. Joseph picked it up and struck the remaining man in the knee. He fell to the deck in pain, freeing Ethan from his hold.

"Aunt Doreh." Joseph turned his face to the balcony where we stood. "Give up. Seraphin will never hurt innocent people. Your plan has failed."

But her plan almost didn't fail. I fell for her coaxing. Did Joseph know all along what her plans were? Why didn't he warn me?

"She will if she loses control." Ms. Z said, too low for Joseph to hear. She closed her eyes and began a seamless chanting of unrecognizable words.

The man holding me grew excited. "Yeah Z! Bring out the big dog. That'll shut 'em up."

There was a disturbance under the surface of the water and a few dozen merpeople shot away from the rising air bubbles. Ms. Z continued to chant. Joseph and Ethan ran to the railing to investigate.

I wanted to be free of the burly man's arms. I sunk my teeth into his arm and then threw my head back into his face. I heard a bone crack. Ms. Z was in a trance—I ran to her but the man threw his arms out, pushing me in anger. My back hit the railing along the balcony. I tried to grab something, but there was nothing to hang on to. Wind rushed around my body; I was falling, the hard wooden deck was five stories below.

Joseph yelled, "SERAPHIN! NO!"

Before I hit, a wave washed over the side of the *George Washington*, grabbing my body and surrounding it; protecting it. I felt Joseph's arms wrap around me and as the wave cleared, I remained in them—safe.

"Joey! That was awesome!" Ethan ran over, helping us to our feet. He was soaking wet having just been engulfed by the same wave that saved me.

Joseph seemed stunned. "I didn't know—I've never done that before. The water just followed me."

It was the same thing that happened the day I saved him from the Sirens. We looked at one another, wondering what else we could be capable of.

The three of us huddled together. "What are we going to do with Ms. *cray*-Z?" Ethan asked, pulling his shirt off and wringing it out. "More importantly, what am I going to tell Dr. Radski? The deck is trashed."

I glanced around; the deck was littered with whale tagging equipment. "Where is everyone else? The crew? The Captain? And what is she chanting?"

Ms. Z remained in a trance as the air bubbles breaking through the surface of the water grew more massive. The merpeople moved further away from the *George Washington*. They pointed at the disturbance and waved their arms in warning.

Ethan and I looked at Joseph as if he had the answers to all our questions. "What is she doing? What's down there?"

"I don't know!" He began to ramble, panic grew in his voice.

"You were just in the water, what were you doing?" Ethan asked; his voice was accusatory.

"They tricked me into leaving the boat." Joseph turned to me. "I thought you were in trouble Seraphin. When I realized my aunt tricked me, I called for help, sending out a distress signal. If she's doing what I think, we need help. We can't handle IT alone. I hope someone heard my call."

A sudden burst of water broke his train of thought. A massive tentacle glided along the surface towards the boat. It was black and covered with scales. Even before Ms. Z said it, I knew where I had seen it before. The creature attached to the tentacle had carried my father to his death.

"Seraphin," her voice was an evil laugh. "Do you want to meet the beast that left you an orphan?"

"No." I whispered too low for her to hear—frozen in terror.

Joseph stepped in front of me. "Get back Seraphin."

The boat began to sway, quickly working its way into a violent tip. Equipment slammed the railings, breaking into pieces. Ethan bent down; picking up a large harpoon with a radar device attached to the end. "What beast?" He shouted; ready for battle.

Joseph confirmed my fears. "It's Leviathan, brace yourselves."

Leviathan rammed the side of the vessel.

"Aunt Doreh, what could you have promised this creature to have so much control over it?" He shouted with disbelief.

She laughed again—standing on the balcony with her arms spread wide. "I will deliver the souls of all those useless human beings."

"And in exchange, what did you get?" I asked.

"I got what I wanted—the most powerful children on earth, all to myself. You belong to me. I took you in when no one loved you—the unwanted son of a worthless ruler. And you Seraphin, I fostered you—guided you. For that, you owe me. I dedicated my life to you.

You will do as I command or Leviathan will deliver every soul on this boat to the gates of Hell."

"What is it that you command?" I asked.

"To flood the Earth so we can have a new beginning; together you will rebuild the population. Seraphin, you will be the mother of all kind and Joseph, the father. Your children will praise you for bringing them into our new world. No longer will we hide, frightened." Her voice was passionate. The man with the tattoo nodded his head in agreement. She turned her focus to her nephew. "Joseph, imagine a life where you can break the surface—breaching higher than you've ever thought possible. A world where there are no secrets, no goonches; only the children of the Guardians, perfect children."

"What about the other merpeople, are we to kill them as well?" I asked.

Joseph questioned me with his eyes.

"Those who pledge their loyalty to us will survive. The rest will have to face Leviathan." She was so sure of herself, thinking I was convinced of her plan as well. "Seraphin, I ask you to call upon your gifts now. Create a storm to end all with waves that cover the desert. Fill the valleys and leave no mountain exposed—wash away the infestation on land so that we all shall live the way we were meant to live. This is what you were born to do."

"Is this the only solution?" It seemed extreme, but I didn't let my opinion be known.

Joseph was puzzled. "Seraphin, you can't possibly be considering—your powers were meant to save."

I laughed. "Let's be honest, Joseph. My powers are destructive; I don't care what you say. Do you really feel that lightening and violent winds can save lives? Do you believe that my lightening and winds compare to your healing abilities?" I wasn't curious. I knew he was superior. I was conducting a test. Where did his loyalties lie? "Joseph, perhaps we were meant to do this? The sea would again be safe for all marine life. That's why we are here, right?"

"Seraphin?" disappointment filled his voice. "You can't do this. I won't join you in killing innocent people—I'll stop you, if I have to."

And that was all I needed to hear. I smiled knowing that I made the right decision.

"Ms. Z, where shall I begin? What will make you the happiest? When will you find peace?" Enthusiastic in my questioning, I controlled my expression—stalling, not wanting to reveal my thoughts until the perfect moment.

"My dear, Seraphin," with outstretched arms she gestured for Leviathan to retreat, which is what I was hoping she'd do. "I always knew I could count on you. You will make me happy—I will find peace and so shall you."

"Do you think?" I moved closer, looking up. My voice was eager.

"NO!" Joseph moved to me, taking my arm. He urged me to reconsider. It was cute that he fell for my deception and I silently praised myself for being a good enough actress to fool even him. "I will go against you if I have to Seraphin. We save lives, not take them."

Finally, I saw Ethan. He raised the harpoon. No one else noticed.

Then I let loose all my anger. It was directed at Ms. Z. "Will I be at peace watching my children grow but knowing that I *slaughtered* others.

Am supposed live with the myself knowing that I was the one responsible for filling their helpless lungs with death while their mothers' lifeless bodies float nearby?"

Ms. Z's expression hardened.

Thunder rolled in the distance. Dark clouds began to circle.

Though my soul ached with rage, I calmly questioned the evil woman that stood on the balcony above me. "Will I find happiness watching sharks enter living rooms and feast on the corpses of dead families?"

Lightning cracked.

Ms. Z caught on to my deception. She lifted her arm and began chanting, calling the monster back to kill.

"Hey old lady, I wouldn't do that if I were you." Ethan stood behind her, the harpoon only inches from her head. He spoke to the man with the tattoo across his face. "If you take one step forward I'll kill her where she stands."

"You don't have the nerve boy." Ms. Z doubted Ethan.

"I don't? Aren't you the one who almost had me tossed overboard? Why don't you try me?" Ethan was furious.

Joseph checked to be sure Leviathan did not hear Ms. Z's call. The surface of the water remained calm.

Completely in control, I willed the storm to do as I commanded. The electricity was building in the air. Flashes danced across the sky, and for a moment, everything remained still. My eyes on Ms. Z; her eyes on Joseph; Ethan watched the burly, tattooed man while he watched Ms. Z. No one would make a move. There's no telling how long we would have remained locked in time, had it not been for

Nasani. With ease and ignorance she stepped onto her balcony, adjacent to the one where Ethan held Ms. Z captive.

It took only a second.

First, Joseph's eyes shifted.

Ms. Z called for Leviathan—she moved her arms, waving them at the water then twisting to point at Nasani on the balcony.

Ethan understood what was happening, he shouted. "Nasani, get inside."

Nasani held Ethan's panicked gaze but didn't move.

The man with the tattoo leaned in, ready to attack Ethan. A bolt of lightning struck—the man collapsed.

Joseph cheered. "Nice work Seraphin!"

Ms. Z's attention turned to me. "You think you're in control girl? You have no idea how out of touch you are with those powers. Try to overcome these emotions," then she confessed to the most horrific crime. "I was the one who had your father killed. I watched as Leviathan crushed him. Oh, but I couldn't have done it without your help."

Rage and fury, those are the only words to describe how I felt.

"You stupid girl, you made it so easy. You brought him right to me. Any protection Orin Bindolestiv placed on him was broken the moment you demanded his attention." Then she mocked. "*Look at me Samuel Shedd!* Yes, look at your daughter while I kill you."

The clip played in my head though I didn't blackout; on the beach; in the water. I wasn't alone. It was so clear. Her eyes were in the water, she urged me to disobey.

Bolt after bolt of lightning struck the balcony where Ms. Z stood. Ethan was thrown onto his back into the penthouse suite. Only she remained exposed.

"Brace yourself, it's coming back." Joseph warned.

Leviathan rammed the *George Washington* again. Nasani was thrown over the balcony but managed to hang on to the railing. The woman with the white hair appeared, reaching her hand to help Nasani.

"Vanita, stay back!" Joseph shouted. "Nasani, let go!"

Nasani dangled from only one arm as the woman approached. "Mother, please help me." She pleaded.

Joseph shouted again, "LET GO!"

Vanita Caro approached her daughter, grabbing her by the arm. Nasani smiled right before her mother whispered, "Sweetheart, Joseph said to let go. I thought you did everything he asked of you? Why stop now?" Then she did the unthinkable and dropped her daughter 5 stories.

I gasped, unable to help.

But Joseph came to her rescue, sending a rush of water that cushioned her fall.

Ms. Z raised her arms—directing them to Nasani.

Three tentacles reached out of the ocean; over the railing of the boat; sliding along the deck to where Nasani was.

"JOSEPH!" She screamed in terror, "DO SOMETHING!"

He grabbed the crow bar and began striking the massive, scaly arms. Leviathan continued, persistent in his mission.

I called lightning from the sky again—blasting the balcony. Finally, the wooden structure could withstand no more. The platform broke free of the suite. Ms. Z fell with it, but instead of crashing into the deck her body turned to water. Clear, with only her angry eyes visible, she poured herself into the ocean.

I feel as though I should defend myself before proceeding. I have always been a cautious person—especially when it comes to electricity. That day, however, my mind was elsewhere. You've got to understand that I had just been told my favorite teacher, a woman I respected, killed my father. Nothing but hatred filled my mind and when she escaped, my anger turned to the beast that did her bidding. True, I wanted to destroy anything connected to Ms. Z—except for one person. I made a terrible mistake and disregarded elementary science.

Metal conducts electricity. Joseph was waving a metal crowbar in the air. I wasn't watching him; I had my eyes on Leviathan. So, when he raised the only weapon he had, hoping to strike Leviathan, lightning struck Joseph—my lightning. And, he was thrown unconscious.

Joseph.

Everything moved in slow motion, including myself. Leviathan's tentacle wrapped around Nasani but she had stopped screaming. She watched Joseph—waiting for a sign of life. His body remained motionless—smoke rising from his skin.

Joseph.

Nasani and I locked eyes. I had to make a choice—she knew. "Save him."

"No." I took a step towards her.

"NO! You can still save him. The world needs the two of you—not me. Even my own father and mother know that." She stopped struggling as Leviathan lifted her off of the *George Washington*. Tears dropped from her eyes.

I ran to Joseph. His heart was still beating. Water flooded the deck—rushing under my feet. I slipped—falling and sliding. The vessel began to tip and the water carried me away from him. When I turned, Leviathan's face had surfaced. It smelled of death and its crust looked like decaying flesh. With the facial structure that mimicked that of the ancient dinosaurs, it let out an earth-shattering roar.

Nasani went limp.

First a loud ringing vibrated through my eardrum then I could no longer hear. Complete silence. I reached up, touching my left ear, blood smeared across my fingers.

The water's had cleared—the injured merpeople knew better than to wait around. Their ears had taken the first blow from Leviathan. A ploy by Ms. Z to fool me into believing human scientists had done harm to them.

Without the ability to hear, my balance was thrown off. I stumbled, experiencing vertigo. Everything was spinning. I tried closing my eyes and crawling, but I only slid further away from Joseph.

Ethan emerged from the broken penthouse—the harpoon on his shoulder. He released, it penetrated the thick scales of the creature and though I could not hear—I felt the vibrations of a painful roar.

Nasani remained entangled in its tentacles.

Ethan held his ears, his mouth wide open. The Petoskey stone flew past my head, hitting the creature's hard scales—doing no damage at all. Ethan would not give up. He disappeared; only to reappear in mid air, soaring towards the creature. Landing on top of the beasts rotting skull, he punched at its eyes and pulled at its rotting flesh—trying desperately to free Nasani.

Then, they disappeared. Leviathan returned to the water with my friends.

The man I was destined to marry lay face down, unconscious.

Why was I the only one left untouched?

Everything and everyone around me was destroyed. Ethan and Nasani were gone—both selfless in trying to save another. Nasani sacrificed herself—Ethan ruthless in his attempt at saving her. And I, the supposed hero—the Guardian—a failure.

How could I have been so careless?

Ms. Z was right. I didn't understand my powers and I was a fool to think I could control them.

The vessel righted itself and I scurried to Joseph. His breathing was weak. Lifting his body, I held him tight and cried. Though, I could not hear my own words, I repeated again and again. *I'm so sorry.* Leaning over Joseph I let out a sad, heartfelt whimper of loss. Picking up his hands, I kissed the burns on his palms where the electricity had traveled into his body. I laid my hands on him, willing my body to heal but without his energy, I was nothing. Just a miserable girl who could make it rain—and rain it did. Large slow drops fell from the sky.

The Petoskey stone was next to me. I picked up the useless rock. The thing was much like I was; we were misplaced objects. I threw it in anger, it hit the flagpole, bouncing back and slamming into the hard deck. A small crack in its surface spread as a burst of blue light escaped from deep inside the stone. It moved around Joseph and me, circling. The air grew warm and my hair lifted, blowing and twisting with the sudden burst of wind. The voice in my head was my father's. He repeated the same lines several times much like a recording.

> *"Trust no one but your mother and the man who is your other.*
> *She'll know not why until you show her the sky."*

The blue light shifted around us, his voice grew weak but not before the Petoskey stone exploded with white, encasing Joseph into a cocoon of light. His body lifted from the ground as healing waves of energy swirled around him.

When he returned to my arms, his eyes opened slightly—just long enough to watch the light retract fully into the glowing stone. He said nothing and smiled. I couldn't return the smile knowing that our friends were dead.

A splash from the surface of the water caught my attention. I watched as a group of mermen carefully floated two unconscious bodies along the top of the black water. They approached the ladder. Laying Joseph down, I hurried to help. My fears were confirmed as the largest of the mermen carried Ethan's limp body onto the deck. Behind him a smaller man held Nasani. I could see movement in her chest—a glimmer of hope that at least one of them would live.

The smaller man spoke but I still could not hear. I pointed to my ear. He nodded his head in understanding. Rushing to Ethan, I began CPR compressions. A gentle touch on my shoulder told me to move.

The small man took my place, violently shoving his fist inside of Ethan's mouth. I lunged forward but the larger man held me back. I watched as the small man pushed his hand deeper into Ethan's throat and when he could go no further, his arm lifted. A stream of ocean water followed. Ethan let out several coughs as he gasped for air.

Tears of joy ran down my cheeks. Clouds cleared and sun burst through the sky. While my attention was on Ethan, Joseph stumbled across the deck. His balance remained troubled until he wrapped his arms around me. I turned to him, burying my face into his chest. He placed his hands on either side of my head, covering my ears. Within seconds I could hear.

Without hesitation, he released me and moved to help Nasani. I bent down, helping Ethan to his feet—he immediately went to Nasani's side. Joseph assured him that she would recover. Her ribs were broken but could be healed easily. Ethan kneeled by her, pushing her hair to the side so he could better see her eyes. She smiled weakly and touched his face.

I took Joseph's side. "I'm so sorry." I whispered.

His arms held me. He let out a laugh. "I should have known better than to wave metal in the air during a lightning storm."

A man cleared his throat behind us and we both turned.

"GIANNI!" I said with excitement, letting go of Joseph and hugging the other man. Lieutenant Gianni Enzio wrapped his arms around me then released quickly, returning to the line where the other mermen stood. The men stood united wearing tight black swim shorts with a purple letter R wrapped around their left leg. They looked like a swim team.

Joseph stepped forward so that half of his body was shielding mine. It was an unnecessary protective stance. His eyes were green, but not with anger.

Gianni didn't speak but instead clenched his right fist and with a stern look, moved his arm across his bare chest, placing his fist over his heart. He slid his left leg forward and locked eyes with me. The other four men did the same. Gianni held my gaze. Together they leaned forward and bowed.

The small man spoke. "We are *The Retribution*, loyal *only* to Guardian Seraphin."

Joseph placed his hand on his chest and returned the bow. "Thank you for saving our friends, Nick."

The man said nothing as they continued looking at me; completely ignoring Joseph.

I stepped around Joseph to Gianni, grateful that the men were able to help. "Thank you."

His expression softened. "Seraphina, I am-a your loyal servant."

The small man continued to explain, "Guardian Seraphin, we are men of the sea who promise to protect and watch over you. You already know Gianni. I am Nicholas Trite."

One by one the men gave their names as I shook their hands. Benjamin Lockzski; Salil Pelqu; Jianguo Li; they finished with a bow.

Gianni stepped forward again. "You ask for me; and-you find us." He took my hand and kissed it.

Joseph stepped forward but said nothing.

I didn't understand what Gianni meant and they gave me no time to ask. Without another word, Nicolas Trite raised his arm and the other men followed. Lining up along the side of the *George Washington*, they dove into the ocean.

Joseph mocked the men under his breath once they left but I watched in awe. They had come to our rescue and promised to do so again. Gianni had yet to show a fault in my eyes.

Nasani and Ethan joined Joseph and I. The four of us gathered together, hugging. We were all speaking at once.

"Did you see Ms. Z turn into water? What kind of power is that?" Ethan asked.

Still recounting my father's words, "was I the only one who could hear my dad when the Petoskey stone broke open?"

"Ugh, I smell like sea monster." Nasani sniffed at her shirt.

"Seraphin, what's with you and Enzio?" Joseph's voice was concerning and his eyes remained green. We stopped talking and looked at him.

"What do you mean me and Enzio?" I asked.

"Obviously the two of you—I mean, did you see the way he looked at her?" He turned his attention to Ethan.

Ethan did not join sides with Joseph. "That guy just saved my life. If he wants to be Phin's groupie, I don't have a problem with it."

Nasani was shaking her head at him. "Not now Joseph."

"Forget it." He changed his tone of voice. "I'm sorry about my crazy aunt—I'm so sorry."

Suddenly, I felt sick. She was responsible for my father's death. "I didn't know. I feel so foolish for trusting her—and for many years."

Ethan placed his arm around my shoulder. "All we can do is focus on stopping her before she kills more innocent people."

"With that monster," Nasani added in repulsion. "Did you see that thing? Its flesh was falling off; it had open wounds—ugh. No wonder the poor thing is so angry. It's probably been stabbed, hooked and netted more times than any creature in the sea. If only it was a little nicer, I would have tried to ease its pain a bit."

"I think it would take more than a few band-aids to calm that thing down Nasani." I added. "I didn't get any sense of threat from it but rather from around it. It was as if someone was controlling it—like the monster was just a pawn." Joseph revealed.

"We can track it." Ethan held up a digital screen. "I harpooned it with a whale tag. From now on, we'll know when it's coming."

Joseph patted Ethan on the back, "Great thinking."

Nasani turned to me. "Seraphin, what did you say about hearing your father?"

Ethan retrieved the broken Petoskey stone—handing one half to Joseph and the other half to me. He explained where we found it. I repeated the rhyme, my voice cracked at the mention of my mother.

Joseph was intrigued. "It's a puzzle. First the poem and now this, your father is leading us on a scavenger hunt. Maybe Orin will know something. We have to ask him."

"That's going to be harder than you think." There was a long silence while Ethan and I traded concerned glances then I finished explaining. "Orin took off—he's gone. The only thing he left behind was a note."

Joseph was irate. "Why didn't I know about this until now?"

I raised my voice. "Excuse me? How could I have told you? You and Nasani were nowhere to be found—telling us nothing of your whereabouts."

Ethan interjected, "we were kind of worried about you guys. I mean maybe you could give us a hint next time you decide to take off for a few days?"

Joseph and Nasani traded glances. She stepped forward and spoke to Ethan. "You were worried?"

He shyly nodded.

"I'm sorry Ethan. When Joseph told me what he suspected his aunt was capable of, I wanted to include my father. Only Joseph and I could go. I thought he could help—big mistake. All he was interested in was Seraphin." Her expression dropped. "He said that if they were really the Guardians then they didn't need his help. The only reason he came aboard was to meet her."

"What about last night? You could have told me then." I tried to ignore Joseph but he wouldn't allow it. He continued. "I would have liked to know that the man who holds the key to so much of our future has disappeared. We need him to translate the Legend."

Until then, Joseph had not revealed that Orin was the one who could translate the Legend. Again, I had been kept in the dark. What else was he hiding?

"I'm just as disappointed as you. I'm sure he'll be back." I said, trying to calm him. My words were false though, I wasn't sure Orin would return.

"We didn't get to ask him ANYTHING!" Joseph would not back down. He acted as though Orin was our prisoner. He was yelling and his face was only inches from mine. "What if he dies? What if he's poisoned again? You should have told me last night! I could have had Dr. Caro looking for him."

"Last night—"

He cut me off. "We've wasted so much time. He could be anywhere by now. Who knows when he'll resurface?"

"You think last night was a waste of time?" I lowered my voice and eyes.

Joseph did not catch on to my disappointment but instead continued to mutter. "We've got to send word that he's in danger. Nasani, get in touch with all your contacts and let your father know that Orin is missing. If we get to him in time, maybe he won't go into hiding again."

What he also failed to see was that Ethan and Nasani were sharing a moment that did not include the rest of the world. They were locked in one another's arms with their lips just inches apart. They whispered words and shared smiles—until Joseph broke in with his demands.

Ethan began to pull away but Nasani held tight. "No." She whispered.

Joseph tried again to draw her attention from Ethan, "Nasani!"

She shook her head. "I will not. I am done."

Ethan whispered something in her ear.

"Don't let him make you feel that way." She said to Ethan, and then finally gave Joseph her attention—but not the kind he had hoped for. Her voice grew loud as she spoke. "I'm done Joseph. I need a break from all this. My Mother was right; I always do what you say and I'm through. Oh, and my father, he showed me how little he cared—only the Guardians—only you and Seraphin are his concern. The son he never had and the daughter he should have been given. I don't fit in to that equation." Her eyes returned to Ethan even though she still spoke to Joseph. "I gave my life for you today—literally. That life is gone; it's buried deep in the sea with Leviathan. I want a new life. I'm ready to be loved again—and an amazing man is ready to love me."

Ethan gave her a sweet smile.

Joseph's face turned to disgust. "You can't just walk away from this Nasani. We need you."

"No. You have Seraphin now. You need each other—AND, I need him." She took Ethan's hand and began pulling him until he followed her into the main cabin. "If my father asks, you tell him that Leviathan took my life. You tell him that I sacrificed myself so you and Seraphin could live—you make me into a hero. Maybe this way he'll finally love me."

Like I said, we should have assured her that her life was worth living the moment her father made her feel like it wasn't. It hurt to see Nasani so angry—but she was right. No longer was she a pawn in whatever Joseph was planning. Though, she was wrong to think I would be his next loyal follower.

It stung to think that he considered the time we spent together, wasted. I was mistaken to think he could be ordinary; his mind returned to the one track it had always been on. It seemed like the only thing he wanted was to become the most powerful man in the sea. I left him standing alone on the deck of the *George Washington*.

I found the rest of the crew locked in the 2nd floor meeting room. There were a few injuries from being tossed around but overall, nothing serious. Just like I had done when Gianni pulled me from the cliff in Taranto, I lied. I told the Captain and Dr. Radski that I didn't know what had happened. Ethan made the same claim. Though, in our defense we certainly did not know how our lives had taken such a dramatic turn and how our high school biology teacher turned out to be so evil.

When she saw the wreckage on the deck of the *George Washington*, Dr. Radski was furious, but was soon after rendered speechless when told that Perrine Canard had fallen overboard. I preferred her speechless, as did Ethan. Without her constant pestering though, he seemed bored. During the next 24 hours, I often found him lingering on the main deck. It wasn't until night fell that I realized what he was doing. Nasani surfaced for just a minute beside the boat. She was following us back to CORE.

Joseph made several attempts to speak with me regarding his upcoming plans but I simply walked away, uninterested. We were preparing to dock when he approached me for the last time. "Seraphin, you have to hear me out. We've got to stay on track. I'm going to search for Orin; I need you to ask your neighbors about your mother."

"No," I refused. My back was turned as I gathered my things.

"Seraphin, being a Guardian means you have to go where you are needed."

"And who needs me?"

"I do."

"Joseph, I don't need you." The second those words left my mouth I regretted them. My parting words were not meant to be so hurtful.

His expression will forever be burned into my memory. The corners of his mouth dropped. "I will no longer be where I'm not needed." He stepped away.

I didn't stop him.

TWENTY

The *George Washington* returned to the CORE campus without tagging a single whale. Everyone who worked the failed mission was granted a few days off to recuperate.

Ethan spent most of those days at my house working on the Gran Torino with Mr. Chesney, the high school auto shop teacher.

Because Nasani no longer had a place to live, I invited her to stay with me. Truth be told, it was nice to have her around. She made herself at home in my grandmother's old bedroom. There was only one issue, she could not actually see the house; luckily it took her only a few days to get acquainted with the neighbors on Briarwood Court. They took turns walking her onto the porch and through the threshold. Her favorite escort, besides Ethan, was Celia. The two hit it off beautifully.

Joseph occupied my thoughts. Even though I was angry and frustrated, I felt incomplete without him. The night we talked in Dr. Caro's penthouse suite played over again in my mind. In his opinion, it was a waste of time, but for me it was the first time I saw Joseph without an ulterior motive, without a plan. And I liked him that way.

Saturday arrived and with it came the Keyes' Market Anniversary Gala. Ethan and Nasani had managed to get an invite. They were excited. I was not. Nasani spent the day primping. She borrowed a dress from Celia's mother. It was a lavender strapless sundress. Of course, she looked stunning.

She tried to help me get ready but her efforts proved difficult. "Seraphin, you are love sick."

I laughed at her accusation.

She pressed further. "It's perfectly normal to miss him."

"Nasani, I'm not in love with Joseph and I don't miss him. Besides, I can assure you that he does not miss me. He knows where to find me and yet he's made no effort." Of course, I was lying. I did miss him.

Ethan spent that day working on my car. Ten minutes before we were to leave he shaved and threw on some clean clothes.

Together, the three of us walked to the beach club where the celebration was taking place. A massive white canopy was draped with strands of twinkling lights and surrounded by burning torches. Twenty circular tables were underneath; each had a white tablecloth and a decorative flower arrangement. It looked more like a wedding than a corner market anniversary party.

Nasani squealed when she saw the lavish decorations. "Am I under dressed? I wish I had my clothes. That dress you wore to dinner with Joseph would have been perfect—" She stopped herself.

Ethan took her hand, assuring her of her beauty.

A string quartet began to play and I wandered away from the lovebirds. The wind was soft and the moon was full. Its light danced atop the gentle waves of the Atlantic Ocean. It was a perfectly romantic summer evening. I felt ashamed when again I began to long for Joseph's company.

Several hours passed. Meaningless conversations were conducted. Ethan, like a gentleman, asked me to dance but I declined.

Mr. and Mrs. Keyes made the surprise announcement that along with the Market's anniversary; it was also their wedding anniversary. Seemingly, out of nowhere a priest appeared and the Keyes renewed their wedding vows after 20 years of marriage. With their closest friends gathered around, they promised their lives to one another. They spoke about how they were like two puzzle pieces that fit together—two parts of a whole.

My mind let those words sink in. It wasn't until I saw that Mr. Rigby and I were the only two not engaged in the moment that I really felt alone. A tear dropped and soon the sky began to sprinkle. Nasani immediately realized what was happening but before she could attempt to cheer me up, I snuck away. I didn't wander far. The party was still within sight.

Love wasn't something I had ever been in and I was certain the feelings I had for Joseph were not that, yet. It was different with him. The Keyes' words repeated in my head—*two parts of a whole*. No matter how difficult Joseph was, I felt partial without him.

My toes touched the water; gently the waves washed over my feet and I admitted. "Joseph, I need you. Come back to me."

Just off the shore a soft blue glow spread across the surface of the water. I watched as a figure emerged—a man. I called to him. "Joseph?"

He spoke, confused. "Seraphin? Where am I?"

My feet carried me further into the water; every inch of progress was instinctual. There was a force that was not my own. It pulled my body towards his. "Have you been following me?"

"Seraphin? Following you where? Up until 30 seconds ago I was in Perth, eating brunch."

"You don't miss me, do you?" I asked, sad.

We were face to face, standing in the cool water. He wore a white button down, long sleeve shirt. It was open at his neck and the sleeves were folded once each. It hung low over a loose fitting pair of tan linen shorts. He was completely dry. His expression softened. "What makes you think I didn't miss you?"

"Obviously you didn't miss me or you wouldn't have been enjoying omelets or croissants or whatever you were eating in Australia," wanting to hear only that he was sulking, not enjoying brunch.

Laughing, he declared, "You are not making sense. You know I would never eat an egg—I mean, sometimes as an ingredient I can't avoid them but I would never just crack open an egg and fry it up."

I smiled, comforted by his sense of humor.

"I'm dreaming," he bent down, touching the water with the tips of his fingers.

"You're not dreaming." I assured him.

"Sure feels like a dream. Look, not a drop of water on me and I just emerged from the ocean. Heck, as long as I'm dreaming, I might as well." His arms wrapped around me and without warning his lips met mine. They were soft and warm. It was our first kiss. We both seemed to relax, comforted by the contact. When he pulled back I moved forward, surprising us both. "Yes, this is definitely a dream."

"You're not dreaming." I repeated, whispering.

"Then why am I here? How am I here?" His lips rested on my forehead.

"I think I brought you here. I have to talk to you—I want to tell you that I didn't mean what I said." Suddenly, he lifted; my feet left the water as he carried me back towards the beach. I continued talking. He said nothing as his lips moved to my neck. I tried to focus on my words but it was difficult. Having trouble forming a sentence, I mumbled the word, "apologize."

"Me?" He questioned. "I'm sorry for anything and everything I've ever done or might do to upset you Seraphin."

"No, I apologize," trying to clarify.

"*Mmmhmmm*," he dropped to the sand, pulling me onto his lap.

"Joseph, what are you doing?"

"I'm having the *best* dream, *ever*." As he kissed my collarbone his hand ran up my leg.

"JOSEPH!" I pushed him back.

"This is not a dream, huh?" A sigh escaped as he removed his hand from my thigh. I remained nestled in his lap. "So, you summoned me here to apologize? And how did you manage to do such a thing?"

"I was standing on the shore and I said; *Joseph, I need you*." When I repeated it a blue glow surrounded us. Again I felt a pull towards his body. "Do you feel that?"

"When a beautiful woman admits her need for you, it's difficult to not feel, THAT."

"I'm serious."

"Oh, I'm completely serious as well. So, what is it then that you need me for?" With sarcasm in his voice, he asked. My cheeks flushed and when I didn't answer right away he let a large smile take over his face. "Oh. I see. You *need* me."

"No. The reason I—"

He stopped me. "I'm so thrown off by you. All this time I expected to find your opposite—someone more like me. A person who's only drive in life is to be a Guardian but instead, I've got you."

"You're going somewhere with this, right?" My feelings were close to being hurt.

"I've got you to remind me that I'm only a man—that I make mistakes and that I'm not perfect. You are challenging, confusing, and difficult—all the things I didn't know I needed, until we met. You are all I think, worry, and obsess about. It's driving me mad to not be with you Seraphin."

"But the time we did spend together, the night in Dr. Caro's suite, it meant so much to me and so little to you."

He held me tighter. "Sometimes it's difficult to balance all the thoughts in my head; most of the time it's impossible for me to turn off and just relax. That night was special to me too and I'm sorry if I gave the impression it was not."

My toes pushed the sand around as his hand mindlessly buried them. "What do we do now?" I asked.

"We go back to school in a few weeks, so there won't be much time for relic hunting." With a mischievous smile he caught my attention.

"You *are* going back to school this coming term," excited that he made that choice.

"Yeah, you were right; I've worked too hard to abandon my studies. I can still be active at CORE and as long as Dr. Caro is doing his best to patrol the waters, I don't see a need for the Guardians to emerge, *yet*." He grinned. "Though, you are wrong about one thing; *we* will be going back to school this fall, not just *me*."

"WHAT?"

Quickly he began to explain. "With your grades it was a breeze, they let you right in—"

"Joseph?"

"Welcome to the University of Maine. You should be receiving your welcome packet in the mail any day now." An innocent smile cracked as he shrugged his shoulders. "We can carpool."

In a way I was thankful that Joseph had made the decision for me. For the first time I felt like I knew where my life was going, at least in the short term. Joseph would be good for me as well. "Okay."

Okay? You're not upset with me?" He asked. "You'll have to live on campus though; the drive is too far to commute. Are you mad now?"

"Is a random storm bursting through the sky?" I answered not thrilled about leaving my house behind for the school year. I reasoned that at least Nasani would be there, it wouldn't sit empty again.

He laughed and kissed the top of my head. "Seraphin, if there is one man that you can rely on, that you trust with all your heart; know that it's me. I promise that I'll be truthful from this point forward. Whatever I know, you'll know."

The music from the string quartet filled the air.

"Just out of curiosity, who were you having brunch with in Perth?" I whispered, holding him to the promise he had just made, wanting to know everything he knew.

Looking back, sometimes things are better off unknown. Sometimes the truth hurts more than a lie and being naive is a blessing in disguise. From that moment on, it was going to be difficult to distinguish between being protected and being lied to.

He moved his lips to my ear and spoke soft, "I was having brunch with your father."

Memoir of a Mermaid
When, At Last, She Could See
By Adrianna Stepiano

Follow Seraphin as she discovers what it means to be a Guardian and uncover a tragic past that even her worst nightmare pales against. Be sure to catch the second book in the *Memoir of a Mermaid* series, January 2013.

About the Author

Following a summer of unexpected struggles and rampant changes in her life, Adrianna Stepiano craved a creative escape. As an avid reader, she found solace in fiction but desired more. For several years the idea of a merfolk based story swam around in her head, inspired by family vacations to coastal states and a life spent along the shores of the magnificent Great Lakes. Finally, a prayer brought Joseph and Seraphin to life by way of the written word.

Adrianna lives in Michigan with her family. She writes for her personal enjoyment, as well as yours.

www.memoirofamermaid.com

Made in the USA
Lexington, KY
29 April 2012